"Bridgie, will you marry me?"

For a moment, she actually considered it.

Thirty-three years without ever being proposed to, and here was her second proposal within a week.

She could marry Tripp Ashby, the romantic figure of her youth. They would make mad, passionate love every day before breakfast, have six or seven lovely, undisciplined babies, and live at the seashore.

Yeah, right. How long had she known him? How long had he been blind to who she really was?

And if he discovered that she had been hot for his body since the age of eighteen, he was likely to run from the room screaming.

Besides, he looked like he was about to explode. It was not the look of a man in the heat of undeniable passion. It was the look of a man pushed into a corner.

"Will you, Bridgie? Will you marry me?"

She took a deep breath. Tripp, wanting *her.* How many times had she dreamed of this happening?

"No!" she cried. "I couldn't possibly!"

ABOUT THE AUTHOR

Julie Kistler has been reading books and imagining herself as part of the adventures since the age of three. She is happy to report that writing books is almost as much fun as reading them, although it's a lot more work! An avid film buff, Julie has a special fondness for old black-and-white screwball comedies; these movies have provided the inspiration for many of her books, including the arranged marriage and mistaken identities in *Once Upon a Honeymoon*. Julie and her husband live in the tiny town of Mahomet, Illinois, with their cat, Thisbe.

Books by Julie Kistler

HARLEQUIN AMERICAN ROMANCE

JULIE KISTLER

ONCE UPON A HONEYMOON

Harlequin Books

TORONTO • NEW YORK • LONDON
AMSTERDAM • PARIS • SYDNEY • HAMBURG
STOCKHOLM • ATHENS • TOKYO • MILAN
MADRID • WARSAW • BUDAPEST • AUCKLAND

ISBN 0-373-16557-9

ONCE UPON A HONEYMOON

Chapter One

There was a nude woman in his shower.

A nude woman *stranger* in his shower. Or at least he didn't think he recognized any of that obvious flesh.

Frozen to the carpet between the bedroom and bath of his modest suburban Chicago town house, Tripp Ashby muttered to himself, "You're dreaming."

After all, he'd only gotten out of bed thirty seconds ago. Of course he was dreaming. What living, breathing, warm-blooded American male wouldn't dream of a mysterious woman popping up naked, dripping wet, in his shower?

But if he was dreaming, shouldn't he be turned on, excited, fantasizing? Well, he wasn't. All that flesh, and he wasn't interested in the least. All he could think of was finding a weapon or an escape route.

He blinked and looked again. But, no, he hadn't imagined her. He still had a very good view of pale pink skin—lots of it—only a little blurred by the frosted glass of the shower door.

Long blond hair. Tall. Lots of curves.

"Jeez," he muttered, only now realizing that his eyes were glued to her body, his gaze zooming like radar through the glass.

It wasn't polite to stare, even if she didn't seem to realize that she had company, even if she was showing off
her birthday suit in *his* shower, happily splashing and
soaping away.

But who the hell was she? And how had she gotten in
there? She would've had to jimmy a lock or two, and
then tiptoe through his bedroom, within inches of his
sleeping body, to get to the shower.

Tripp raked a hand through short, sleek brown hair
that was already moist from the steamy bathroom. He
didn't need this. It was difficult to think this early in the
morning. But even when his brain was firing on all cyl-
inders, he doubted he'd know how to behave when
confronted with a nude bather who might be a burglar.
Or maybe just a psycho.

Was this an invitation to jump in with her? Or maybe
a ploy, to divert him, while her burglar pals ripped off
the whole apartment?

As he turned toward the door, deciding retreat was
the better part of valor under these circumstances, the
shower door opened, and she stepped out—naked as the
day she was born.

"Hi," she said breezily. "How are you, Tripp?"

She knew his name. She knew him. His mind raced
with questions, but it also automatically supplied the
appropriate reply—appropriate for a tea party at his
mother's house, anyway. "Fine, thank you. And you?"

"Oh, I'm great!" she returned, widening her smile.
She flicked wet hair back over one shoulder, but still she
lounged there, careless and unconcerned. "I just love
the morning, don't you? I'm always so *perky* early in
the a.m."

Trying to avoid looking at what exactly might be
perky, Tripp turned hastily, grabbing a large bath sheet.

"Here," he mumbled, holding it out in her general vicinity.

"Okay. But you know, I really enjoy not wearing anything. I have a great bod, you know? And I feel like, what's the big deal?" She began to rub herself down vigorously. "I mean, it's nothing anybody hasn't already seen. Except better. Right, Tripp?"

He really didn't like the sound of his name on her lips. "How did you get in here?"

She giggled. "It was great. I called this locksmith guy and told him I locked myself out. No prob. I mean, geeky guys are always falling all over me. They'll believe anything I tell them."

"Right." Burglary, fraud, deceit . . . and conning a poor, harmless locksmith. And this bimbo was proud of it.

"So then I just sort of sneaked past where you were sleeping." She shrugged, offering him a smug smile. "You're cute when you're asleep. So I thought I'd surprise you when you woke up. And here I am!"

"Lucky me," he said, deadpan.

He was used to women finding him attractive. Decent looks, a certain athletic prowess, and a family that traveled in the right circles guaranteed his popularity. He didn't pretend to understand what the big deal was, but he'd been living with it long enough to accept it. Yes, women had always found him attractive. But no one had ever gone to this kind of extreme just to get near him.

He opened the door into his bedroom wider, letting in a rush of cool air to clear his head. "Tell me, have we met?"

"Sure."

"We have?"

"Like, *duh!* Would I be here if we hadn't?"

"I don't know," he managed. "Would you?"

"You remember!" she insisted. "It was the big hospital benefit at the Hilton. We danced."

He vaguely recalled the black-tie affair she was referring to, but that was as far as it went. "I don't think so—"

"Oh, come on. Of course you remember." She fluttered her eyelashes at him. "We danced a tango, and you told me I had beautiful eyes."

I tell everyone they have beautiful eyes, he thought desperately. What could he possibly have done at that damn benefit to provoke this kind of crazy stunt?

"Look at my eyes," she coaxed. "Don't you remember?"

His gaze flashed up to her face, which he hadn't really given much of a glance so far. He'd been occupied elsewhere. But, no, her features rang no bells.

"Kynthia Chipton," she said impatiently. Finally, almost angrily, she consented to cover herself with the towel, twisting it around her. "My parents are H. H. and Buff Chipton, as in, you know, the Chipton Bank in the Loop. And Mummy is on all the best boards. Surely you've heard of them."

"Of course," he responded, even though he couldn't remember. He had a very short-term memory where Chicago's society folk were concerned. But... "Did you say your name was Kynthia?" How could he have forgotten someone whose name was Kynthia?

"Uh-huh. It's Greek. You do remember, don't you?" she declared, peering up at him with vacant blue eyes that hid, he felt sure, an IQ no larger than her bust measurement.

"But what are you doing here?"

She smiled coyly. Or what someone named Kynthia's version of coy looked like, at any rate. "I came to visit. To jog your memory." She tapped a fingernail against his chest, playing with the V where his robe gapped open.

Tripp caught her hand. He was right the first time—she was psychotic. So was it better to boot her out coldly, or be kind until the men in the white coats arrived?

His normal reaction was kindness, but this time he chose cold. With her hand placed firmly away from him, he backed out into his bedroom, getting them both out of the steamy bathroom. "It's time for you to leave, Kynthia. Where are your clothes?"

"But, Tripp!" She pouted. The effort of it almost made her drop her towel. She flapped it coyly, obviously trying to flash him some skin. She must've forgotten he'd already had a good look at what she was offering, and made it as clear as he knew how that he wasn't buying what she was selling.

"I heard you were lonely, and..." Her words were as stilted as if she were reading aloud from a personal ad. "And ready to settle down into a meaningful relationship."

Tripp stopped dead in his tracks. "You heard what?"

"That you were just dying to find a girlfriend. Well, really a wife." She giggled. "That is just so cute, that a guy like you would be so shy when it comes to... well, you know, connecting. And I'm single again, and you've always been such a hunk. You know, drool city." She giggled again. "So I thought...why not do us both a favor and give poor, lonely Tripp a dream come true?"

"Oh my God," he groaned. "Where did you hear this?"

"Well, from Babs Newton-Parrish. It was at the club where I play racquetball. I was in the locker room, and I overheard Babs telling her sister, Muffin, and that cow Mary Eleanor Beekerman, that your mother had told her, hush-hush, that you were simply desperate to find—"

"Desperate? My mother said I was desperate?" Kitty Belle Ashby. The world's most difficult, manipulative mother. And she was all his.

He should've known.

If stories were going around that he was on the prowl for a "meaningful relationship," Kitty Belle had to be at the bottom of it. She'd been trying to marry him off to anything that moved—or at least anything with the right pedigree—since he turned twenty-one. His mother said she wanted grandchildren. She said she wanted the right sort of bloodlines to carry on the almighty Ashby name. And Kynthia Chipton and her pals had exactly the sort of connections and cash Kitty Belle loved best.

"So when I heard Babs going on and on about how she was going to act like your one-woman life preserver, to save you in your time of need, well, I knew I could get the jump on Babs." Kynthia made a "hmph" noise. "After all, I'm much smarter than Babs Newton-Parrish."

From what he'd seen of Kynthia—and so far he'd seen plenty— that didn't bode well for Babs. "Look, I'm sorry you've gone to all this trouble." He scanned the floor of his bedroom, looking for her clothes. "But my mother is mistaken, and so is anyone who listened to her. I'm not looking for Ms. Right, okay? I'm not looking for anybody."

"But—" she began, as he took her elbow and steered her out into the hall.

"Where are your clothes?" he asked again, making sure he said the words slowly and clearly.

"What's the rush?"

"Here they are," he said with relief, pointing her toward the heap of expensive sportswear tossed negligently on the love seat in his living room. "You can dress in the kitchen."

"In the kitchen?" she huffed.

"Sorry." He tossed her a silk blouse, the top item on the pile of clothes. "But I'll be needing my bedroom and bathroom. I have to get going, or I'm going to be late to work. You can let yourself out, okay?"

"Let myself out?"

There was a definite echo in the living room. "So long," he offered, already on his way back down the hall.

"Well, no wonder you have trouble getting a girl," she shouted after him. "You're really rude."

He refrained from pointing out the relative rudeness of traipsing into someone else's shower uninvited. As he cleared the bedroom door, he heard the front door slam, and he released a sigh of relief. "Good riddance," he muttered under his breath.

His only hope was that Kynthia was so annoyed, she would bad-mouth him back in the locker room and scare away Babs whoever and Mary Eleanor Beekerman.

He still couldn't quite believe that Kitty Belle had announced open season on her only child. Even for her, this was pushing the edge of the envelope.

Maybe it was a mistake or a misunderstanding, he mused, as he blasted himself under the force of the shower that had so recently held Kynthia. Maybe Kitty Belle had made an innocent remark to somebody else's mother, a remark that had picked up something in the translation. Maybe the worst was over.

After all, even if Kynthia thought he was a great catch, the others would know better, wouldn't they? Okay, so they thought he was cute—a hunk, as Kynthia put it. While flattering, as well as mildly annoying, it was hardly enough to get women running to the Marriage Mart.

And as for his general eligibility, he didn't think it was any great shakes.

How could he be eligible when he had no money?

Oh, the Ashby name was distinguished enough, and Kitty Belle certainly considered herself the cream of society. But everyone knew the Ashby wealth had gone with the wind a long time ago. More precisely, it had gone the way of the horse-drawn carriage.

In its time—a slower, more gracious time—the posh Ashby Carriage Company had put plenty of coins in the family coffers. But ever since the advent of the automobile, ever since their luxurious horse-drawn carriages got run over in an onslaught of Fords and Buicks and even Volkswagens, the Ashby family had begun its slow decline.

By the time Tripp hit adulthood, all the Ashbys had left was a town named after them, an almost-defunct business that put out a few high-class bicycles instead of carriages and a lot of pretense coming from Kitty Belle's side of the house.

But Tripp himself was living well below Kitty Belle's standards. He attended only the benefits she forced him to, and he steered clear of the rest of that high-priced life-style. His own life was modest enough, he thought, with more than a touch of self-mockery. Who'd want him?

For the first time in his life, it actually cheered him up to be poor. Shaking his head, Tripp jumped into his car and took off for the office. But his good mood didn't last long. Not even long enough to push open the door.

It was a small office in a small building, barely big enough to house him, his secretary and a small collection of antique sporting equipment on the walls as a dubious attempt at decoration. Mostly it was just a place to work out of, but no great meeting space. He could never recall having six people, let alone six women, waiting for him when he got to work.

His business, called Touch the Sky, designed and marketed fiberglass poles intended for world-class pole vaulters, as well as a variety of other specialty sporting equipment. As a general rule, there weren't a whole lot of women beating down the door to buy poles.

"What's going on?" he asked, but one glance at his secretary's harried, sullen expression convinced him he was better off not knowing.

"I'm first!" shouted a nubile redhead who looked vaguely familiar. She jumped to her feet and leapt out in front of the receptionist's desk.

"I was ahead of you," another one interrupted, elbowing the first one aside. Wearing a fluffy fur coat and baring a lot of teeth in a determined smile, this one brought to mind a grizzly bear on the prowl for plump campers.

"First?" cried an anorexic young thing with a severely asymmetrical haircut. "I'll give you first!"

And then they all started to fuss and whine, edging closer, pushing up to him, until it was all he could do to wedge himself around them and escape into the inner sanctum of his office.

Tripp slammed the door shut between him and them. Debutantes on a rampage. It was terrifying.

He could hear them scuffling and shouting out there, and somebody knocked hard on the door, but there was no way he was going to open it.

As he stuck a chair under the door handle for good measure, and then retreated back around to his desk, he realized he had no idea what to do to extricate himself from this thorny situation. Not a clue. He'd played every sport in the book, in every kind of pressure-cooker situation, but this was worse than any of them— worse than trying to penetrate against the press, worse than trying to find your footing on a muddy track, worse than being slammed into the hardwood by a three-hundred-pound center.

Tripp had no idea what to do. But then, there was no rule book for dealing with marriage-mad society women.

One of his friends, a good ole boy named Deke, could've charmed them all right out of the office without batting an eye. Besides, Deke had bucks to burn, so maybe he could've waved a few greenbacks and led the women out by their rich little noses. But unfortunately, neither Deke nor his bank account was here to help out at the moment.

Lost in his thoughts, Tripp jumped when the phone on his desk rang.

He was almost afraid to pick it up. "Hello?" he asked tentatively. The noise in the background clued him in. It was Rosa, his secretary, calling from the outer office.

"Good morning, sir," she began, in a fakey sort of voice. "I was hoping you could help me with a problem I'm having."

"Don't even ask, because I don't know what to do with them," he muttered. "I guess I could see them one at a time, try to reason with them..."

"No way," Rosa shot back quickly. She dropped her voice. "Are you nuts? You let any one of them in and the others will go ballistic. And I'll be out here trying to fend them off."

"So you think I should I come out there?"

"That's even worse! They'll tear you to pieces."

Tripp sighed. "What do you think they want, anyway?"

"They've made that pretty clear. *You.*"

A wanted man. It was ridiculous.

"Do you know what started this?" she whispered. "What did you do? Take out a personal ad in the Society Register? 'Hot to get hitched—call Tripp Ashby'?"

"It's all my mother's fault," Tripp said tersely. "And I'm going to kill her."

First Kynthia and now six more just like her. Rich, vain and vapid. It was ridiculous. Why would Kitty Belle pick these women? She couldn't seriously think he'd go for any of them. Could she?

The worst part was that, even if he got rid of this bunch, there was no guarantee there wouldn't be six or seven more arriving on their heels. There was no telling how many eligible young women Kitty Belle had revved up.

He groaned out loud.

Meanwhile, he had a potential client—a slick, influential sports agent he occasionally golfed with—due to show up within the next half hour. If Tripp was lucky, this meeting would generate enough income to keep his business afloat for a few more months. But how could there even be a meeting when he had an office full of whining bimbos?

If there was one thing that made him crazy, it was the threat of public embarrassment. And if superagent Marv Monroe caught sight of all those marriage-hungry women, Tripp wouldn't be merely embarrassed. He would be humiliated.

So what was he going to do?

"Let's see," he mused darkly. "I don't suppose we could get the police to cart them all off."

"Okay." Rosa sounded a lot more cheerful, as if she really liked that idea. "I'll call right away. But what do I tell them, you know, to get them to come?"

That I'm such a stud, I've got rich girls six-deep at my office, all clamoring for my attention, and I need protection from them?

Tripp Ashby, stud of the western world. What a joke. Okay, so he and his college friends had called themselves the Studs for a while way back when, but they were never serious about it. At least he didn't think any of them took it seriously.

"Listen," he told his secretary, "there must be some way—"

Even as he spoke, someone behind her with a very loud, very high-pitched voice demanded, "Is that him? You're talking to Tripp, aren't you?"

Quickly Rosa mumbled, "Gotta go," and hung up on him.

He sat there, staring down at the dead receiver. Next he supposed some crew of lovestruck debs would be hiring bulldozers to crash through his wall.

"What did I ever do to deserve this?"

I told you so.

There was no one in the room, but he could still hear the words as clear as day. His old friend Bridget Emerick might as well have been right there in the room with him, giving him one of her simmering lectures.

With one hand on her hip and fire in her eyes, Bridgie would say, *You wanted to be a Stud, didn't you? I told you it was demeaning and sexist. I told you women were going to treat you like prime beef on the hoof. But you had to be a Stud.*

Tripp smiled to himself, enjoying the mental picture of Bridgie on her high horse. Even in the middle of this mess, the thought of Bridgie—earnest, fierce, smart as a whip—was pretty amusing. She was only medium height, rather slender, with a pretty heart-shaped face and long, straight, dark hair. As a matter of fact, Bridget looked like any other standard coed of the late seventies. It wasn't her physical presence that was intimidating to members of the opposite sex—it was her attitude. Studious, driven, with a sense of responsibility worn like a mantle around her shoulders, Bridgie always seemed older and a lot more serious than the other college students.

While they were partying and fooling around, Bridget was applying for special extra-credit internships in Washington. While they were planning keggers, she was writing position papers on sexual harassment on campus.

He could still remember how irate she'd been when she'd first found out about the innocent little club he and his buddies had formed. Steve, Tripp, Ukiah and Deke—Studs by virtue of their combined initials. A quartet of college kids who'd thought it was amusing to call themselves Studs.

It's downright disgusting! she'd fumed.

And, as usual, he'd pled innocence. He simply hadn't understood what all the fuss was about.

But Bridgie had been livid. *Someday, Tripp Ashby, this thing is going to backfire on you. You're going to be very sorry you ever wanted to call yourself a Stud.*

Trust Bridgie to call that one right on the nose.

Back in the old days, when he was an aimless jock who constantly hovered on the edge of ineligibility, he had trusted her. The other guys thought she was a drag, but he knew he could trust her to yell at him when he was being an idiot, to stay up until 4:00 a.m. to help him write his anthropology paper, to bail him out of jail when he got picked up for violating curfew, to go through *Hamlet* with him, line by line, until he got the sense of the damn thing.

Good old Bridgie. His ally through thick and thin.

''Bridgie,'' he said suddenly, sitting up straighter, reaching for the Rolodex. She was a woman. She understood how they thought. Surely she could get him out of this mess.

His other friends were scattered all over the place, but Bridgie was downtown at a stuffy law firm in Chicago's Loop, only thirty miles away from his suburban office. Good old Bridgie.

Her phone picked up on the first ring.

''Niles, Tweed and Sternham. This is Ms. Emerick's office,'' a cool voice answered.

That was definitely not his old friend's voice. ''Is Bridgie in, please?''

"Ms. Emerick," she said in a disapproving tone, making it clear she would not bend far enough to recognize a nickname, "is meeting with a client. Is there some way I can help you?"

"Do you know how long she's expected to be in the meeting?"

"I really couldn't say."

He sensed a definite chill coming from the other end of the receiver, but he had no idea what he'd done to deserve it. *Women.* They were either too hot or too cold—nothing in between.

The noise level in his outer office suddenly accelerated to a roar. What was going on out there? It sounded like a riot.

"Is there something I can help you with?" the woman in Bridgie's office asked again, with a frostier edge this time.

You can help me by getting Bridget out of the damn meeting, he wanted to yell. His situation was getting desperate here. He spun his chair around on its casters, as far away as possible from the source of the disturbance in the outer office, and then spoke quietly into the receiver. "The minute she comes out of her meeting, please tell her that Tripp called. I'd like her to call me back as soon as she possibly can."

"Would that be Mr. Tripp?" the woman on the other end asked suspiciously.

"Tripp Ashby. But I doubt she knows more than one Tripp."

"And this is regarding . . . ?"

"A private matter," he said plainly. "Please just give her my message, okay?"

"And would she have your number?" the woman asked doubtfully.

"Yes, she would."

"I think I should write it down anyway. She might not have it handy," she droned on, as he began to worry whether debutantes wielding antique tennis rackets and baseball bats were going to come crashing through his office door at any moment.

"She has my number," he said abruptly. "Thank you."

Having difficulty maintaining his temper, Tripp slammed the receiver back into its cradle. First he had to fight off a bunch of society bimbos, and now he was forced to be polite to a snotty receptionist who didn't want to take his message.

He'd no sooner dropped the phone than it rang again. "Bridgie?" he asked eagerly.

"No, it's me," Rosa, his secretary hissed. "I got the police to come out. But when I told them what was wrong, they started laughing too hard to arrest anybody. Plus your friend Mr. Monroe just got here, and..."

Tripp covered his eyes with his hand. The police, the women and his influential client, all out there in the lobby, slugging it out. He saw his life over, his business washed up.

Rosa's voice dropped even lower. "Mr. Monroe is making it even worse! First he tried to get the cops to lay odds on which one of the women would get to you first, and then he used my phone so he could call some of his friends and get them in on the betting pool. The Tripp Ashby Matrimonial Sweepstakes, he's calling it, with choice of dates and possible brides.'' There was a pause. ''So what should I do?''

''Bet the farm on no wedding and no bride,'' Tripp said grimly.

The Tripp Ashby Matrimonial Sweepstakes. Could things get any worse?

Chapter Two

Bridget Emerick was having a very good day.

With some canny negotiating and a push in the right direction, she'd swung a 1.5 million-dollar settlement for a very important client, a client she had persuaded to hire Niles, Tweed and Sternham. And she'd done it without ever setting foot in court. Not one motion, not one deposition, and her client was a millionaire. Well, he was already a millionaire, but now he was even richer.

And her firm took in a cool one-third. All for about a week's worth of work.

"Just call me Ms. Rainmaker," she said with satisfaction. This would make the senior partners sit up and take notice.

With a smile on her face, she sailed into her small, but exquisitely decorated office. She was all prepared to put her pumps up and look out the window at the Chicago River, which she could see a tiny corner of if she craned her neck. And then she could relax for, oh, maybe ten minutes.

Life was good.

Until she saw her brand-new, and very officious secretary, Marie, lying in wait, blocking her path.

"Your phone has been ringing off the hook," Marie said sourly, waving a thick sheaf of little pink slips in the air. "I thought you'd never get out of that meeting."

Bridget gave the woman a quelling stare. Marie had only been here for two weeks, and already she was a major annoyance. Gossipy, officious, smug and superior, Marie drove everyone crazy. It was difficult for Bridget to make the most of her authority; she really didn't like having to yell at people to keep them in line. But Bridget was getting very close to singeing her secretary down to her shoelaces.

"Who called?" she asked quickly, running down the short list of people whose messages she was always sure to return ASAP. "Rogers? Hayworth? Barry Chase?"

"Oh, no, no, they're all from—"

"Oh, no. Jay." Bridget frowned. Jay Philpott, her fiancé as of yesterday, had had his secretary launch this sort of phone assault when he couldn't find her and he thought it was important. Jay simply didn't know how to take "no" for an answer when he was on a roll. Of course the things Jay dealt with—urban renewal, universal health care, getting himself elected to the Senate—really were extremely important. But so was her 1.5 million-dollar client! "Are those messages from Jay?"

"No, they're not from him. These are from some other man, who took a very personal tone if you ask me." Marie's lips pursed in a severe line. "I don't think these are business calls. He keeps calling you Birdie or something. Every time, I answer very carefully, 'Ms. Emerick's office.' And every time, he calls you Birdie. I just hate that, when people don't understand when you try to be professional and businesslike."

But Bridget tuned out everything after the word *birdie*. *He keeps calling you Birdie.* Not Birdie. Bridgie. She began to feel a funny fluttering in the pit of her stomach. Only one person called her anything besides Bridget.

Tripp.

"Please, Lord, not Tripp," she whispered.

The funny fluttering turned into major league bells and whistles. Alarms. Sirens.

She did her best to ignore it. *Calm, steady, in control,* she told herself. She was going to marry Jay, and they would create beautiful, bright, socially committed children. She was going to make senior partner at Niles, Tweed and Sternham, successfully juggling family, career and a husband in the Senate. Everything was all set—all perfect—all normal and safe and perfectly placid.

But not if larger-than-life, reckless, irresponsible, golden-boy Tripp, the center of her life and the focal point of her dreamiest fantasies since the impressionable age of eighteen, decided to come careening back into her life, disrupting everything one more time.

A note of panic threaded her voice. "Tell me it wasn't Tripp. Not today."

"Oh, yes, that's exactly who it was." Marie peered down at the pink slips. "Seven messages. All from this Tripp person, all within the last two hours. And Tripp is a really stupid name for a grown man, if you ask me."

"It's a family name," Bridget said stiffly. "Thomas Michael Trippett Ashby. The third."

"Well, la-de-da. So who is he? A friend of yours? An old boyfriend, maybe, hmm?"

"No, no, not at all," she said quickly. She had to get Tripp and "boyfriend" out of the same sentence immediately. "He's a friend from college. We keep in touch every so often. But he's never been what you might call consistent about that sort of thing."

Or consistent about anything, for that matter. Except in the way he created havoc in her life.

Yesterday, when she had finally decided to marry Jay and set sail for the future, she had made a vow—she would no longer spare so much as a corner of her life for this ridiculous attachment to Tripp Ashby, who was too good-looking and too careless and too...everything for his own good.

Bridget sat down abruptly, taking the nearest chair without even looking. Her mind was far, far away from the stuffy offices of Niles, Tweed and Sternham.

Tripp. Always Tripp.

When she'd first met him, back at small, private, tree-lined Beckett College in upstate New York, she'd hated him on sight. Him and his friends. Every one of the self-styled Studs was a hunk and a half, and Bridget Emerick had no time for that sort of vain, spoiled college creep.

She had goals, ambition—the steely-eyed determination to be somebody, to go places, to make a difference in the world.

She was, by choice, totally immersed in her studies, so smart and so unhip they called her Egghead Emerick, and Tripp was definitely not the kind of guy she imagined herself hanging around with. He had his pick of cheerleaders and sorority babes, and every time she saw him, he had a different one on his arm. Stud, indeed.

But then she was assigned as his tutor. The money she could earn was more important than her scruples at that moment in time, so she took the assignment. Grumbling, feeling very superior, she'd arrived with the complete works of Shakespeare in hand, ready to be smug and unpleasant and disdainful of Tripp Ashby, boy jock.

But the more she found out about Tripp, regardless of her lofty principles about her place in the world, the more of a mystery and a fascination he became. And the deeper she fell.

She was young and foolish. He was gorgeous. And even more than his looks, she found herself absolutely mesmerized by the air of dark, wounded vulnerability that clung to him. To an impressionable English major, Tripp Ashby seemed like Heathcliff, Hamlet and Lord Byron, all rolled into one.

Mostly she loved trying to figure him out.

He was very intelligent, yet he did poorly in his classes, too bored or too negligent to apply himself. He never had more than a few quarters in his pockets, and he was at Beckett on an athletic scholarship, yet he had closets full of cashmere sweaters and expensive tweed jackets that he never wore, all sent by his mother. He hated making a spectacle of himself in public, yet he starred on the basketball and track teams. He had a wickedly funny sense of humor, yet he kept his mouth shut around all but his closest friends.

Tripp was always dancing on the edge of trouble, and Bridget was always pulling him away from the cliff just in the nick of time.

Heathcliff. Hamlet. Lord Byron.

Well, no more. She squared her shoulders. *That was then, and this is now.* As of yesterday, she was operating under new rules. And those rules forbade any contact with Tripp Ashby.

She snatched up the pink phone slips and marched back toward the privacy of her own office, ready to throw out the messages and forget he'd ever called.

But then the phone on Marie's desk began to ring.

As the secretary sprinted over to get it, making a big show of how fast she was moving, she muttered, "I'll bet that's him again. Well, at least this time you can talk to him yourself."

"No!" It sounded a little too loud, a little too panicked, even to her own ears. Faced with a phone that might have Tripp on the other end, her knees went weak, her heart pounded, she felt faint....

This was exactly what she was trying to avoid.

"Tell him I'm in a meeting, or in conference or indisposed. Tell him I'm really, really busy and I can't call him back. Tell him anything," she said in a rush. "But don't, on pain of death, *do not* ring him through!"

As she scrambled toward her office, she heard Marie say, "Ms. Emerick is in conference. May I take a message?"

She paused. Maybe it wasn't him.

"I can hardly hear you," Marie complained in her usual put-upon tone. "Could you speak up please? What was your name again? Could you spell that for me?" She shot Bridget a meaningful glance. "*T-r-i-p-p.* Yes, I've got it."

Bridget jumped into her office and slammed the door shut, flattening herself against the back of it.

She knew she was behaving in a completely irrational manner, and she didn't care. Batten down the hatches—bar the doors—she was willing to do whatever it took to keep away from Tripp.

WHY HADN'T SHE CALLED him back? He depended on her. He needed her. It wasn't like his pal Bridgie to leave him hanging out to dry like this. It wasn't like Bridgie at all.

Wasn't she the no-nonsense queen of personal responsibility? She shouldered her burdens, she met her deadlines and she always returned phone calls. Until today.

Meanwhile, his plucky secretary, Rosa, who was going to get a major raise as soon as he could afford it, managed to convince the police and Marv Monroe to leave, and to take several of the women with them. Then she told the holdouts that Tripp had sneaked out the back door. Although there *was* no back exit, they all went flying out to find him, and Rosa locked the door behind them.

Finally, calm was restored to Touch the Sky.

And Bridget still hadn't returned his calls. "If I didn't know better," he mused, "I'd think she was trying to avoid me."

But just then Rosa shouted, "All clear."

"You're sure they're not lying in wait outside the door?"

"I'm sure. I saw the last one roar off in her Range Rover. But I'm warning you, Tripp, if any of them come back tomorrow, I'm not fooling with them. I'm outta here."

"Take the day off tomorrow, just in case. Right now, *I'm* outta here."

He really shouldn't be celebrating, since he'd lost in all the brouhaha both a potential client and what he'd hoped would be a very big sale. But he still felt triumphant, just to get rid of all those crazy women.

Without wasting any time, he hightailed it out to his car, ready to race home where he could hide out in relative comfort.

But he'd no sooner turned out of the parking lot than he heard a suspicious rustling in the back seat. Unwilling to take his eyes off the road for more than a second in the usual crush of heavy traffic and crazy drivers, he hazarded a quick glance back there.

"Oops," a slinky young thing said in a husky voice. "I guess I'm busted."

Tossing aside a blanket, she sat up all the way and scooted up right behind him. The twenty-something brunette, who wore enough makeup to do a TV soap proud, dangled herself over the seat and began to play with his hair.

"Do I know you?" he demanded, batting her hands away. Déjà vu all over again. Hadn't he spent the better part of the day asking strange women who they were?

"Oh, you naughty boy! I know you remember me. From the club. You were playing tennis," she drawled, sidling herself in closer, breathing right in his ear, "and I was drooling all over your little white shorts."

He groaned, remembering. What was her name? Something with an F. Felicity or Francesca or Fifi or something. She'd kept making lousy jokes about the kind of love match they could play, and how much she admired his "strokes." At the time, he'd just figured she was very young and very bored, and he hadn't taken any of the crude remarks seriously.

But it was a different matter when he was whizzing along a major highway at fifty miles an hour, trying to drive and get her tongue out of his ear at the same time.

"Stop that!" he ordered.

But she paid no attention. As she took it into her head to get even closer, clambering over into the front seat, a speeding minivan careened by, honking all the way. Trying to avoid a collision, Tripp swerved sharply to the right, dumping Fifi and her minuscule jeans into the steering wheel, and almost sending all of them up over the curb and through the front window of a Chicago Red Hots franchise.

"Find a seat and stay in it," he growled, skewering her with the nastiest look in his repertoire. He'd been brought up on the doctrine that an Ashby was polite and charming, no matter the circumstances, but today his manners were definitely fraying around the edges.

"Oh, come on—" she started, already scooting over his way.

"Just sit there and shut up." Tripp held her off with one hand while he drove with the other.

He took the first turnoff, into the parking lot of a small strip mall, the kind that lined every highway and byway in suburbia. This one boasted a variety of outlet stores.

He pulled the car to a stop. "Look, I don't know what you thought you were doing, stowing away in my car..." She started to speak but he held up a hand, cutting her off. "But I can make a pretty good guess. Did you happen to talk to my mother yesterday?"

"Well, yes, I did. When she told me how you're always talking about me—"

"Talking about you? I don't even know your name!"

"Oh, sure," she said with a giggle. "There's no point in trying to hide it anymore, Tripp. Your mother told me all about this major torch you've been carrying for me." Pursing her lips into a kiss shape, she reached over to pinch his cheek. "Once I knew about it, I had to do something. You are so cute, and I am such a romantic. So here I am, Tripp. Take me—I'm yours!"

"Oh my God," he muttered. How did he tell her he had no intention of taking her anywhere but home? As kindly as he could, he said, "I appreciate the interest, but I have to tell you—my mother is wrong. As a matter of fact, I think my mother is out of her mind."

But the woman in his passenger seat just smiled. "I don't believe you."

"I don't even know your name," he protested.

"Of course you do."

"Look, where do you live? I'll drive you home."

Her smile grew more smug. "Not telling."

"Don't play games with me," he said darkly. "I'm not in the mood."

"Not telling."

There were little flares of anger sparking in his brain. Tripp Ashby never lost his temper, but he was perilously close at the moment. He had had a truly awful day, and it was barely noon.

"You won't tell me?" he tried again, and she shook her head stubbornly. "Okay." He leaned over her and shoved open her door. "Then you can get out here."

"Get out? Are you kidding?"

"I've never been more serious in my life."

Her mouth hung open. "You—you're *dumping* me?" she sputtered. "Here? This is a *discount* mall! What if I see someone I know?"

"I don't know. I don't really care. I just want you out of my car."

"No way," she said, crossing her arms over her chest and hunkering down in her seat.

"Come on. Game's over. You can run right into one of these places and call for daddy's limo." He gave her a thin smile. "Or better yet, you can call my mother and tell *her* to come and pick you up."

"This is outrageous!" she stormed.

He figured he could last as long as she could. Finally, after several long moments of glares and curses, she got out.

And Tripp was free. For the time being. But who knew what the next stunt was going to be?

Quickly, under a good head of steam, he used his car phone and dialed his mother at home in Ashbyville. Arguing with Kitty Belle was about as satisfying as going one-on-one with a will-o'- the-wisp, but enough was enough. Time to get some satisfaction from his mother.

"Ashby residence," the butler droned.

"Get me my mother," Tripp said tersely, steering with one hand as he held the telephone with the other.

"I'm sorry, sir, but your mother is not in at present."

"When do you expect her back?"

"I'm not precisely sure, sir. She's gone out of town."

Tripp set his jaw. Leave it to Kitty Belle to set him up and then take a powder. "Where is she?"

"I believe she went to Minnesota, sir. Rochester, Minnesota."

Rochester, Minnesota? Who in the world did Kitty Belle know there? Palm Springs or Lake Geneva, he might've expected, but Minnesota? This was a new wrinkle. "Have her call me as soon as she gets back, all right?"

"Yes, sir," the butler said, politely dropping the receiver.

Damn it anyway. Now what was he going to do?

He had been planning on heading home, but the idea of some other crazy young woman—singing in his shower or camped out in his kitchen or playing hide-and-seek in his closet—dissuaded him. Where to?

Deciding suddenly, he took a sharp right turn and got off the highway, headed for the tollway into the city. He headed for Bridgie.

BRIDGET PUT ASIDE the paperwork for a contract offer she was working on, leaning back in her big leather chair. She filled her mind with all those lovely zeroes in the settlement offer, trying to recapture the joy she'd felt in the meeting with her client and the opposition lawyers. *Ahhh, yes.* She smiled to herself, repeating a simple mantra.

Calm. Collected. In control.

But then the door to her office crashed open. She looked up, and her heart stopped.

"What are you doing here?" she cried, popping back up so fast, she almost fell out of her chair.

Didn't he know he was supposed to go away gracefully when his phone calls went unanswered?

Oh, God. He looked like a warrior. He looked wonderful. It was as if Zeus had just stepped down off Mount Olympus and shown up on her doorstep.

Conflicting emotions—a little joy, a little fear, the overwhelming need to smooth his perfect hair away from his perfect face—swept through her.

But then the righteous indignation hit. *Damn you, Tripp Ashby. How dare you do this to me again?* He was a ridiculous childhood crush, and he had no place in a mature woman's life.

"I tried to stop him," Marie said smartly, wedging herself around him and into the doorway.

But Tripp ignored the intrusion. Speaking directly to Bridget, he announced angrily, "You wouldn't answer my calls. I knew you weren't in a meeting this long. I knew you were lying to me.'' He slammed a hand down on her desk, with a sharp crack that made her jump in her seat. ''Everyone else is acting crazy today—certifiable. And now you, too. Don't do this to me, Bridgie!''

She closed her eyes, pretending she hadn't heard. That nickname. It was so familiar, so friendly, so cute. She hated it. He was the only one who ever called her that, and she couldn't bear to hear it.

Of course, she'd never heard it spoken in quite that way, in that tight-lipped, seethingly furious tone. But then, she couldn't recall ever seeing Tripp mad before.

She thought she'd seen him—and memorized him—just about every way he came, from the champion athlete, glorious and beautiful as he smiled through his sweat, to the cynical student, giving her a lifted eyebrow or a sardonic glance to puncture the pretensions of higher education.

She'd seen him in his skimpy track uniform, in jeans and a sweatshirt, in his graduation cap and gown. She'd even seen him in a suit and tie, like he was wearing today.

But she'd never seen Tripp in a real, fit-to-be-tied, mad-as-a-wet-hen, full-blown, passionate rage. Not directed at her, anyway.

''Well?'' he snarled. He stuffed a fist into his jacket pocket, ruining the line of his suit. ''What's going on, Bridgie? What's wrong with you?''

His tall frame and broad shoulders seemed to overwhelm the small space of her office. His body vibrated with power just barely held in check, and his blue eyes were so dark and so angry, she flinched under his gaze. The Tripp she knew was easygoing, laid-back, cool as a cucumber. And his handsome, aristocratic features never, ever looked as fierce as this.

"You've never been to my office before," she said lamely. It was all she could think of.

"What's wrong with you?" he asked again, leaning in on her over the desk.

"Wrong? Why would anything be wrong?"

"I've been calling you all day. I've left ten or twelve messages."

"Eleven," Marie piped up helpfully.

Tripp retreated long enough to neatly close the office door in Marie's face, and then he turned back to Bridget. "So why didn't you return my calls?"

Bridget stood up, bracing herself on her desk, trying to muster up some dignity in the face of this onslaught. She was still about a foot shorter than Tripp, so it didn't balance the relative inequity of their positions, but it somehow made her feel a little better to be up on her feet.

She retreated to competent attorney mode. "I work here," she said crisply. "They pay me to *work*, not to return personal phone calls."

"Eleven messages," he fumed.

"I was busy!" she fumed right back.

"You couldn't possibly be that busy!"

"Yes," she said, "I was."

"Bridgie! I'm in the middle of an emergency." Leaning in on her from the other side of the desk, so close she could feel the warm puffs of his breath on the tip of her nose, he looked deep into her eyes, giving her a puzzled, searching gaze. "You're my last hope, and you won't talk to me. This is so unlike you."

"Oh, please!" She spun on her heel and marched out from behind the desk, turning her back on him, pretending to look out at the view. There was no view, but she didn't care. "As if you would know what I'm like or unlike," she said under her breath.

"I heard that." He sounded wounded. "Of course I know. I've known you for fifteen years."

"Sixteen," she corrected automatically. At thirty-four, she'd known Tripp just shy of half her life. God. Was she already thirty-four? How had that happened? She was supposed to be so much farther along her life plan by now, but somehow, things had just slipped away....

Well, no more.

"Okay, sixteen. But all of a sudden, you think I don't know you? What is this all about? Bridgie, I am a desperate man. My life is a disaster. I don't have time for this. Will you please tell me what's going on with you so we can get past it and get on to the real problem?"

His life was a disaster. She felt like a creep and an ingrate. She felt like the worst sort of traitor. But enough was enough!

"Maybe I just don't have time for this anymore," she tried. "Maybe I'm tired of running around looking out for you when I have better things to do."

Tripp just stood there for a long pause, not saying anything, and she was dying to turn around and look at him. But she knew that's exactly what he wanted, and she absolutely refused to give in and do things his way. She had some gumption, after all.

She wasn't going to look at him. She didn't want to look at him. If she looked at him, she'd weaken. If she looked at him, if she let herself drink in that straight, classic nose and that clean, beautiful jawline, those dreamy blue eyes and...

Oh, hell. This was far worse than just looking.

Steeling herself, she spun around. Yes, he was still there. Yes, he was still Tripp.

Still trouble with a capital *T.*

Chapter Three

Stiffly she asked, "Well?"

"Well, what?"

"Why aren't you saying anything?"

"Maybe because I'm stunned," he said, in a tone so bleak and so hurt, it was like a knife in her heart.

The man was really very good at this. Manipulative should've been his middle name.

"Don't think I'm buying this," she told him.

"Buying what? I'm not selling anything, Bridgie."

"Don't call me Bridgie," she muttered. "It makes me feel about five years old."

One side of his mouth lifted in a mocking smile. "I'll bet you were cute when you were five."

"Oh, Tripp..."

He was getting to her, just like he always did. What kind of a creampuff was she? *Calm, collected, in control,* she told herself. She looked him straight in the eye. A mistake. Tripp had the most beautiful blue eyes this side of Mel Gibson. She looked away.

"So what's the scoop, Bridget?" he asked, drawing out her name to make the point that he was deferring to her wishes. "Why are you mad at me?"

"I'm not mad at you," she returned. "But I told you—I'm very busy right now. I don't have time to fool with you. Not today. And not within the next year and a half."

He raised an eyebrow.

"It's true," she protested. "In case you didn't know, I am extremely busy here. My billable hours are number one in the firm. And besides that, I've taken on a new project. A political project. And it's going to keep me tied up for a long time."

"Congratulations," he said with a small smile.

"Thank you." Stiffly, twisting her new diamond ring around on her finger, she added, "Because, you see, I got engaged yesterday."

That got his attention. "Who to?" he demanded. "Not that Philpott guy? Is that what you meant by a political project? He's running for something, right? Aw, Bridgie, tell me you didn't."

She refused to pay attention. So what if Tripp didn't like Jay? Who cared what Tripp thought? He didn't run her life, or choose her fiancés. He was nothing to her— nothing. And the sooner she got that across to both of them, the better off they'd be.

"Yes, as a matter of fact, I did." She held her chin high. "Jay loves me very much. We're going to get married and accomplish great things together. I have it all planned."

Tripp's steady, devastating gaze held her. "Good luck," he said finally.

"Thank you. But I'm not going to need it."

"Uh-huh." He set his jaw, still watching her, still giving her the once-over, as if he were trying to see inside her head, right into the workings of her brain. "And so this new engagement, that's what made you decide all of a sudden that you don't have time for me?''

"Well, yes." Somehow the ring on her finger felt huge and clumsy, as if it were weighing down her whole hand. She stuck both hands behind her and stood up straighter. "Surely you can understand that with all this going on in my life, it's just not appropriate for us to...for me to...for us to go on with the way things have always been between us."

There was a pause. "You know, you've really changed," he said finally. His eyes narrowed. "I can't quite figure out what it is."

She didn't appreciate him staring at her like that. It was unnerving. "I, uh, got my hair cut," she said quietly. She ruffled the blunt edges of her short, dark bob. "That must be it."

"No, it's not your hair." His eyes were pensive and very blue as he considered her. "It's cute, though. But it's not your hair. No, there's something else. Like your attitude."

"That's silly." She crossed her arms over her chest and looked away, anywhere but at him while he gave her the once- and twice-over.

"No, it's not silly. I mean, you've always been so serious—"

"So I'm even more serious now, because I've signed on to be a political wife, is that it?" She sighed. "Don't start with me, Tripp. You're always needling me to lighten up. It hasn't worked yet, and it isn't going to work now."

She wondered whether she had become even more serious. Maybe she had. All her ducks were in a row, and all it would take was one more step to be the person she had always wanted to be. Perfect. How dare

Tripp think she needed to lighten up? How dare he look at her like that, as if he'd never seen her before?

"I never noticed how..."

"How what?" she asked quickly. She was sure it wasn't going to be flattering.

But Tripp surprised her. "How beautiful you'd become," he said softly. "I guess I always looked at you and saw the girl I met in college, good old reliable Bridgie. But you've really changed. It seems a pity to waste you on Philpott."

Bridget breathed in cool air. This was truly bizarre. Tripp was treating her like some femme fatale or something.

"Nothing has changed," she said awkwardly. "Except the haircut."

"I guess that must be it, then," he returned lightly. "Pretty cute."

Suspicious of this softer side of Tripp, she asked, "Is this some new tactic to get around me? Because it isn't going to work. I know you too well."

"Tactic? I'm crushed."

"Yeah, well, you're the king of tactics. I ought to know." Hand on hip, she demanded, "How many times have you talked me into taking a day off work to run down to Saks and buy your mother's birthday present because you forgot?"

"Once?" he ventured.

"At least three times. And that doesn't count Christmas gifts or Mother's Day." She gave him a dark look. "Your mother hates me, and I end up picking out all her gifts, all because of you and your tactics."

"She doesn't hate you. She just doesn't like you all that much," he said evasively. "But who cares what

Kitty Belle thinks? And it's not *all* her gifts.'' He smiled, obviously trying to curry favor. "Just most of them.''

"Putting Kitty Belle aside for the moment,'' Bridget continued, "there's also the matter of that horrible pole vaulter person I had to pick up at the airport because you were stuck in Cleveland—''

"He was an Olympic gold medalist! I thought you'd like him.''

"He was a creep!''

"Come on, Bridgie—''

"No, Tripp, I'm serious. I've done your taxes, wired money when you got mugged in Australia, flown to your hospital bedside in Aspen when you were dumb enough to break your leg skiing—and that's just the past few years.''

"And who took away your mousetraps so you didn't have to look at the poor, dead mice? Who shoveled your car out of a snowbank?''

She didn't have to listen. She'd heard it all before. Every time they got together, it was the same litany of who'd done what for whom and who owed favors to whom.

"And,'' he finished up triumphantly, "I cooked dinner for your entire family.''

She hated it when he brought that up. "One little Thanksgiving dinner!''

"It was *not* little. It was twelve people, two turkeys, cranberries, sweet potatoes—the whole thing. It was a lot of work.''

Sheesh. One lousy dinner and he expected her to be indebted forever. Feeling sensitive, she declared, "That was a special favor, Tripp. You knew I didn't know how to cook, and you knew my whole family had somehow invited itself to my house for Thanksgiving, and I was desperate."

"And when you didn't want them to know you weren't cooking your own dinner, didn't I sneak in and out through the kitchen window? I cooked the whole thing, I got no credit and I didn't say a word." He smiled, obviously pleased with himself. "That's what friends are for."

Oh, terrific. Piling on the guilt. "But one dinner doesn't even balance out college."

"Oh, no, she's bringing up college again," he groaned.

She ignored him. "Of course I'm bringing up college. That's when this cycle started! Four years of working my tail off to keep you in school. I drove to— where was it? Philadelphia?—when that bimbo you were dating dumped you under the Liberty Bell. I stayed up all night writing the English paper you didn't have time to, just to keep you in the big game."

"That was team spirit, for good old Beckett College."

"Puh-leez," she scoffed. "I did it to keep you from flunking and ruining your life, and you know it. And what did I ever get out of the deal?"

There was a pause. When she looked up, she saw that his expression had changed. Softly Tripp said, "I don't know. I never did. What did you get out of it, Bridgie?"

Oh, God. His words spun dizzily through her brain. What did she get out of their arrangement? A chance to be close to him, of course. And in the old days, that was enough.

"Bridgie," he went on, in that same slow, sexy voice, "I've known for years that I can never repay you. You kept me in college. You kept me sane. You know that. I do appreciate it, Bridgie."

She took a deep breath. "I know you do," she said quietly. She tried not to be bowled over by the emotional tidal wave that Tripp had always represented in her life, but it was a losing battle.

"If it will make you feel better, I'd be happy to do Thanksgiving dinner again. For you and that feeble Philpott fiancé of yours. Only this time I insist on sticking around and eating some of it."

"Tripp, will you please stop insulting Jay? He's anything but feeble, as you well know," she insisted. "Unlike some people I could mention, Jay is ambitious and committed, and he's determined to change the world for the better."

"Unlike me, is that what you're saying?"

"Well, no, but since you mentioned it..."

"Right. Forgive me," he said sarcastically. "Some of us are just regular folks. It's tough to compete with Saint Jay. What's he up to this week? Inventing a new rocket fuel? Or maybe negotiating world peace in his spare time?"

"That's really unfair! Just because he cares about people, and about the world, you're making fun of him." Bridget was on firm ground here. It really was difficult to criticize Jay, who happened to be a truly noble, selfless person. "As a matter of fact, he's had to scale back some of his work while he campaigns for the primary next March. But he still volunteers at a soup kitchen twice a week, and plants trees in disadvantaged neighborhoods every Saturday."

"He's a real prince all right," Tripp muttered.

"Yes, he is!"

Tripp shook his head. "He's perfect. I admit it. But he doesn't need you. I do."

He moved up behind her, bracketing her shoulders in his hands, leaning in very close. "Bridgie," he whispered in her ear, "I'll do anything you say, anything you can think of. But you have to help me. I'm desperate."

She'd heard that tune before. But he sounded so sincere, so sweet, and she really couldn't resist when he was touching her and breathing on her this way. Closing her eyes, she leaned back against his hard, welcome warmth. "What is it this time?"

"A nightmare." His voice grew grimmer. "My mother has apparently told every debutante from Milwaukee to St. Louis that I'm desperate to get married."

Bridget opened her eyes. Her getting married was one thing, but she had never considered that Tripp might. "Are you?" she asked quickly.

"God, no."

"So why did Kitty Belle tell a bunch of women you were?"

"Hoping one of them would strike a spark, I guess."

"Strike a spark? You mean she's throwing women at you, trying to find a match? Has it worked?"

"Of course not!" Shaking his head, Tripp released her. Hands jammed in his pockets, he turned his back to her. "You know my mother's been hassling me for the past ten years about getting married and carrying on the high-and-mighty family name. I guess she finally got tired of being ignored."

For the first time since he'd mentioned the word *marriage,* Bridget relaxed.

She knew him well enough to know that he always did the exact opposite of whatever his mother wanted. It was a game he and his mother played, a battle of wills, and Tripp had never given in yet.

"So what's the problem?" she asked dryly. "Kitty Belle tries to interfere in your life, and you ignore her. Sounds like business as usual to me."

His brows drew together darkly. "Except for the fact that I'm up to my neck in marriage-crazed women. I can't figure out why they're behaving this way. They act like they're sharks, circling, while I give off the scent of fresh blood."

Poor baby. Couldn't beat them off with a stick. Bridget smiled cynically, glancing down at her watch to indicate she didn't have all day. "Gee, Tripp, that's really rough."

"There was one in my shower when I got up this morning. In my shower!" he said with disgust. "And then there were six or seven more at the office. They were awful, screeching and clawing at me. My secretary threatened to quit, and I lost a client who was more interested in laying odds on who would catch me than buying vaulting poles."

"Who won?"

He turned, confused. "Nobody won."

"Oh, of course. Nobody's caught you. Yet."

"Well, one did stow away in my car. She practically tried to sit in my lap while I was driving. I dumped her at a strip mall in Schaumburg. Let her find her way home from the wilds of suburbia." He ran a hasty hand through his hair as Bridget tried hard not to laugh at his distress. "I don't think you're taking this very seriously, Bridgie. I'm a desperate man."

"Sure you are," she said sweetly.

"Are you going to help me or not?"

"What can I do?" she asked with a laugh. "Call them all up and threaten to break their kneecaps if they don't leave you alone?"

"Do you think that would work?" he asked hopefully.

"No."

But Tripp pulled her hands into his, giving her his most soulful gaze. "You have to think of something to get me out of this mess. They're at my house, in my office, in my car... I have nowhere to go."

"Tripp, I do not see this as a major problem." Bridget yanked her hands away. Even at her weakest moments, she had always steered clear of any involvement in his romantic life, and this certainly qualified. "They can't make you marry them. And if you wait long enough, they'll go away."

"Can't you think of anything to do in the meantime? I'm losing my mind!"

With a decidedly sharp tone, she said, "Well, you could always give in and pick one. Tie the knot. Have some kids. That would make Kitty Belle happy."

He shuddered. "I'm not getting married. And especially not to any of them."

Good, she thought before she could stop herself. She could've smacked her subconscious. What did she care if Tripp married a society bimbo hand-picked by his mother? She was marrying Jay and riding into the sunset, wasn't she?

"Okay, well, I only have one other suggestion." As his expression brightened, she offered, "Call Kitty Belle. Tell her to find a way to get rid of them. After all, it's her fault."

"I tried," Tripp said grimly. "She's skipped town for a while."

"How convenient."

"Short of taking out an ad in the *Tribune* that says I'm not responsible for my mother's insane delusions, there's nothing I can do," he mused.

"An ad. I like that." Bridget smiled with satisfaction. "'Hear ye, hear ye. All those acquainted with Kitty Belle Ashby draw near and pay heed. The aforementioned Mrs. Ashby is a menace and a meddler and should be treated as such. Steer clear, citizens of Chicagoland!'"

Tripp raised one eyebrow. "You've made your feelings on the subject of my mother perfectly clear."

"She," she said plainly, "never liked *me.*"

"She never said that." He took her hand in his and squeezed it gently.

She wished he would stop touching her. It was driving her crazy. And it was making it hard to think. But she could hardly snatch her hand back from that sweet, soothing clasp for the second time in five minutes without looking like an idiot.

Pretend you don't care that his hand is warm and strong. You don't even notice. Calm. In control. Think of calm, controlled things. Think of Jay—your fiancé.

But perfect Jay would never take the hand of a woman who didn't ask him first. And perfect Jay would never make her tremble, either.

"I—I never had anything against Kitty Belle," she said quickly, trying to get her defenses back in order. But it was tough when he was fondling her hand, rubbing his thumb tenderly across the backs of her fingers, sending little sparks of pleasure all the way up her arm.

Concentrating on a mental image of his odious mother helped, however. It also gave her the courage to take her hand back once and for all and hide it in the pocket of her suit jacket.

Bitterly, she declared, "I tried to like her. Really I did. In those days, we were all fighting with our parents. But your mother was the worst. And when she looked down her nose at me, and announced—right to my face—that you shouldn't hang around with trash or it would scare away the quality people, well, that was enough for me."

"That's not what she said," he tried.

But Bridgie was implacable. "Close enough."

"She never used the word *trash*. She wouldn't do that."

"Okay, so she implied it. I knew what she meant."

"Besides, she never liked any of my friends. Steve was blue-collar, Ki was pushy, Deke was a hick . . . And your blood wasn't blue enough to suit her. She wanted me to pal around with Rockefellers and Vanderbilts." He shrugged. "She's nuts. What can I do?"

"Have her committed?" Bridget suggested.

Dryly, Tripp commented, "But I'd still be stuck with the bimbos she left behind."

"Well, that's all the advice I have to offer." She scooted back behind her desk and tried to look businesslike. Seated, she folded her hands neatly, covering her engagement ring with her other hand as she gave him a cool stare. "If I were you, I would pick up this phone right now, and order Kitty Belle in no uncertain terms to call off the dogs and the debutantes. Problem solved."

"That's what you think," he muttered. "Even if I could find her, I'd really be inviting trouble to trust her to fix things. If she agreed to call off the Chicago contingent, and I sat with a gun to her head and made sure

she did it, she'd just expand her search with the next
breath. She's very cagey."

"It's worth a try."

He shook his head again, gazing down at Bridget in
disbelief. "And that's the best you can do?"

"Tripp, I'm not Wonder Woman." Even though that
was always what she'd tried to be—for him. Rather than
hazarding meeting his eyes, she fiddled with a stack of
papers on her desk, pretending to be absorbed in the
fine print. "I'm sorry, but you're on your own this
time."

"Okay. I get the message. You're busy. You're going
to marry a senator. You're too busy for old friends like
me."

His face was cold and hurt as he wheeled and
stomped out of her office.

As soon as the door closed behind him, she sagged
with relief. She couldn't help it. Catastrophe—in the
form of Tripp Ashby and his devastating effect on her
life—had been averted one last time.

"You did it, Bridgie," she told herself. "He's gone."

So why did she feel as if she'd just sold her heart
down the river?

"I LIKE THE GREEN," Jay said thoughtfully. "And it has
good environmental significance, too. Not a bad message to give to our guests."

"I suppose so," she returned, trying to keep the
doubt from her voice. "But, unfortunately, I don't look
good in green. And I do think the color scheme at my
own wedding should be something I look good in."

"But your dress will be white." He crinkled his forehead. "Why does it matter if you look good in green if
you're wearing white anyway? You have to consider the

importance of the statement against the sacrifice you have to make.''

Bridget shot up to her feet, recklessly throwing down the huge notebook of fabric swatches. ''I really do not want my whole wedding to be the color of broccoli, no matter how politically correct it is!''

''Darling, please. Don't upset yourself.'' Jay gave her an encouraging smile. ''If you don't want green, we won't have green. And I'm sure you'll look wonderful no matter what you wear.''

Bridget tried to relax. She knew it must be torture for him, trying to appear interested in all these wedding preparations. As usual, Jay had a million obligations and demands on his time. And she'd offered several times to make all the arrangements herself. Yet he'd chosen to sit here at her dining room table, leafing through bridal magazines, venturing his well-thought-out opinions on everything from his-and-her matchbook covers to the style of her wedding veil. Infinite patience, exquisite taste. Jay was as thoughtful about empire waists and beaded headpieces as he was about economic sanctions in the Balkans. He took it all very seriously. So why was he driving her crazy?

''And we have to be very careful about the menu and the flowers, as well as the dishes and the linens. No paper products unless they're recyclable. And ask Lawrence to give you the list of boycotted products from countries with human rights violations. I know Iranian caviar is on it,'' he said calmly, looking down at a list.

''Iranian caviar. Okay.'' Life was extremely complicated when you were required to be environmentally, socially and economically aware at all times.

If only Jay weren't so perfect, maybe she could relax a little, too. But she was always afraid of making some major faux pas. Would it ruin his reputation if anyone found out his wife-to-be had an alligator handbag, when alligators were endangered?

"What do you think, darling?" he asked, handing her a list of possible sites for their reception. She recognized the handwriting. His campaign manager had come up with the list of choices for *her* wedding. She glanced down at them. All very grand. All very large. And not at all what she'd had in mind.

"Lawrence says we need to get this squared away ASAP," Jay interjected.

"But the wedding's not till a year from June! Surely we have some time—"

"Yes, dear, of course." Jay patted her hand. "But we have such a large guest list that we have to plan ahead. Lawrence thinks we need to have a place, signed and sealed, right away."

"Such a large guest list?" Bridget echoed. "I thought last time we talked, we were thinking around a hundred people."

"Sorry, sweetheart. I guess I neglected to update you." His smile was fond, but firm. "I've come to realize that this will be a terrific chance to say thank-you to a lot of big contributors. The timing is such that there would be a lot of noses out of joint if I didn't invite my major campaign supporters. You see that, don't you, sweetheart?"

Bridget chewed her lip. "How many people are we talking about?"

"No more than two thousand."

"Two thousand?" She felt her jaw drop. "We're jumping from one hundred to two *thousand?*"

"No, darling, be reasonable," Jay said in an even, unhurried tone. "This has become more than just our wedding. It's as if it were a celebration for all the little people who are working so hard." He nodded. "I know it's hard not to be selfish, when it comes to something like our wedding. But you have to remember, a big part of both of us belongs to our constituency now."

"I can hardly forget," she said slowly. But what about her dream of a small garden wedding, with family and friends? This was going to be some kind of extravaganza.

"Jay," she tried, "it's not too late to keep this under control. We can still have the kind of wedding we want, and then maybe do some big monster reception later, for all your people. What do you think?"

"I wish I could say yes, darling." He stood up from the table, dropping a quick kiss on her cheek. "But you and I have a responsibility to the people working so hard to get me elected."

"But this is my wedding," she protested.

"It will be beautiful and you will be beautiful." His teeth flashed white and even in a bright grin, the one that looked so good on the six o'clock news. "Trust me, darling. It will be wonderful."

"But—"

"Look, it's getting late," he told her. "I hate to go, but I've got a bunch of paperwork waiting for me." He took her arm, leading her toward the front door, where he winked at her. "I'd love to stay, but with my luck, there'd be a hundred reporters waiting to snap my picture sneaking out of your apartment at the wee hours."

"Can't look bad for the voters," she said. She tried for a playful tone, but it came out a little harsher than she'd intended.

"Sorry, darling. I know you're disappointed." He gave her a comforting squeeze. "But right now, the voters have to come first. I have to get elected before I can make waves.''

''I know.''

''Love you. Don't forget to pick a site off that list, will you? Just call Lawrence and tell him which one you want.'' And after a quick kiss good-night, Jay was on his way, back to his paperwork and his campaign manager, back to saving the world.

Alone at last. She massaged her temples, trying to stave off a headache.

But tonight, with Jay, had been really awful—she felt guilty that she didn't want green bridesmaid dresses, she felt guilty that she didn't know about Iranian caviar, she felt guilty that she didn't want to share her wedding with two thousand people she didn't know, and she felt guilty keeping him away from his real work.

Jay was so good and kind and selfless . . . sometimes it was really irritating. Sometimes she just wanted him to eat a greasy cheeseburger pumped full of preservatives and carelessly throw the foam container on the ground.

''Oh, God, Bridget,'' she moaned out loud as she fell into bed. ''Are you really going to be able to pull this off?''

If she was this cranky after just one evening, if she couldn't even commit to environmentally aware bridesmaid dresses without getting fussy, how could she possibly marry Jay?

She wondered idly if any local convent needed a new nun.

But then she regained her composure, sat up, smoothed the quilt over her lap and tried to be rational about this. ''So you had a bad night. You lapsed. It won't always be like that. Jay is a good person, and he loves you, and he will understand if you're not always as strong as he is. Once he's elected, things will relax, and he won't even notice that you don't always remember to recycle your pop cans.''

The effect of her calm words lasted about ten seconds. "I want out," she wailed, ducking down under the covers. "I'm a coward and a wastrel and an abuser of fluorocarbons—and I don't think I'm strong enough to get married."

Not to Jay Philpott, anyway.

And then the phone rang. It was muffled by the blankets over her head, but it was definitely the phone.

"If that's Jay, asking me if he can add a thousand more people to the list, the engagement is off," she muttered, thrusting a hand out from under the bedclothes to feel for the phone. "*Finito*, expunged, over and done with, dead as a doornail."

"Hi, Bridgie," a deep, sweet voice murmured in her ear. "Did I wake you?"

Her heart leapt to her throat. Hope blazed inside her.

"Tripp," she whispered.

She was feeling very vulnerable, and the sound of his wonderful voice in her ear tipped her right over the edge into surrender.

Tripp—her savior! He would send Jay and his lofty ideals packing, and then he would sweep her up in his arms, telling her that he loved her, that he had always loved her. He would carry her down the hall to this very bed, where they would make mad, passionate love amid the tumbled quilts, and their hearts would beat as one. And then her life would be perfect. . . .

Except, of course, that that was never going to happen. He might be willing to thrash Jay, just on principle, but the sweeping business was a pipe dream.

Nonetheless, she pulled the phone under the covers with her, cradling Tripp against her shoulder and snuggling back into the bed.

"It's good to talk to you," he said in his sweetest, most sincere tones, and she melted a little bit more.

"You, too," she told him. "I've missed you."

"Oh, Bridgie, I'm so glad to hear you say that. Listen, I'm sorry about the other day, in your office." His voice dropped, taking on a huskier edge. She sighed and sank down into her soft bed, enjoying the feel of his voice ruffling her nerve endings. "I would never hurt you for the world, Bridgie. You know that, don't you? I don't want to lose your friendship. It means everything to me."

"Oh, Tripp..."

"Still pals?"

"Still pals," she whispered. How could she hold out? He'd called just when she needed him most. "Where are you? You sound really far away."

"I'm in Tahoe, at the cabin."

"The Studs cabin?"

Her cozy dreams began to curl up around the edges. That damn cabin. Every year for as long as she'd known him, he'd trekked to that cabin to drink beer and carouse with his low-life, studly friends. And if that wasn't insulting enough, he had never, not even once, invited her to the stupid place. Boys only. Off-limits.

So what was this, a drunken prank or something, in the middle of an all-night party? Although the connection was very bad, she thought she could hear music in the background. For a second or two, it boomed very loud, and then it died out completely.

"So," she said frostily, "what are you doing at the cabin? I thought the Studs' annual rendezvous was in the summer. Don't tell me you called a special meeting? Just couldn't wait till next year to toss back a few brewskis with the boys?''

"I'm here alone. Refuge." His voice crackled over the line, and she had to hold very still to make out the words. "Refuge from the bimbo brigade. It was the only place I could think of where they couldn't follow. Bridgie, can you come here right away? I need you."

Her heart twisted. She'd always wanted him to ask her to the cabin. For a long time, she had been insanely curious about just what it was like, and why they returned so faithfully, year after year.

But why was he asking now, after so much time had passed? "Tripp, you've never invited me up there. I thought it was a boys' club kind of thing."

"I know. But I need you now. Only you. You won't let me down, will you, Bridgie?"

She sat up and pushed the quilts aside. "What's wrong, Tripp? You sound terrible."

"I am terrible. Will you come? I'm begging, Bridgie. No questions asked . . . for old times' sake."

"I don't know. I don't think I can. What is it? What's wrong?"

But as she pressed closer to the receiver, anxious to get his answer, all she heard was a series of high-pitched, outrageously stupid giggles. And then the line went dead.

She just sat there, looking down at the phone. What was this all about?

From his tone, she would've thought he was in mortal danger. Mortal danger from a giggling bimbo? Had one of them tied him up to torture him?

Replaying their conversation over one more time, Bridget made up her mind. This might be her last Tripp Ashby rescue mission, but she was going to go for it.

She had precious little time left in which to act silly and irresponsible, to go gallivanting off tilting at windmills. Soon enough, she'd be the staid, respectable wife of a senator, whose wildest activity was pouring tea for Girl Scouts.

So she was going to Lake Tahoe. Going after Tripp.

At last she'd get to see the lair of the Studs, that off-limits den of iniquity. And she would pry that anonymous, giggling no-brain off Tripp while she was at it.

Chapter Four

"Plane to Reno, rental car to Tahoe," she repeated to herself, poking into her pocket to make sure she had the reservation slip for the car and the directions to the cabin. When she traveled, Bridget was in the habit of checking her travel documents every five minutes whether she needed to or not.

After satisfying herself that it was where it was supposed to be, she refolded the all-important sheet of paper with the directions on it and slipped it safely into the outside pocket of her briefcase.

That document was precious. Without a phone number for the cabin, she hadn't been able to call Tripp back to find out how to get to him. Information provided a number, but when she dialed it, the recorded message told her it was no longer in service.

No longer in service? She began to worry. Maybe something dire really had happened to Tripp. She remembered the maniacal giggling just before the phone cut out, and she made a reservation on the next flight.

But she didn't have any idea where she was going, and that was going to make a rescue difficult. Finally she gave up and called one of the other Studs. She figured Steve Chambliss, the most settled of the four, would hassle her the least, and she'd been right. Steve had been curious, but otherwise perfectly willing to come across with the info she needed.

She had the niggling suspicion that maybe the Studs cabin wasn't such a big-deal secret after all.

Winging her way west from Chicago, over scenery that had grown increasingly beautiful the farther they flew, Bridget buried her nose in the Nevada guidebook she'd picked up on her way out of the airport.

Under the general heading of Lake Tahoe, she skimmed through information on the Donner Party, the 1960 Winter Olympics, a casino where the dealers wore togas, and last but not least, the Cupid's Arrow Chapel of Perpetual Motion, where you could get a ski-by or jog-by wedding, depending on the season, all on the spur of the moment. Not only that, but they had an Elvis impersonator on staff to perform the ceremony!

"This is some place I'm going to," she murmured. "The Donner Party and Elvis weddings, all in one state. At least all those quickie wedding chapels will be handy if Tripp takes a liking to one of the bimbo brides."

"What did you say, dear?" asked the sweet little old lady next to her, who was clutching a copy of *Reno Rules: Winning Strategies for Serious Gamblers*.

"Nothing," she said weakly. She was only now aware that she was entering a different world.

Meanwhile, she knew the average rainfall and temperatures for most of Nevada, she knew what highways to take from the Reno airport to Tripp's remote cabin on the shores of Lake Tahoe, and she knew where to find a cash machine or a wax museum if she should need one. But she had no idea what she was going to do once she got to Tripp's place. None.

Somehow, she had expected a plan to come to her. No such luck.

"Fasten your seat belts," the pilot announced, and Bridget dug in for the landing.

And then she was caught up in the bustle of finding her luggage and dragging it out to her rental car, or more precisely, rent-a-rugged-little-thing-with-a-ski-rack-on-the-top. It was apparently what people drove when they went skiing.

Bridget was the first to admit she knew very little about such things. Even though she was on her way to Ski Land U.S.A., she had no parka, no boots and definitely no skis. If she couldn't get by inside, she wasn't going to do it.

"I can't think of a more idiotic sport than skiing," she muttered, as she fumbled with the map with one hand and drove with the other, navigating the winding road heading south out of Reno.

Skiing was exactly the sort of daredevil stunt Tripp had always loved. A naturally gifted athlete, he thought hurtling down mountains at the speed of light was great fun. And he'd had the broken limbs to prove it.

Bridget had tagged along on a ski trip exactly once, on a college-sponsored outing to Vermont. While Tripp learned to balance his moguls and his ski bunnies, Bridget spent all her time holed up in the chalet, doing a slow burn over her hot chocolate.

"That was probably the first time I swore never to speak to him again," she reflected. It certainly hadn't been the last.

But she couldn't stay grumpy, not when all around her the scenery was so spectacular. Snowcapped, craggy peaks, impossibly tall pine trees, clear blue skies... It was truly beautiful.

No wonder the Stud boys had looked forward to escaping here. Calm and serenity, the two things she found herself struggling to achieve, seemed to come with the territory.

Although there was a bit of a chill in the crisp autumn air, the sun was beaming brightly, and Bridget rolled down the window of her bouncy little vehicle to better commune with nature. It wasn't long before she eased over a hill and into view of Lake Tahoe itself. Crystal blue water, stretching off to forever, lay in a huge, flat bowl carved out of the mountains.

But there was no time to gape at the scenery. Following the rather cryptic directions she'd pried out of Steve, Bridget headed for the turnoff onto the tiny, private road that led to the cabin. She went past it the first time, threw the car into reverse and backed up on the highway for about a mile, and finally wheeled in.

"Oh, well," she said under her breath. "There was nobody coming."

The private road to the cabin was lined with deep ruts, and she was glad her rugged-little-thing came equipped with four-wheel drive. At first she thought she must have made another mistake. This couldn't be leading anywhere, could it? But after climbing up and winding around through trees thick enough to count as a forest, she finally came to a clearing.

And there it was—the mysterious Studs cabin.

It was a simple A-frame, two stories tall, made of weathered wood that glowed golden in the afternoon sun. A snow-dusted evergreen stood sentry on one corner, and a small wooden sign with the name Ashby etched into it told her she was definitely at the right place.

It looked perfectly normal, like any cabin on a mountain. It was also very quiet.

No wild parties. No giggling girls hanging out the windows. No beer bottles strewn around the grounds. Not even one dumb blonde running out the front door in her underwear. In fact, it looked very little like the Animal House of her imagination.

Gazing at it over her steering wheel, Bridget approached cautiously, trying not to spin any dirt or make any noise. Two cars—both jaunty red, both four-wheel drive, exactly like her own rental car—sat parked near the house. One for Tripp, and one for the *bimbo du jour.* The odd thing was that the hoods were up, and there were wrenches and tools scattered on the ground, as if both cars were in a state of disrepair.

She could've just barged right in, but she still wasn't exactly sure what she was getting into. If Tripp was in there fighting off the advances of an amorous woman, she really didn't want to see it. If, on the other hand, Tripp were in there succumbing to the advances of an amorous woman, she felt it was her moral duty to break it up.

So what should she do? Knock on the door? Start a fire? Call the police?

Tempting, but also temporary solutions. She had to think of something better, something more permanent, to get Tripp out of harm's way.

Bridget pulled her little red vehicle off the road, squeezing between two fir trees, killing the motor only when she knew she was out of sight. And then she pulled out her suitcase and her briefcase, and crept carefully toward the front of the cabin.

There were wide windows across the front, but the drapes were drawn. After dropping her luggage off to one side, Bridget tiptoed closer to the windows. At the far end, she could see that the window had been cranked open from the inside, and the curtains were blowing inward. By hunkering down and peering in just above the window ledge, she could get a fairly decent view of the living room of the cabin.

She felt like a Peeping Tom. "It's for a good cause," she reminded herself.

From her awkward position, she could see that it was a big, open room, mostly done in whites and creams, with some exposed beams and a large stone fireplace on the opposite wall. Furniture was minimal—a comfortable sofa in a nubby oatmeal fabric and a couple of cushy chairs—plus a fluffy white bearskin rug lying in front of the fireplace.

"Typical," she muttered. "A bearskin rug for fireside seductions."

The words had no sooner left her mouth than Tripp came charging into the living room, dragging with him a curvy blonde in a tight ski outfit. He had lipstick all over his face. He also had at least a day's growth of tawny brown beard, and a very frantic expression.

Bridget narrowed her eyes.

"You have to leave," he said roughly, as the blonde dug in her heels and clung to his arm.

"But how?" she protested. "The phone's not working, and both cars are out of commission."

Well, wasn't that cozy. *And I bet I know how the phone and the cars went kaput,* Bridget thought unkindly. *Miss Ski Pants knows how to pull wires with carefree abandon.*

"You can walk down to the minimart," Tripp tried. "It's only a mile or so, and I think old Jedidiah has a truck."

"I can't walk that far," the blonde cried, suddenly going limp and collapsing on top of Tripp. They both toppled onto the bearskin rug. "I seem to have sprained my ankle."

"Oh, please," Bridget snapped.

"Did you hear something?" Tripp asked as he tried to get himself out from under the blonde.

"Bears!" she screamed, plastering herself to his chest. "I told you I couldn't go out there. There are bears!"

"Look, I'll walk down to the minimart. I'll get the truck."

"Watch out, Tripp. Your ankle's next," Bridget said under her breath.

"You can't leave me!" the woman wailed.

Bridget had seen enough. She had half a mind to rap loudly on the front door and announce that she would be happy to drive Miss Ski Pants off a cliff somewhere, but she refrained. If the blonde was that good at inventing excuses, a cranky woman at the front door would be small potatoes.

No, she preferred to sneak up on them, from inside the cabin.

Grabbing her stuff, she hightailed it around to the back of the place, which was larger and more spread out than she would've suspected from the front. A long deck ran the length of the second level, and a shorter, wider one, complete with hot tub, spanned the ground floor. Practically the whole back side of the cabin was glass—there were windows everywhere.

Skirting the spa, she headed for the back door. Locked. Charming. Who locked the back door of a mountain cabin in the middle of nowhere?

Next, Bridget tried the nearest window, one that ran along the outside wall fairly low to the ground. Thankfully, it had been left partially open, too, just like the one in front. It seemed Tripp had a taste for fresh air. With Miss Ski Pants breathing down his neck, Bridget didn't blame him.

Once she had the window pushed open, it was easy work to hoist herself over the low sill and into the cabin. "If you can do it to make my Thanksgiving dinner, I can do it to save your skin from being mounted on Miss Ski Pants' trophy wall," she said. And then she glanced around at her surroundings.

A bedroom. Tripp's bedroom, from the looks of it.

Bridget straightened. She swallowed. Tripp's bedroom. The images that conjured up were enough to stop her dead in her tracks.

She recognized the clothes tossed casually on the bed, and she could still smell his distinctive scent, lingering faintly on his shirts and his robe. Her brain fed her an image of Tripp peeling off that shirt, carelessly casting aside that robe, baring his beautiful, bronze skin to her hungry eyes.

And it didn't take much to envision him, half-naked, sleepy, wound up in the creamy white sheets on that old brass bed.

Her breath caught in her throat.

She sat down on the bed, clutching the silky robe, pulling it up to rub the sleeve against her cheek. Tripp's bedroom. How many years had it been since she'd set foot in Tripp's bedroom?

And why did she have the insane desire to just snuggle right in and never leave?

But there was a loud squeal from the other side of the cabin, and she knew she had to shake off all those lascivious, inappropriate feelings. She had to help Tripp, not moon over his clothing.

But at least it furnished an idea. Stripping down to her skivvies, she tousled her hair, shrugged into his robe and threw some of her own clothes around the room. She even left her hairbrush on the dresser, and dangled a slinky nightgown she couldn't believe she'd brought with her across the end of the bed.

And then she took a deep breath and wondered if she really had the guts to pull this off.

"Hell, yes," she said out loud. It was for Tripp, after all. For his own good.

After a quick glance to make sure Tripp's bathrobe was positioned properly, exposing enough of her skin, Bridget sauntered down the hallway toward the living room. She didn't bother to be quiet, but the loud voices from the living room convinced her nobody knew she was coming, anyway.

And when she passed the kitchen, she got an even better idea. With a smile, she grabbed a bottle of already opened wine off the counter, and took a big sip. Fortified. With the bottle in one hand and two glasses in the other, she was ready to make her grand entrance.

"Darling?" she called out, trailing the bottom of his robe behind her as she peeked around the corner into the living room. She gave them a little leg first, and then popped into full view.

Tripp and the blonde both froze.

Miss Ski Pants found her voice first. "Who are you?" she sniffed.

"You mean he didn't tell you?" Bridget asked in her sultriest voice. Up until this exact moment, she hadn't really been aware she had a sultry voice, but she did her best.

"Tell me what?"

"About me, of course." Tripp was still standing there, openmouthed, as Bridget sidled right over and handed him a glass. "I got tired of waiting, darling. I thought you were never coming back to bed."

It was a gamble, of course. There were lots of ways the blonde could figure out that Bridget was lying. But somehow, Bridget didn't think the woman was a rocket scientist.

"Sweetheart," Tripp said, with a sexy little growl in his voice. He held the glass while she poured, and then silently saluted her. He was smiling, and she loved every minute of it. "I've been trying to get rid of her, darling. Believe me, I wanted to get back to you. It was just . . . awkward."

"Yeah, but . . ." Looking utterly confused, Miss Ski Pants flashed her gaze from face to face. "Yeah, but I thought it was all part of the game. Your mother said you liked really aggressive women, that no matter what, I shouldn't take no for an answer."

"His mummy doesn't always know what's best for Tripp, does she?" Bridget whispered. His lazy smile widened.

The blonde sputtered, "She said you might fight it, you know, as part of your little game, but that the surest way to your heart was to hang on and not let go. B-b-but, she didn't say anything about some other woman. She said you had a major crush on *me*. So who is this?"

Only the rigid set to Tripp's jaw clued Bridget in to the tension he was really feeling. He kept staring down at her, doing a very good imitation of being absolutely dazzled by her nearness.

And then he reached down, took away the wine and her glass and set them on a nearby table. Taking her hand in his, he brushed a small, soft kiss right into her palm.

"My robe looks better on you." And his blue eyes flickered over her, licking her with fire.

God, she thought, *this is sweet.* She didn't have to pretend at all. Standing there, basking in the warmth of his gaze, with Tripp treating her as if she were some kind of sex kitten, made her want to purr and sink into his arms.

As she enjoyed these bizarre, amazing feelings, Tripp turned her hand over, and dropped another kiss right under Jay Philpott's horrible engagement ring.

And Bridget's bravado began to falter. She remembered, all of a sudden, that she wasn't a siren or a femme fatale. She was Egghead Emerick, and she would never pull this off. Never.

"Who is this?" the other woman demanded again, stamping her little foot in frustration.

Bridget flushed, more ill at ease and out of place than she'd ever been. Scrambling for an answer, she began, "I—I'm—"

"My wife," Tripp finished. His arm was strong and sure behind her, offering courage. "We're newlyweds. We just got married—"

"At the Cupid's Arrow Chapel of Perpetual Motion," Bridget said dimly. "We skied by."

Tripp's beautiful blue eyes were dancing with mischief as he murmured, "That's right," and drew her closer.

His fingers brushed her hair. His gaze held hers.

And then he bent down and kissed her.

Chapter Five

He had kissed her before, once, on New Year's Eve, with a friendly peck on the cheek, maybe even brushing past her lips. But that was nothing like this.

Nothing like this.

This was hot and hard and demanding, as if they really were newlyweds who couldn't get enough, of each other. Her arms tightened around him, forcing her closer. He slanted his mouth across hers, her lips parting, deepening the kiss, delving into her luscious warmth.

God, it was intoxicating. If he'd had his wits about him, he would've pulled back immediately, let her go, ended this craziness. But the moment his lips touched hers, the second her tongue danced past his, some irresistible impulse took over. As he bent her backward, as she wound her arms around him and pressed herself into his embrace, Tripp forgot about where he was and who she was. He gave himself up to the seductive, powerful feeling of kissing Bridget senseless.

She tasted wonderful. She felt wonderful. Her hair and her skin were soft and smooth under his fingers, and he wanted to touch more of her, to unpeel that slinky, shadowy robe and see what she was hiding. In another minute, he'd push them both down onto the bearskin rug, and there would be nothing between them but a lot of bare skin.

The incredible, overpowering need to make love to her—now—leapt to life from out of nowhere.

But first... First, it was her mouth—her soft, hard, wet, deep, sweet, mysterious, greedy mouth—that drew his attention. Serious, reliable, dull? Ha! Kissing Bridget was like throwing gas on a raging fire.

Without allowing himself to think, he dipped his tongue deeper, and slid his hands down to her hips, urging her closer, fitting her up against him.

She moaned a little, clinging to him, and that sound rippled under his skin, making him feel even more restless and aroused, even more out of control.

"Well, you don't have to slobber all over her in front of me, even if she is your wife!"

The screechy tones penetrated his misguided brain, and he felt Bridget stiffen in his arms.

Good God. He was kissing Bridgie. More than kissing her, he was practically eating her alive, as if she were Little Red Riding Hood and he a grade-A wolf.

What was wrong with him? This was *Bridget.* But it appeared Bridget had changed. And so had his reaction to her.

"Sorry," he murmured. He released her slowly, reluctantly. And then he traced the curve of her cheek with one finger, and gave her a soft half smile. He reminded himself that this was all part of a convenient plan to get rid of a bimbo. Nothing more. He willed his pulse back to a more normal level, and his body to relax and behave itself. He manufactured a superficial smile. "I forget myself when I'm with my wife."

Bridgie stepped back, looking a little dizzy, and she gulped audibly. Those words on his lips were as shocking to her as they were to him.

"I can't believe you're already married," the blonde fumed. "But then why was your mother pushing me so hard to come out here and get you?"

"Well, you see—" Bridget began.

"My mother doesn't know," Tripp said quickly. "We've kept it a secret."

He squeezed her hand, trying to let her know how much he appreciated her rescue attempt, and her willingness to create this ruse in the first place. But the moment his fingers touched hers, electricity arched between them, and he dropped her hand pronto. What the hell was going on?

He knew why he'd kissed her like that—sort of, anyway. It just happened, that was all. But why had she kissed him back? Why had she put her heart and soul into it, scorching him like that?

What a mess. What a way to say thank-you. What a way to screw up his friendship with Bridgie and send her racing back to Chicago.

"A secret? But why?" A lightbulb lit up over the blonde's head. "Wait, I've got it figured out. Mom doesn't approve, right? And she won't come across with the bucks. Everybody in Chicago knows you're coming into major bucks when you get married."

The jumble of words passed him right by; Tripp heard what the woman was saying, but he didn't quite take it in.

"So, you gave up the money for true love, huh?" She made a snorting noise. "What a waste. Let me tell you, you were the hottest prospect on the market. Looks, money, the name—you had the whole package, hon.

But you gave up the cash for love. Wow. What a comedown. And when word gets out you're already taken, there is going to be hell to pay. Wait till I tell Sissy Worthington!"

"Please do," Tripp said quietly, as she gathered up her parka and made a quick run for the door.

"I thought your car was broken," Bridgie called after her, but they heard it roar to life outside the cabin, and then spin away down the road.

And they were alone. He wasn't prepared for this part, for the reckoning.

Oh, God. He'd kissed her. He'd kissed her with such heat and hunger, the memory of it would be branded on his brain forever. Now what were they going to do?

Knowing Bridgie, she'd probably slug him. His only hope of salvaging this for either of them was to make light of the whole thing before she had a chance to kill him.

"Well," Tripp murmured, "you're very good at this undercover stuff, Bridgie. Maybe you have a future as a spy."

"I sincerely doubt it. I've never felt more ridiculous in my life."

His smoky gaze made a leisurely pass up and down her body. "Ridiculous? I don't think so. It's a new look for you, but it's not bad. Not bad at all."

He could read it in her face; she suddenly became very aware that she wasn't wearing a whole lot. As hot color suffused her face and throat, she pulled together the robe, clutching the fabric in clumsy hands.

"I'm really sorry." She cleared her throat awkwardly. "It was the only plan I could come up with."

He could see how uncomfortable she felt, and he went back to the familiar plan: tease it away. If he was joking, they'd both know how to deal with it. "And why are you sorry?" A grin curved his lips. "I enjoyed it. In fact, I thought it was a lot of fun."

"Sure. Loads of laughs." Looking self-conscious, she folded back the cuffs on his robe. And then she seemed to reacquire the moxie she usually had. With one hand on her hip, she lifted her chin and dressed him down. "Pretty sad, Tripp. Making me fly all the way out here just to kick out one grade-D female. So why couldn't you take care of it yourself?"

Now this was a Bridgie he recognized. He shrugged. "I tried everything I could think of. When Nina—the one last night—ripped out my phone, I knew I was in trouble. If these were guys, I could just punch them. But what do you do with women?"

"So who's Nina? I take it she's not the blonde. Thank goodness it was a different person, or my story never would've held water." When he raised an eyebrow, she added, "About being here with you, in bed, I mean."

And then she realized what she'd said, and she blushed prettily, suffusing her cheeks with rosy color. Adorable. Tripp smiled. Absolutely adorable. He wondered if she blushed every time the word *bed* came up. And if she was actually in bed, her soft, supple body curled beneath him, how much of her would take on that rosy hue?

Definitely worth thinking about. His mind was just about to wander even farther into treacherous waters, but he caught himself in the nick of time. What the hell was he doing, thinking Bridgie was adorable? One damn kiss, and all he could think about was jumping her bones. It was disgusting. It was a betrayal of their friendship.

He clamped down hard to stop this nonsense in its tracks.

Meanwhile, Bridgie went on, scrambling through some kind of explanation. "I mean, if Miss Ski Pants had been here overnight, she would've known you weren't sleeping with me."

Sleeping with her. God, he wished she hadn't said that.

What was wrong with him?

Taking a completely different tack, he asked dryly, "Miss Ski Pants, huh?"

"Well, they were awfully tight. It was the most obvious thing about her."

"Uh-huh."

Adorable again. But Bridget wasn't paying attention to his overheated glances. Thank God.

"So what was that about someone ripping out your phone?"

"Nina Sherrard. We were in the same dancing class twenty years ago." He shook his head. He didn't want to think about the bimbos anymore, especially here, where his sanctuary had been invaded. It was galling. "I came here for peace and quiet, a chance to think about what to do about all this, and what happens? I'm not here five minutes before Nina Sherrard and her personal chef arrive, sent by my own mother."

"A chef?" Bridget echoed. "That's a novel approach."

"It was ridiculous. He was out in the kitchen making flaming crepes, and Nina was unpacking china and silverware before I had a chance to say, 'No thank you.'"

Tripp reached for the wineglass he'd set aside earlier, taking a long swallow. After a moment, he said, "I ate the dinner, I politely asked her to leave and she laughed at me. She told me she had Gypsy violinists coming down from Reno to serenade me. Serenade me, do you believe it? I feel like I'm in an old Doris Day movie, and *I'm* playing Doris Day," he said in disbelief.

Bridget laughed out loud. "Even at your worst, I don't think anyone would mistake you for Doris Day."

"Yeah, well, I hope you're right. When Nina went to let in the Gypsy violinists, I pushed her out the door and locked it." Tripp smiled with satisfaction. "Hardly subtle, but it got the job done. And then I called you. But before I turned around, Nina had sneaked in through the kitchen door and was climbing all over me."

Bridget's expression grew a bit darker. "That must have been the giggling I heard."

"Yeah. I hate gigglers. She ripped the phone out of the wall after I called you—do you believe it?" He was starting to get angry again; he could feel it rising. He hated the position he'd been put in, but even more, he hated his own inability to control these women. "I tossed her out again, and this time I locked all the doors so she couldn't get back in. I thought maybe a wolf or a moose would get her. She pounded on the door for hours, but finally she went away. Maybe the Gypsies gave her a ride."

"Oh, Tripp!" she said in a disgusted tone. "I can't believe you have to go through all this nonsense. Why can't you just tell them you're not interested?"

"Don't you think I've tried? I've said every mean, hostile thing I can think of. But they don't go away. My mother has them all primed—they think I'm playing hard to get." He winced. "It's part of my charm."

"Uh-huh," Bridget said doubtfully, as if she didn't believe he had charm at all.

"And I had no sooner gotten rid of Nina than this afternoon's blonde showed up." He raked his fingers through his hair. "Thank God you got here when you did. She disabled my car!"

"Tripp, I don't mean to malign your appeal or anything. I mean, I think you're..." She paused. After a moment, she said, "Of course I think you're wonderful. But still, it's not like you're the last man on earth. I mean, they all act like you've got magic charms in your underwear or something. What is going on?"

Magic charms in his underwear? "Excuse me?" he choked.

She blushed again, a more scarlet shade this time. "Okay, so maybe that wasn't the best way to put it. But what are you doing to cause this kind of a fuss? Why would all these women go so crazy trying to catch you?"

"My mother."

"What about her?"

"It's what she's telling them." He sighed. He didn't know which was worse, his mother's perfidy, or the fact that all these women seemed to buy it, hook, line and sinker. "It's so stupid, and yet they all believe the same story. Each one thinks I've been secretly in love with her, from afar. And they also think—courtesy of my mother—that I'll be a millionaire as soon as I get married."

"But..." She gave him a very funny look. "I thought you were, well, poor."

Trust Bridgie to cut right to the chase. "Not exactly poor," he said fiercely. "But let's just say there hasn't been any major money in the Ashby family since about 1935.''

"So why did Kitty Belle...? Oh, I see." Bridget nodded. "She wanted to up the ante, to really make you an attractive target. A millionaire who looks like you would be quite the prize."

That was a surprise. He knew he was reasonably attractive, but coming from Bridgie, that idea was pretty shocking. "Looks like me? What do you mean? You've never said anything about my looks before."

"Well, I—" she started to say, but she was interrupted by the sound of the front door being forcefully pushed open.

"Not another one," Tripp grumbled, already on his way to catch the next entry in the bride-wannabe sweepstakes before she could get into the cabin.

But this time, when the door swung open, it didn't reveal any nubile young heiress.

No, this time, it was Kitty Belle Ashby. His irascible, infuriating mother.

"Oh, good heavens!" she cried, carrying her perfect pale pink suit and her perfect ash-blonde coiffure into the small cabin. She fixed accusing eyes on Bridget. "What is *she* doing here? And dressed like that? Tripp, have you no shame?"

Bridgie's face went pale.

"Sorry," he muttered into her ear. "Relax, okay?" But her arm felt stiff and tense under his hand.

Since he was fully aware of the effect Kitty Belle always had on Bridgie, and since he didn't want warfare to break out in the living room, he decided to hustle his old pal out of the line of fire as quickly as he could. "Bridgie needs to change her clothes. Don't you, Bridgie?" he tried.

"Oh, yes, of course."

Kitty Belle arched a narrow, golden eyebrow. "Of course she needs to change. No lady would appear in public in that disgraceful outfit."

Tripp flashed his mother a severe look, but she didn't take the hint.

"Disgraceful," she said again. Lifting a hand to her brow, she crumpled gracefully into a chair, showing every sign of sticking around awhile. Good. That would give him plenty of time to have a serious, meaningful discussion with her. If he didn't kill her first.

"This is hardly public," Bridgie said, bristling. "And I only wore it to get Tripp off the hook and out of the clutches of that dim-bulb ski bunny you sent up here."

"I beg your pardon?"

"It's just my robe," Tripp protested.

"I'm fully aware of what it is. But what's *she* doing in it?"

"I borrowed it, okay? I know it doesn't look good, but don't worry, there's no hanky-panky going on."

"Of course not," Mrs. Ashby scoffed. "I hardly think my son would consort with the likes of you."

"That's enough." Tripp glared at his mother. "Although it's none of your business, I would be honored to consort with Bridgie. The question is whether she would be willing to lower her standards enough to consort with the likes of me."

"Oh, my heavens. This is outrageous. To speak to your own mother like this. Where are your manners, Tripp?"

"You're a fine one to talk about manners, the way you've behaved," Bridgie shot back.

"Ladies, ladies," Tripp interceded, turning his back on his mother, pushing Bridgie ahead of him out of the room.

She was stubborn, but he managed to propel her all the way down the hall and into his room. But as he closed the door, he got a good look at the chaos in his room.

"What's all this?" he demanded. He picked up a lacy black nightgown slung over the foot of his bed. His eyes went wide as he held it up, mentally matching its skimpy outline to Bridgie's body. "Is this stuff yours? Bridgie…" He cleared a throat that had suddenly gone dry. "I find it difficult to picture you in something like that."

But that was the problem. It wasn't difficult at all. God. He was losing his mind.

Bridgie snatched it out of his hand. "You think nice girls don't wear black lingerie?"

"Of course they do. I mean, who knows? I never thought about it. But not you, anyway."

"Tripp, sometimes you are the most infuriating person." She stuffed the nightgown down into her briefcase.

"Infuriating? What did I do?"

"You're making such a big deal of this. What's the problem? It's not like you, Mr. Stud, haven't seen women's underwear before. But if it's mine, it's suddenly too risqué for words." Steam was practically coming out her ears as she smashed things back into her luggage. "I was just trying to put on a good show for your bimbo."

"And you did that, didn't you?" What did she think he was, a eunuch? "Throwing your lingerie all over my bedroom, waltzing out into the living room wearing a robe slashed open down to your navel—"

"My navel?" she cried. "It was not!"

"It still is," he said grimly.

She followed the path of his eyes, flushed crimson as far down as he could see, which answered one question about where she was capable of blushing, and then muttered some nasty oath as she grabbed the lapels of the robe together up to her chin.

"*You* kissed *me*," she reminded him, "which was totally uncalled for."

"What do you think I am, a eunuch?"

"What's that supposed to mean?"

Hell, he had no idea. "Whether it was uncalled for or not, you didn't seem to mind at the time." Mind? She'd practically torched him with the heat of her response. He still had sparks left over.

"Oh, yes, I did mind!" she insisted, but the hot light in her eyes belied her words. "I just...went along, for the sake of the story, to get rid of that thing in the ski pants. And then, after I hauled myself all the way to cannibal country—"

"Cannibal country?" he interrupted, utterly mystified.

"I read in the guidebook about the Donner Party... Oh, never mind!" she broke off. "What's important is that I bailed you out one more time, and for what? So you and your mother could both insult me!"

He hated arguing with Bridgie. She always won. And no matter what had gone on before, no matter who kissed whom, she was right that his mother was the real menace in the story. "Look, I'm sorry she was on her high horse again." And then he told her what he should've said a long time ago. "Thanks, Bridgie. I really mean it. I appreciate you coming to my rescue."

He took her chin in his hands, and dropped a quick kiss on the tip of her pretty little nose. It was weird how his hands kept reaching out for her. Now that he'd held her, he kept wanting to do it again, to prove to her, and to himself, exactly who was most affected, exactly who was trembling with this outrageous, unexpected attraction. But that would only make things more complicated, and far, far stickier. He backed away instantly. "So, listen, I owe you," he said unsteadily.

"I know you do," she returned tartly. "Big-time. Now go back there and read your mother the riot act. This is your chance."

But he wasn't thinking about his mother as he went back to face her. No, he was still trying to deal with the image of Bridgie lounging in his robe, with just enough bare skin to make his mouth water, the feel of Bridgie's soft, eager mouth under his while her small hands clutched his back, the idea of Bridgie decked out in that tiny lace nightgown.

Was he sick? Was he running a fever? Or was this sudden heat due to the startling discovery that Bridgie was a woman?

It was too bizarre. Turned on by Bridgie, of all people. Serious, studious, reliable Bridgie. How could he have never noticed what was underneath that sedate, somber shell?

One touch, one kiss, and Miss Priss had turned into a living, breathing, hot-blooded femme fatale. *Watch out,* he told himself. He had plenty of women skirting around the edges of his life, but only one friend like Bridgie. And if she vaulted over into the "woman" category, he was in deep trouble.

A moment's aberration, he told himself. A sudden, inexplicable impulse that would never come again.

As long as she was dressed.

Striding back into the living room, he found his mother still there, although she had moved to the couch, where she was sort of lounging, with her eyes closed. That was odd.

Usually, Kitty Belle was too nervous, too high-strung to sit down, let alone recline like that. She preferred to flit around, lighting here and there for a second or two, sort of like a hummingbird. In fact, with her sharp little face and plump body, she sort of resembled a hummingbird.

And now, awaiting a confrontation, normally she'd be up on her feet, bursting with energy, battle plans ready, raring to go. But she was dozing. Yes, this was very odd.

"Are you all right?" he asked.

"Now, why do you ask that?" She sat up quickly, giving him her most imperious stare. "Well, son? What was that Emerick girl doing here? And what do you have to say for yourself?"

She must have been resting only to store up energy for the fight. "Me?" he demanded. "Mother, you're the one with explaining to do. What you've done is unforgivable."

"Oh, pish posh. It was for your own good," she argued, waving a heavily ringed hand. "I did what I had to do to find you the right sort of wife. The Ashby name must go on! And now you've run off all my best hopes. Oh, Tripp, how could you? But perhaps you can still go after one of them and make things right."

"I don't think you're listening." With increasing heat, he faced her down where she reclined on her sofa.

"How could *I*? How could *you*? How could you lie to all those people? How could you put your own son in this terrible position?"

Kitty Belle regarded him with a stunned expression. "Tripp, darling, you're shouting at me!"

"Not yet, I'm not," he returned, tight-lipped. "But I'm going to start very soon."

"Oh, Tripp," she cried, crumpling, bursting into tears. "You mustn't be angry with me."

"Give me one good reason why." He found a box of tissues and awkwardly offered her one.

"Darling, what choice did I have?" she sniffed.

"You had lots of choices." Pacing on the bearskin rug, he told her, "You could've talked to me. You could've waited patiently when I told you I wasn't ready to get married. Couldn't you wait until I found the right woman on my own, without your interference?"

"Well, no. It simply wasn't going to happen," Kitty Belle persisted, dabbing at her mascara. "I gave you lots of wonderful opportunities, and what did you do? You ran right to that odious Emerick girl. No wonder you're not married yet. Playing games with the likes of her."

"Leave Bridget out of this," he growled. Now he was really mad. "You were wrong, Mother, very wrong to make up these stories and throw women at me. And your attitude toward Bridgie is terrible. Unless you apologize to her right now, and promise to clean up your act where she's concerned, you'll force me to choose between you. And I'm telling you right now— I'm choosing her."

"You can't choose her—I'm your mother!" she cried.

"She's a lot more useful and a lot less destructive than you are."

"Oh, no, no, no. I'm going to have to tell you everything. I see that now," she whispered. She gave him a moist, emotional gaze. "Tripp, darling, it's my health. I'm afraid it's...it's very bad news."

"Bad news? What kind of bad news?"

"Darling, I didn't want to tell you. But..."

Silence hung in the room.

"Tripp, dear, you have to understand. I'm dying."

Tripp just stood there, too stunned to react. "What did you say?"

She took a few seconds to compose herself, and then she repeated, "I'm dying."

"Dying? You mean you're really..."

She nodded.

"But you look fine, the same as always. When did this happen? *What* happened?"

Carefully removing another tissue from the box, she blotted her brow with a trembling hand.

She was pale, perspiring, shaky. Kitty Belle never showed signs of weakness. Never. For the first time, he began to really look at his mother. Was she ill? Was it possible?

"Mother, tell me what it is."

"I... Well, it's difficult to speak of. It's really been nothing major so far, and that's the confusing part. A few dizzy spells, a few migraines, but nothing more."

"Then when did you find out? How?"

"Well, I went to see Dr. Garland about the dizziness, and he thought I needed new glasses." She smiled weakly. Tripp knew her longtime physician, and he also knew that Kitty Belle bullied him like she did everyone else.

"So what happened?"

"It wasn't my eyes." She shrugged. "He ran a lot of tests, and he began to suspect that it was bad. It was so very shocking, because he said I should've had more symptoms than I've had. Every person is different, you see, but most people have much worse headaches or even fainting spells. But I had none of that. Just to be sure, to see, you know, how long, he sent me..." She paused, took a deep breath, and added, "To the Mayo Clinic."

"The Mayo Clinic." But wasn't that for...no, it couldn't be.

"In Minnesota," she went on. "I was there just before I came here."

Minnesota. He'd thought she was taking a vacation to elude him, and she'd been undergoing tests at the Mayo Clinic.

"Once I knew for sure what the prognosis was, well, it made me even more positive that what I was doing was right. If I have only a few months to live, I really do want to find you a wife before I go."

He kneeled at her side, not sure how to comfort her. Kitty Belle, dying? It wasn't possible. "What about treatment, Mother? Surely there must be something they can do."

She became very, very quiet. Finally she said, "It's inoperable, dear. I'm so sorry. I know how you are, always wanting action, but there's nothing that can be done. They said they could try drugs and radiation and horrible things like that, but it would only prolong things a few months at best. And this way, if I just go gracefully, I can feel well up to the very end. Please." She patted his cheek gently. "It's what I want. No chemicals, no machines, no hospitals."

"This is all such a shock," he whispered.

"I know, dear. I really don't want to discuss it any further, if it's all right with you. Maybe later, when I'm feeling stronger. Or you can call and talk to Dr. Garland. He can give you all the details, all the medical mumbo jumbo, and the chances of one versus the other. You'll see that I've made the right choice. This way, I have two or three months of feeling just fine, and the other way it's maybe six months of feeling just awful."

"All right," he said softly. "I'll talk to Dr. Garland later."

"Yes, later. That would be good. But you see now why I wanted so desperately to see you married, Tripp, before I go. Won't you please reconsider, for my sake? Won't you give me this last wish?"

This was more than he had bargained for. He didn't know what to think.

Kitty Belle, dying. Kitty Belle, desperate to see him married, settled, before she left him forever.

"Oh, God," he whispered. No wonder she'd behaved so irrationally. She was dying. He felt shamed, that he had considered the discomfort of a few days more important than his mother, when she was carrying the burden of this terrible secret all by herself.

"Tripp, darling, please..." She reached out for him. "Tell me you'll get married before I—"

"Let's not talk about that. First we need to talk about you and what you need to get through this. Better doctors, better care. Surely there's something we can do."

"I've tried, Tripp," she said gently. "It's no good. We must learn to accept the inevitable."

"But—"

"All I want is this one small thing. Will you do it, Tripp? For me? Will you pick one of those lovely girls, and get married?'' She fastened him with a hopeful, trusting expression.

"I don't know. How can I?"

"Please?"

"I don't know."

But it didn't take long to make up his mind.

There was a huge roaring sound in his ears, and he felt as if he were standing in the deadly calm eye of a tornado. Without saying another word to his mother, without giving himself a chance to think about the enormity of what he was about to do, Tripp strode to the bedroom and threw open the door.

He caught Bridgie in middress, wearing only a long T-shirt and her underpants. And then her head snapped up, and her expression was astonished, confused.

"What are you doing here?"

"Sorry. I didn't mean to barge in like that." He wavered in the doorway. "I need to talk to you."

Quickly she grabbed a pair of jeans and hopped into them. "Okay. Talk."

He struggled to find the words to begin.

"Tripp, what is it?" she asked. "Are you all right?"

But he didn't answer. He almost turned and left right then.

Instead, he came into the bedroom, slowly, deliberately. He opened his mouth, he considered what he wanted to say... and said nothing.

He tried again. Nothing.

Oh, the hell with it. Swearing under his breath, at the end of his rope, he finally just looked her in the eye and cut to the chase.

"Bridgie," he said savagely, "will you marry me?"

Chapter Six

For one starstruck moment, she actually considered it.

Thirty-four years without ever being proposed to, and here was her second proposal within a week.

Out with the senator's wife. In with reckless lust.

She could marry Tripp Ashby, the romantic figure of her youth. They would make mad, passionate love every day before breakfast, have six or seven lovely, undisciplined babies, become itinerant artsy types and live at the seashore.

Yeah, right. And the Easter Bunny was bringing a basket with her name on it.

How long had she known him? How long had he been blind to the fact that she was more than just a bookish brainiac? A very long time.

Great mysteries of the universe didn't solve themselves overnight. And Tripp Ashby wasn't going to wake up and take off the blinders after one little kiss.

And if he did discover her secret—that she had been hot for his body since the age of eighteen—he was more than likely to run from the room screaming. Look at what had happened after he'd merely seen her nightgown! It seemed clear Tripp was uncomfortable with the idea of her as a sex object, in even the most innocent of circumstances. So this proposal was not based on anything as earthy or interesting as that.

Besides, he looked as if he were about to explode. His jaw was held so tightly, she wondered how he could breathe. His hands were clenched into fists, and his whole body was tensed, on edge, ready to boil over or blow up at the slightest provocation.

This was not the look of a man in the heat of undeniable passion. This was a man pushed into a corner.

As he advanced on her, rubbing his hands together nervously, she backed up all the way to the window.

"Will you, Bridgie? Will you marry me?"

She took a deep breath. She looked at him. Tripp, wanting *her*. How many times had she dreamed of this happening?

"No!" she cried. "I couldn't possibly!"

"No, of course not." He began to pace back and forth, wearing a hole in the rug between the bed and the door.

"Tripp, what is wrong with you?"

"It's not what's wrong with me," he muttered. "It's my mother."

"Well, that's no big secret. We know what's wrong with her. She's nuts! She's a vain, stuck-up, elitist—"

"Please, Bridgie, don't," he begged. "You don't understand."

The haunted look in his eye finally penetrated. "Wait. Are you saying something . . . something else is wrong with your mother?"

"She's dying."

"She's . . . ? Are you serious? But she can't be."

"But she is," he said, his voice hardly a whisper.

"Oh, come on, this is a joke, right? Another of her tricks?"

"She just came from the Mayo Clinic," he shot back. "Would she do that on a lark?"

"Well, I guess not, but with your mother—"

"It's not a trick. When I came back into the room, she was lying down. With her eyes shut."

"You're kidding." That was more serious. Kitty Belle never displayed signs of weakness. She'd rather die than let anyone know she needed to lie down. Bad choice of words, but still . . .

"She was very pale," Tripp went on. "Trembling, sweaty. She said she's been having dizzy spells."

"So, what is it? Has she seen a doctor? Oh, that's stupid. Of course she has, if she was at the Mayo Clinic."

"She didn't say exactly, but I got the idea it was a brain tumor." Tripp shook his head. He really looked like he was in shock himself. "I'm supposed to call her doctor and get more information later."

"Okay, well, that's a good idea."

Bridget dropped to the bed. Kitty Belle? It seemed impossible. If anyone was too mean to die, it was Kitty Belle Ashby.

Immediately swamped with guilt, Bridget put a hand up to her mouth. What a horrible thing to think. If Kitty Belle was dying, and Tripp was obviously shook up about it, then Bridget was going to have to be kind and sympathetic.

"Tripp, I'm so sorry," she managed. Tripp and his mom were always in conflict, but she still knew him well enough to realize that he was very attached to his irascible mother. He might not show it, but his feelings for Kitty Belle ran deep. Awkwardly, Bridget ventured, "I know it's been just the two of you for a long time."

"Since my dad died," he said bleakly. "Right after college."

"Did she just . . . I mean, did you just find out?"

He nodded. "She didn't want to tell me, but she had to, to explain why she was doing all these crazy things to find me a wife. When I think," he whispered, "when I think of how angry I was, and all the time, she was dealing with this. This terrible news."

"So she was pushing women at you because she knew she was dying?" What sense did that make?

"Yeah." He sighed wearily. "She wants to see me settled. She wants to see me married."

"And that's why you just proposed to me?"

She'd almost forgotten Tripp's offer. Almost, but not quite. And she had been foolish enough, for a whole three seconds, to think he was proposing because he'd discovered he was in love with her, or at least in lust with her.

Wrongo. He'd proposed because his mother wanted him married before she shook off this mortal coil.

And Bridget was the only available female when he got the urge. "Any port in a storm," she whispered.

"What did you say?"

As lightly as she could manage, she offered, "I said it's too bad that Nina and Miss Ski Pants blew their timing. Just think, one of them could've been the lucky girl."

"Not even for my mother would I ask either of those twits to marry me," he said flatly.

"I suppose that's good to hear." She ranked higher than someone, at any rate.

"Bridgie," he murmured, in that low, persuasive tone he always used when he wanted something. He joined her on the bed, and he gazed deep into her eyes. "Will you at least consider it? It wouldn't be real. Just good enough to fool my mother, to give her the one thing she wants most in the world.''

"Tripp, you can't be serious. A fake wedding? A pretend marriage? The whole idea is immoral, not to mention degrading.'' She shook her head firmly, twisting away from him. ''Never.''

But he pulled her back around to face him. "Listen—''

"I don't want to listen! For one thing, I'm already engaged. What do you think Jay would say if I suddenly up and married someone else?''

"But—''

But Bridget had a better argument all ready to go. "Plus there's your mother. If this whole scheme is for her benefit, you have to consider how she feels about me. Even if I were willing to consider this, which I'm not, I don't think bringing me into the family would make Kitty Belle's last days happy ones.'' He flinched and she added, ''Sorry. I didn't mean to say that part about the... you know.''

"Last days. Well, I'm going to have to face it.'' He let out a long, sorrowful breath.

Bridget couldn't help it; she lifted her hand and softly brushed his cheek. He looked so sad.

"I wish I could make it better for you, Tripp.'' But a note of panic threaded her words when she insisted, "But there's no way I can marry you. You, of all people.''

He caught her hand. "I didn't say we would actually go through with it. I'm just asking for an engagement—a temporary engagement—not a wedding. And your Philpott guy would never even have to know. If my mother only has a few months...'' He stopped, gazing down at their intertwined hands. "If she only has a few months left, then we could tell her we were engaged, but there wouldn't be time for a wedding."

"She hates me, Tripp," Bridget reminded him gently. "She's not going to want you engaged to me any more than married to me."

Tripp frowned. "I know she doesn't approve of you. And I'll admit, it would be better if your father were a banker instead of a plumber."

"So—"

"You didn't let me finish. If she wants me married that badly, she's going to have to make a few compromises."

"Are compromises a good idea when it comes to dying wishes?"

He smiled then, and it was so reckless, so beautiful, it took her breath away. He really did know how to flip her switches. "I may be willing to fake an engagement for her sake, but I at least get to pick my own counterfeit fiancée. There is no one I would even consider doing this with—except you."

"No one except me?" She began to melt a little.

"If you refuse, it's over," he said firmly. "No bride for Kitty Belle."

Still she hesitated.

"Come on, Bridgie. Take a chance. We already know we get along, and we know each other better than anybody. And that will make the whole scheme a lot easier, a lot better. Besides, I trust you," he said earnestly.

He trusted her? Was he saying he trusted her not to get caught up in the intimacy and forget it was all a fraud? But that was exactly the problem. She didn't trust herself.

"But I'm a terrible liar," she told him. "I don't think I could—"

"You did just fine pretending to be my wife in front of Miss Ski Pants, didn't you? Same thing exactly."

"But Jay—"

"We won't tell him."

"What if he finds out?"

"He won't find out."

"You can't be sure of that."

"I'll make sure. Trust me."

"But if he did, if the reporters did, it could ruin his campaign," she protested. "I mean, he won't even spend the night because he's afraid he'll get caught. How's he going to feel if his fiancée is engaged to someone else, and it gets splashed all over the papers?"

"But it won't. Why would anyone find out?" He smiled. "This is just for you and me and Kitty Belle. Nobody else."

"But I won't know how to act, or what to say. Your mother will know in a minute it's not real."

"Oh, come on. You're already engaged to Philpott. So you have experience at acting like somebody's fiancée." He smiled encouragingly. "Just treat me like you would Philpott, and we'll be fine."

Bridget almost choked. Treat Tripp like Jay Philpott? What a disaster!

She might as well treat a mountain lion like a house cat and see how far it got her. As a matter of fact, at least a big cat and a little cat appeared to share the same species. She wasn't all that sure about Tripp and Jay.

For her, Tripp was all reckless passion, all smoke and mirrors. Jay was steady, reliable, a real paragon of virtue. She could push him to the wall and he'd never lose control. But Tripp... What would happen if she kissed him again, or if she told him that in her eyes he was the epitome of hot sex appeal on wheels?

Say something like that to Jay, and he would laugh, amused. But with Tripp... Well, she had a feeling she would feel the heat before the words were out of her mouth.

"I can't treat you like Jay," she mumbled.

"I know. Because you don't feel about me the same way you feel about him. But that's okay," he said gently. "I'm prepared to deal with it."

Oh, brother.

But Tripp was really on a roll, and Bridget felt her objections withering away. She lifted a weak hand to her forehead. He was too good at this, and she was unprepared to fight back.

But who would've ever expected to need arguments about why she shouldn't marry him? Talk about out of the blue!

"How long would this last?" she asked warily. "I mean, I'd have to be sure it would be over well before I needed to campaign for Jay. Otherwise, your mother would see my picture in the papers as his fiancée, and that would look very strange."

There was a long pause. "She said a few months." He shook his head. "Only a few months."

I must be as insane as he is to be considering this. Am I considering this? Oh, God, I am considering this.

"Come on, Bridgie," he said, with more of his usual infectious charm. "It will be fun. We'll hang out together for a few months, we'll let my mother think whatever she wants to think, and once she's..." He took a deep breath. "Once she's gone, we can fold up our engagement and put it away, and no one will ever be the wiser.''

She didn't answer. She was so torn. He made it sound so simple, yet she knew it would be anything but. He made it sound so reasonable, when pretending to be engaged to him was absolutely absurd.

"Would you do it for me?" he asked, and she remembered he was the son of a master manipulator. "I know I have no right to ask you to put your life on hold for a few months, just for the sake of our friendship. But I hope you'll do it, Bridgie. For me. And for my mother. I know she's not your favorite person, but even Kitty Belle deserves a last wish.''

Bridget nodded. Deep down, she knew she couldn't let his mother die unhappy if there was something within her power to make it better. But this was such a big favor....

In the secret, selfish reaches of her heart, she knew she had another reason for considering his offer. If she said no, he might be forced to look up one of those other women who were so eager to lasso him. Sure, he said he'd only do it with her, but who believed that?

When someone as antimarriage as Tripp began to look for a bride, things had to be desperate. Who knew what he would be reduced to?

If Tripp was going to be spending long hours in someone's company, pretending to be in love, she couldn't stand the idea that it would be some brainless rich girl. If it was going to be anyone, she decided it had damn well better be her.

Besides, there was also the matter of one last, reckless flirtation with irresponsibility before she married Jay and settled down to a life of being perfect. One last time, she could throw caution to the winds and do something outrageous. It didn't hurt that she'd get to do it with Tripp, either.

"Okay," she said quickly.

"Okay? So you're saying yes?"

"Yes. I'm saying yes."

"You won't regret this," he promised. He pulled her over and gave her a quick kiss on the mouth.

A quick kiss. And already her senses started to reel. Already, she was ready to panic.

Backing off considerably, trying to breathe, Bridget put a finger to his lips. "I said yes. For now. For fake. And that's it."

"Of course." He gave her another mischievous grin as he offered a hand to help her to her feet. "So, are you feeling brave enough to share the happy news with Kitty Belle?"

"I don't think I'll ever be brave enough for that."

"Oh, and Bridgie?"

"Yes?"

"Could you take off Philpott's ring? If you're going to be engaged to me now, you probably shouldn't be wearing his ring."

Wordlessly, with a curious sense of relief, Bridget slipped Jay's ring off her finger and wedged it deep into her pocket.

"No, I SIMPLY WON'T hear of it!"

"You don't have a choice, Mother."

Kitty Belle moaned and Kitty Belle whined. She tried fireworks and waterworks, but Tripp remained firm.

"I love Bridget," he said quietly. "We discovered about a year ago that our friendship had turned into something a little more serious, and we've been together ever since." He flashed her a quick, encouraging wink, telling her to go along with the story he was making up on the spur of the moment. "We would've gotten married anyway, eventually."

He was really a very good liar. Hearing him spout this sentimental, plausible story, Bridget had to fight to remind herself it was just a fairy tale.

And the cozy way they were sitting on the nubby sofa in the living room, with his arm casually draped around her shoulders, their hands clasped in her lap, they really did look like the kids next door, popping in to tell Mom and Dad the good news.

Except it was all a lie, and Bridget already felt the mammoth hands of guilt pressing down on her shoulders.

"You might as well get used to it, Mother—Bridget is the only woman I've ever felt this way about, and she's the only woman I will ever consider marrying."

"But why didn't I know the two of you were involved?" Kitty Belle demanded. "You've always insisted you were just friends. Why, just a few moments ago, she was swearing there was no hanky-panky going on!"

"Well, of course she said that. What do you think she's going to say?" Tripp asked, his brows drawn together darkly.

"But why didn't you tell me?" his mother persisted.

"I asked him not to," Bridget improvised. "It was my idea."

In her ear, Tripp whispered, "I told you you were a natural at this."

Oh, great. Her talent for lying was getting as polished as his.

He leaned over and kissed her on the cheek, just to put on a good show of tenderness between them.

"And why did you want him to keep this involvement a secret?" Kitty Belle asked.

Under her prospective mother-in-law's disdainful eye, Bridget explained, "Well, it was obvious to both of us that you wouldn't approve—of Tripp and me, I mean—and I didn't want to cause any disharmony in the family. So I asked Tripp not to tell you that we had, um, gotten together."

"I see," Mrs. Ashby murmured. "But now you're perfectly willing to cause disharmony, is that it?"

"Mother, please. This is what you wanted." Bending forward, closer to Kitty Belle's chair, he started to launch his persuasive powers in her direction for a change. "You said your fondest wish was that I find someone I love and get married. Well, I'm doing exactly that. Bridget and I are willing to set up the timetable a bit, and announce our engagement now, to defer to your wishes. Can't you be happy you're getting what you want?"

"Oh, Tripp!" she wailed, reaching for the tissues again. "If I only thought you would be happy...."

"I will." He patted Bridget's knee fondly, and she closed her eyes, asking God to forgive her for this travesty. "We both will. Won't we, honey?"

She swallowed. "Of course, um, honey," she managed.

Tripp had never called anyone "honey" in his life. Surely Kitty Belle would notice how phony it sounded. Surely she would call the betrothal police and have them both carted away for impersonating an engaged couple.

"I'm so ill," Kitty Belle whimpered. She leaned back into the sofa, took several deep breaths and mopped her damp brow. "I simply don't have the will to fight you,

Tripp. I just want to be sure that you're happy before I have to leave you."

She did look pale and tired, and Bridget was suddenly struck with a wave of empathy. She was almost sorry for all the years she'd disliked Tripp's mother. Even if the woman was a royal pain, Bridget would never have wished illness on her.

"Please don't worry, Mrs. Ashby. I love Tripp with all my heart," she said in all honesty. "We've known each other for so many years that there certainly won't be any surprises between the two of us. And I promise you, he'll be very safe with me."

Safe? She wasn't even sure *she* was safe with herself these days.

"All right," her prospective mother-in-law said, sighing. "I will accept her as your wife, Tripp. If I must." She shook her head, which, for the first time in Bridget's memory, did not have a perfect coiffure. As a matter of fact, there were several moist tendrils escaping the swept-back sides. More evidence of her illness, Bridget supposed. Kitty Belle prided herself on looking just so, no matter what was going on—appearance being everything in her real world—and it must really be torture for her to lose her fierce grip on her hairdo. "I still feel she isn't the most suitable choice, to be the wife of an Ashby, after all. The disparity in your backgrounds and in your breeding . . . Well, I can't pretend to be satisfied. But better her than no one, I suppose."

"What a ringing endorsement," Bridget murmured.

Tripp rose from the sofa, looming over his small mother. "I am trying to do the best I can for you, Mother. But that is the last time I ever want to hear anything about anybody's breeding, do you hear? I want nothing disparaging about Bridget coming from your lips. Ever.''

He was very cold, and quite furious. Bridget sat up straighter. There was something to be said for hearing a man defend her so aggressively. She kind of liked the idea that Tripp would spring to her defense.

''I love Bridget,'' he continued. ''I respect her. I love you, too, Mother, but I will not accept your belittling comments about the woman I intend to marry.''

''Why couldn't you have liked one of the others?'' Kitty Belle grumbled. ''Why not the Chipton girl, or Nina Sherrard? Both lovely, smart, *rich* girls. They would've been such an asset to the Ashby family.''

Tripp's blue eyes were steely, unmoved. ''I'm not looking to pad the family assets. I'm looking for someone I get along with. No more of this, Mother.''

''All right, all right.'' Kitty Belle waved them away. ''I'm feeling unwell, and I think we've discussed this quite enough for one night. I said you had my approval. Isn't that enough?''

Tripp nodded, and Bridget tried to find a smile. Step one of the Great Fake Engagement Plot was apparently complete.

''I'd like to go back to my hotel now,'' Kitty Belle said in a small, quavery voice. ''Will you call Powell in from my car and tell him I'm ready to leave, please?''

''You're staying at a hotel? But there's plenty of room here, Mother,'' Tripp offered.

Please let her turn him down, Bridget silently prayed. The idea of sharing a roof with Kitty Belle's prying, disapproving eyes was more than she could handle.

''Oh, heavens, no,'' Kitty Belle returned, and Bridget allowed herself a sigh of relief. ''I've never slept in a cabin in my life and I don't intend to now. I'm sure I'll be much more comfortable in a hotel. Also more privacy, of course. I find it difficult to keep up appearances as I used to."

"If you're sure."

"I'm sure. Leave me now, will you? Powell will see me out."

But as Tripp and Bridget made their exit from the living room, hand in hand, still hiding behind their young-couple-in-love guise, his mother took a parting shot. She muttered it under her breath, but Bridget heard it plainly, and she was pretty sure Tripp did, too.

"There was nothing wrong with any of those women, except that I approved of them. Ever since he was a little boy, he's always chosen whatever it was I didn't want him to have."

Bridget winced. Even though she hated buying into anything Kitty Belle said, she detected the ring of truth this time. No matter what he'd told her, Tripp wanted her as his partner in this fake engagement for one reason only—because choosing her would annoy his mother. Who better to pick than the one woman he already knew his mother despised?

She was being used as a weapon in his lifelong battle with Kitty Belle.

She felt like slapping him. She felt like running from the damned Studs cabin and never speaking to Tripp again.

How many times had she sworn him off? And how many times had she found herself right back at his side?

"I think I need therapy," she whispered.

"You?" Tripp laughed. "You're the sanest woman I know."

Coming from him, it wasn't all that comforting a thought.

"PLANS MUST BE MADE," Kitty Belle announced over the breakfast table.

Although there were still traces of her illness in her less-than-flawless hair and ashen coloring, she had clearly made an effort to get herself together this morning. As she held court in her palatial suite at Harrah's Lake Tahoe, she was rather heavily made up, and exquisitely dressed.

Tripp supposed she was trying to hide her pallor under all the makeup, although it didn't really work. Poor Kitty Belle. As vain as she was, a devastating illness really hit her where she lived.

"Plans?" Tripp set his fork down next to the Belgian waffles he was toying with. He hated fancy breakfast food, but his mother had taken the liberty of ordering before he and Bridget arrived. Waffles for everyone. Neither he nor Bridgie had taken more than a bite. Just one more thing they had in common, he supposed. "What kind of plans?"

"Your wedding plans, of course."

"Surely we have time for that later."

"Time, my dear child, is the one thing I do not have." His mother pulled two plane tickets out of a folder and slapped them down on the table next to the silver coffeepot. "We'll need to get you both back to Chicago right away. A romantic proposal out of town is one thing, but we must do the formal announcement at home."

"Formal announcement?" Bridgie's face took on a pinched look.

"Of course. When an Ashby marries, all the right people want to know." Frowning, Kitty Belle flipped open a small leather notebook. "Let's see. We'll need photos for the *Tribune* and perhaps *Town and Coun-*

try. Of course, the Ashbyville *Gazette* will want to do a bigger write-up than the others. It's been years since the last Ashby wedding, and we're practically royalty in that town. They'll want to make a big splash, I'm sure.''

"Isn't this moving a little quickly?" he asked.

"Not at all. There's not a moment to lose."

Bridget began to fidget. "Tripp, may I speak to you for a moment, please?" She slipped away from the table, walking briskly over to the other side of the suite.

He saw the panic in her eyes, and he knew he was going to have to do some damage control. Joining her, approximately a football field away from the breakfast table, he said, "Don't worry. I'll take care of it."

"But all these announcements? What about Jay? What about the people at my firm? If they see announcements—"

"They won't. I promise."

"Tripp, we have to tell her the truth now. If she gets the gossip mills going, or worse yet, starts sending out press releases, it will be too late."

"Don't worry." He glanced over at his mother, busily making notes while she waited for them, and then back at Bridgie. With a confidence he wasn't sure he felt, he said, "I can handle my mother."

"Oh, right," Bridgie shot back in a heated whisper. "That's why you're engaged at the moment, right?"

"I can handle her," he repeated steadily. "I promise you there won't be any wedding announcements in the paper, and the only people who will know are a small circle of Mother's best pals. Philpott doesn't know any of them and they don't know him. So don't worry, okay?"

"But how—"

"I'll just tell her that we're keeping a low profile on this, that we're both private people, so we're going to have a small, quiet wedding, and all this fuss isn't appropriate. That sounds good, doesn't it?"

"It *sounds* good," Bridget muttered, "but I don't believe for one minute it will ever work."

"Do you two have any thoughts about where to have the engagement party?" Kitty Belle called out. She fluttered her lashes at them. "Who's going to stand up for you, dear? I'm thinking, oh, ten or twelve bridesmaids. Be sure to choose someone for your maid of honor whose family home has a ballroom. It will make things so much easier if we can count on the maid of honor for one of the parties."

"A ballroom?" Bridget echoed in evident horror. "Ten or twelve bridesmaids?"

"Hold on," Tripp started, but his mother was already rolling right along.

"And of course you'll use Henri. He's catered all my affairs for years. He's expensive, but worth every penny."

"A caterer?" Her fingers dug into Tripp's arm. "We have to call it off," she whispered anxiously. "Your mother is going to have us contracted for services to most of greater Chicagoland before we turn around. And no matter whether we have a wedding or not, we'll still have to pay for all that stuff!"

"Mother, we need to discuss this—" he began.

"I think green would be nice for the color scheme," Kitty Belle mused. "Those miniature topiary trees, festooned with pink roses, are lovely. Then a soft green for the bridesmaids, with lots of green and white and just a hint of pink in the ballroom. Don't you just love green, Bridget?"

Kitty Belle beamed, while Bridgie began to make little choking noises at the back of her throat.

His so-called engagement was less than twenty-four hours old, and already Tripp was caught between a rock and a hard place.

Chapter Seven

"Hellooooo," Kitty Belle called, trailing her mink and her chauffeur behind her. "Tripp, dear, where are you?"

Home sweet home. He hadn't actually lived in the big house in Ashbyville since high school, but there was something about the lemony smell of its polished wood floors, the deep *bong* of the grandfather clock in the downstairs hall, the long, tempting curve of the front stairway banister, that still spelled home to him.

Feeling a tad cynical, he idled in the front hall, his hands in his pockets, as he waited to greet his mother. Just like old times. He might've been in high school again, waiting for Mom to get back from her garden club, waiting for Dad to come home after a long day trying to make something out of nothing at the Ashby Carriage Company.

"There you are, darling. It's so lovely to have you at home, even if it's only for a few days." She stretched way up to kiss him on the cheek, and then she wafted into the drawing room, leaving behind a trail of expensive perfume.

He had given up and closed his town house, as well as his business, for the duration of his "engagement."

Things hadn't been going all that well anyway—he never had been much of a salesman—and trying to keep Kitty Belle from driving Bridgie crazy was a full-time job. This way, moving back to the house in Ashbyville, he could take the brunt of the wedding plans himself, as well as spend some time with his mother.

Supposedly. So far, he'd seen her for a total of about ten minutes, and they'd spent the whole time wrangling over wedding plans. He'd never seen Kitty Belle so animated, so excited. She still tired easily, but while she was up, she was very up.

Once she found out what Kitty Belle was up to, Bridgie was going to be pretty excited herself. So excited she'd blow a gasket.

He followed his mother into the drawing room, where she was stripping off her gloves and poking into her purse. "Voilà!" she said brightly. "My list."

"What list is it this time?" he asked, with a sense of foreboding. He'd already had to dissuade her from sending out engraved engagement announcements to three hundred of her closest friends, and from sending his picture to the society columns of every major newspaper in the country.

"Floral designers, caterers, couturiers," she said, ticking them off on her fingers. "I'm only considering the absolute best of the best. I'm going to make it all spectacular. For you, darling."

"But I don't want 'spectacular.'"

She dismissed him with a wave of one hand. "I know you want the wedding to be very small and private. I understand that your fiancée is not wealthy, and isn't able to afford anything lavish."

That was the cover story so far. "Exactly."

"You said hands-off, and hands-off it shall be. For the wedding itself. But the engagement party is something I can do," she said sweetly. "I'm having Mariata Francatta design Bridget's dress. Something simple. I'm thinking ivory or maybe navy blue slipper satin, cut on the bias. Navy has really become *the* evening color."

He had no idea what any of that meant, but he knew Bridgie wasn't going to like it.

"Mother, just this morning, you promised you would not be broadcasting this wedding to the seven-state area. We came up with an acceptable list of the people you were going to tell, and that was it. Remember?"

"Well, yes. So?"

"So having an elaborate engagement party is going to be a major clue that there's a wedding going on, don't you think?"

"I want to have this party," she said stubbornly. "What's the point of being engaged if you can't tell anybody?"

"We've already been through this," he argued. "Bridget wants it all kept private. Besides, Mother, I don't think you should be spending all your money on things like this. Your medical care has to be expensive, and we don't need—or want—that kind of party."

Under normal circumstances, he wouldn't have brought up her financial situation. He knew she was very sensitive about the fact that she felt obligated to keep up appearances, while she had precious little funds to do it with.

The once-famous Ashby Carriage Company had creaked to a near-standstill a long time ago, eking out just enough with its line of bicycles to keep Kitty Belle supplied with the bare necessities of a fashionable life.

Certainly not enough for the kind of fabulous party she was planning.

"Tripp, you know I never discuss anything as vulgar as money with you." She gave him a reproving glance. "But I do need to speak with you about a few other things. Please sit down for a moment, will you?"

Making a mental note not to forget to quench her party-giving spirit before their conversation was over, Tripp stretched out in a chintz chair. "Okay. What's up?"

"It's you and Bridget, dear."

He waited for the other shoe to drop. "What about us?"

"You just don't seem all that enamored of each other."

"Mother—" he sighed "—we've been through all this—"

"No," she said pointedly, "we haven't."

"If you're going to disparage Bridgie again—"

"But I'm not," she swore. "I've given that up completely. You were very forceful on that issue and I told you I would accept her gracefully."

"So what's the problem now?"

With a very motherly tone, something that was new to Kitty Belle, she informed him, "This marriage is never going to work when you two show such a lack of amorousness with each other."

"Amorousness?" What the hell did that mean?

"Why, you've never even kissed her as far as I can tell."

This was downright embarrassing. He couldn't believe his mother was angling for more public displays of affection. That wasn't her sort of thing at all.

"Trust me," he muttered, "we've kissed."

"Well, you ought to do it more often."

"Mother, please."

"You are a very virile young man."

He groaned out loud. The word *virile* and his mother didn't belong in the same hemisphere, let alone the same room.

"And I want grandchildren!" she snapped. "That's very important. The Ashby name must go on. But how are you going to beget sons if you never touch each other?"

"We touch each other, just . . . not around you," he finished lamely.

"I saw you at the airport, when we flew back from Tahoe," Kitty Belle put in. "You stuck her in a cab with her luggage and off she went. No kiss, no tender goodbye. I was appalled."

"We were tired. It was late."

"Hmph. Why, anyone would think you weren't in love at all, but merely pretending."

He sat up straighter. "That's crazy."

"Well, this love affair of yours certainly popped up out of nowhere, didn't it?" Kitty Belle's gaze was shrewd. "I would hate to think you were trying to fool me. It would be a terrible thing to lie to a dying woman, Thomas Michael Trippett Ashby."

"Don't call yourself that," he mumbled.

"Well, I am dying, and we might as well admit it."

"But I'm not lying to you." He stood and shoved his hands in his pockets. "I wouldn't do that. Bridget and I are a perfectly normal couple, in every way. Including . . . well, *that* way."

"I certainly hope so. But if that's true, this is the most peculiar love match I've ever seen," she huffed.

"You're here in Ashbyville, and your bride-to-be is in the city, fifty miles away."

"She has a job!" he protested.

"Well, she doesn't work twenty-four hours a day, does she? I don't understand why you aren't pining to be together every free moment." Her stare was level, as if she were discussing the newest color of chrysanthemum. Who'd ever have guessed she was dissecting her son's love life, of all things? "I have seen no evidence of any lust on either side."

"Lust?" he sputtered. "Lust?"

"Well, of course. And I blame you, Tripp. You should be wooing the girl, sending her flowers, arranging a romantic tête-à-tête now and again. I've seen you with women before. I know you can do it—and quite well, from all the gossip I've heard." While he was still digesting that piece of information, Kitty Belle coolly announced, "If you want to make a success of this match, you'll have to turn up the heat in your romance."

"Turn up the heat?"

"Exactly. Why, when your father and I were engaged..." Her eyes took on a wistful glow. "We nearly had to be pried apart by our fathers. There's something very stirring, very provocative, when you first make the promise of a life together. It's intoxicating. Every time I looked down at my ring, I got a little tingle, to know that I would soon be married to your father. I felt so romantic, so loved."

"Things are different now," he tried. "It's a new era."

"Some things never go out of style," she said flatly. "And lusting after your fiancée is one of them. And that reminds me. You have to get her a ring. I'm ashamed of you, not even remembering to buy an engagement ring for your new fiancée."

He could hardly protest that Bridget already had an engagement ring and didn't need another one. "All right," he muttered. "I'll take care of it."

"I certainly hope so." There was suddenly a new sparkle in her eye, and she clapped her hands together happily. "I'll tell you what, Tripp. Since you don't want the engagement party I was planning, I will scrap the whole thing."

"No party? But that's great, Mom."

"Provided, of course, that you take the initiative. You can arrange a small, intimate dinner, just for the two of you, and present her with the ring over dinner. That will give the two of you a chance to be alone." She pressed one eyelid down in a very heavy wink. "To be *alone,* if you catch my drift."

"I've got it," he said darkly. She might as well have written Make Love To Bridget on a ten-foot banner and hung it from the chandelier.

"Good. Have fun, darling."

And then she was gone, sliding out of the drawing room as slippery as an eel, before he could grab her and tell her he couldn't possibly do what she was asking.

Bridgie was going to have a fit.

BUT BRIDGIE WAS ALREADY having a fit.

"Tripp," she murmured into the phone. "Is that you?"

"Yes. Why are you whispering?"

"Because I'm at the office and I don't want my secretary to hear me."

"Bridgie, you're the boss. You can say whatever you want."

"Will you cut me some slack here? This is important." She paused, and he imagined her checking her phone for wiretaps. "Tripp," she started again, in that same harried, suspicious whisper, "I found out that Newman Niles, the senior partner—the most senior partner—knows your mother. His wife is on some board or committee with her or something."

"So?"

"So, if your mother tells his wife, Niles will know! But he already knows I'm engaged to Jay. Everyone in the firm knows. They think it's fabulous that one of their own is going to marry Jay Philpott, the most promising senatorial candidate to come out of Chicago since Carol Moseley-Braun. I'm big news here! But if your mother tells his wife, and Niles knows I have two engagements going, the whole damn firm will think I'm cheating on Jay—"

"Slow down a minute, Bridgie. My mother won't tell your boss, okay? Problem solved."

"How can you be sure of that?"

He felt a certain triumph when he said, "I scored a major coup. I got her to agree to tell only people on the approved guest list. And that's her relatives in Alabama, a few harmless people in Ashbyville, my three best buddies from college and our household staff. And that's it. A total of about fifteen people."

"You're sure she won't tell anyone else?"

"She promised."

"Okay." She breathed a sigh of relief. "I guess if it's only that many people . . . I mean, what are the chances one of them would say anything that would get back to Jay, here in Chicago? And there's even less of a chance of my family in St. Paul finding out, which is certainly good. I mean, I already told my dad and my sisters that

I was engaged to Jay, so they would be very confused if suddenly I was engaged to you, too. Or instead. Or whatever.''

"Bridget, you're babbling," he said kindly. "Have you had a bad day?"

"Of course I've had a bad day! I've spent the whole day worrying myself sick about this stupid engagement you talked me into. I'm a nervous wreck!"

"Relax, sweetie. There's nothing to get excited about."

A long pause hung on the phone line. "Did you just call me sweetie?"

"Yeah, I guess I did." Women got fried about the most bizarre things. Was there something wrong with "sweetie"?

"And you wonder why I'm a nervous wreck!" she returned. "Tripp, please don't make this worse than it already is."

He shook his head hard. Had he missed something? Or was Bridgie acting completely irrationally?

"I can't take this," she murmured. "I'm losing it. Here I am, trying to think up excuses to keep Jay away, because I don't want to tell him where I was all weekend—not that he would ask, because he trusts me, of course. Even though maybe he shouldn't trust me after this fiasco, and even though he would be really, really mad at me for doing this with you, since he has this tiny little spot of jealousy where you're concerned—"

"He's jealous of me?" Tripp smiled, enjoying that idea.

"Well, maybe more like impatient. He just doesn't understand why I still hang around with you."

He'd only met Jay Philpott once, but he was less than impressed. In his admittedly biased opinion, Philpott was too good to be believed. He was handsome enough, in a bland, political way, and he had a plastic smile that women voters seemed to love.

Philpott knew facts and figures on every issue under the sun, and he seemed to spend a lot of time and effort making it look as though he really cared about whales and screech owls, migrant workers and Haitian refugees.

He didn't take insults personally, always turned the other cheek, paid his taxes on time and had never been caught in any kind of indiscretion.

But nobody, *nobody* was really that good. There had to be a skeleton in the closet somewhere.

"Why would he be jealous of me?"

"Maybe because I'm always leaving him in the lurch while I run off and rescue you," she said cynically. "There might be a hint there about who goes where on my priority list."

"Yeah, well, the guy's not good enough for you, anyway. If he hassles you about where you were, just dump him."

"Oh, that's charming! I'm the one who agrees to be engaged to somebody else while I'm wearing his ring, and if he says a word about it, I'm supposed to dump him."

Tripp smiled. "Sounds good to me."

"You're impossible. Listen, I have to go. Jay's coming in a few hours to pick me up, and I have to think of what I'm going to tell him. Oh, no," she cried, "I left my ring in the pocket of the jeans I was wearing in Lake Tahoe. And I can't leave work and go home to find the stupid thing. What will I tell him if he sees my naked finger?"

"Just tell him you forgot to wear it. Big deal."

"You don't understand. Jay is perfect. He would never forget his ring. How can I tell him *I* did?"

"He'll forgive you."

"Oh, I know he'll forgive me. He always does. But sometimes, you know, I just hate needing to be forgiven."

"Bridgie," Tripp tried again, "I really think you should forget trying to live up to Philpott's standards. He's inhuman. You're not. You make mistakes. That's life. But speaking of rings..."

"Yes? What? Hurry, will you? I need to get off the phone."

He reconsidered. Maybe Bridgie would find it more amusing if he gave her the ring as a surprise. He smiled. He found he liked that idea a lot. Even if it was only a sham, even if it wasn't a real engagement, he still thought she'd enjoy knowing he'd picked out something pretty just for her, and then gone to the trouble of arranging a romantic dinner.

"Listen," he said slowly, "did you say you were having dinner with Philpott tonight?"

"Yes. Why?"

"Because you can't. You're having dinner with me."

"Tripp, I can't. I have plans."

"Get rid of him," he ordered. "I'll wait for you at your apartment. Can you make it home by seven? Will that give you enough time to get rid of Philpott?"

"Well, it would, if I were going to, but—"

"You will unless you want him to run into me. I'll be there, waiting."

"Tripp, don't—"

"Do you want Philpott to come into your apartment and find me there?"

"God, no!" She shuddered, and Tripp took that to mean she wasn't planning on letting the two of them meet up. Good. "But you can't wait for me there," she told him. "You don't have a key."

"Just be there at seven. And don't worry—I'll take care of everything."

Why did it seem like he had said those words a hundred times in the past few days?

EVERYTHING WAS READY. And he actually felt nervous.

He'd had to run around like a crazy man to find a ring he liked, get to the gourmet grocery store he liked and then talk Bridgie's doorman into letting him into her apartment.

"I'm her fiancé," he'd said sheepishly. And once he'd flashed the ring at the guy, he was inside without a whimper.

Dinner was now well underway, and as far as he knew, everything was perfect. He'd whipped up a simple fettuccine Alfredo, which he knew was one of her favorite dishes, plus he'd brought salad, wine and a two-layer chocolate cake with fresh fall flowers arranged on the top.

For the final touch, he set the ring box neatly in the middle of the flowers.

The last time he'd been this nervous about a date, he was eighteen years old. She was the captain of the cheerleading squad, a bona fide older woman of twenty-one, and he was so jumpy, he'd almost hit her with the car door when he held it open for her.

But there was no time to think about the women in his past. The woman in his present was about to come home, and he wanted to impress her.

He lit the candles on the oak coffee table, and then turned off all the rest of the lights. Bridgie's living room was now lit with a romantic glow, aided by the lights of Chicago's skyline visible through the window.

"Very nice," he allowed, just as he heard the door twist open.

"Tripp, are you here? Why is it so dark in here?" she called out. "Oh, there you are." She looked around at the candles and the cutlery, she looked at him and she said, "Oh my God."

"Do you like it?"

She swallowed. "What is this for?"

"For you, of course." Tripp edged over to take her coat and her briefcase, but she jumped back the second he touched her. "Bridgie, what's the matter?"

"Nothing," she said, but her voice was shaky, and her pupils were huge.

Bridgie had the prettiest eyes—they were a deep, dark brown, so dark they almost looked black. Her eyes reminded him of darkness, of mysteries, of nighttime. Why hadn't he noticed that before? Her black, thick lashes seemed to make the color even more striking, especially against her pale, creamy skin.

She was wearing a dark suit with a white blouse. In another place, her attire might have seemed severe. But here, in the flickering glow of the candles, she was a study in light and shadow. Shadows played across her face, softening the line of her cheek and her mouth, fading into the whiteness of her throat, where her blouse gapped open at the top button.

He lifted a hand to cup her cheek, a thumb to brush below the curve of her lashes. She was so still, so quiet. So unlike his Bridgie.

He wanted to kiss her. His mouth ached with the need.

All it would take was a small push forward, and he could take her in his arms, he could lower his lips to hers, he could bury himself in her sweetness, in her goodness, in her trust.

He wanted her. Tripp couldn't ever remember wanting anything more, and it rocked him down to the core.

No matter how often this damn animal attraction kept pushing at him, he was determined to push it right back. Bridget was his friend, and she trusted him. How could he stand here, wanting her so badly, it made his jaw clench? Talk about betrayal. Talk about taking advantage. Talk about ruining everything.

He couldn't let this happen. Not with Bridgie.

Immediately he backed off, reaching for her coat and her briefcase. Under cover of shoving her things in the closet, he tried to regain some semblance of self-control.

"It smells great in here. What are you making?" she asked, but he started speaking at the same moment, trying to break the looming silence.

His question— "Do you want to change your clothes before we eat?" —came out on top of hers.

And then she said, "Sure, I'll go change," just as he answered, "Fettuccine Alfredo," in response to the wrong question.

"Fettucini Alfredo is my favorite."

Politely, he responded, "I know."

And they both laughed self-consciously.

Damn. How could things be so damn clumsy with Bridgie? That was what was so special about her, about them, that there was never an awkward moment between them. Until now.

Thankfully, she seemed more able to handle things than he was. She excused herself to change out of her business suit, and he served the food for lack of anything better to do.

When she came back, dressed now in a long, white silk blouse over skinny black jeans, he had everything ready.

They sat on the floor around the coffee table—he'd somehow thought the floor would be more fun than the dinner table—and at least the food furnished them with plenty of ammunition for small talk.

"So how did you manage to get in here?" she asked, taking a long sip of her wine.

He finally cracked a smile. "Your doorman was pretty agreeable. He buzzed me right up. I guess he figured I couldn't be too dangerous if I was carrying a couple of bags of groceries and a bakery box."

"I'll have to speak to him," she said severely, but she was smiling, too, so Tripp figured it couldn't be too bad.

"And how did you get rid of old Philpott?"

Bridget flushed. "Could you call him Jay, please?"

"Sure." Tripp leaned back against the sofa, stretching out his long legs. With a measuring gaze, he asked, "So how did you get rid of old Jay?"

"I was terrible." She bent over her plate, fiddling with a stray strand of pasta. "I told him I had a headache. Straight off a 1950s sitcom. I said I was going to take some aspirin and go right to bed. He wanted to come up with me, you know, tuck me in or something, but I talked him out of that, too."

"He wanted to tuck you in?" Tripp didn't like the sound of that. He suddenly had the overwhelming need to rearrange Jay Philpott's features.

"I blew him off. I lied to him," she murmured. "I'm a terrible person."

"You're not a terrible person. Hey, it got him out of your hair for one night, and there's nothing wrong with that."

"I know, but..." Bridgie's eyes shone large and dark across the table. "I hate being so dishonest. How can I carry on this charade with you and not tell him?"

"Did he give you a hard time about the ring?"

She shook her head. "Of course not. He even offered to buy me another one if I couldn't find it. You know Jay. Always thoughtful. Always perfect."

"You can't marry that guy, Bridgie, do you hear?" His voice was deliberate, dangerous. "Over my dead body."

"Two fiancés, and you don't want me to marry either of them," she said mockingly.

"Neither of them are good enough for you."

His gaze held hers, across the table, across the candlelight. He wished he knew how to read her expression. He wished he'd thought to wonder what she was thinking years ago, so this wouldn't all be so new to him now.

"Did you like my little surprise?" he asked softly.

"The dinner, you mean? It was great." She licked her lips. "Although I'm not quite sure I understand the point of it."

"We're officially engaged. I thought we should celebrate."

"Oh, I see." She cocked her head to one side, sending the dark, glossy waves of her short pageboy spilling to one shoulder. "Sometimes, Tripp, you are such a mystery to me."

Ditto, he thought, but he rose from the table rather than pursue the question.

"Ready for dessert?" he asked, carrying in the cake.

"Wow. A cake, too? Chocolate, of course. You really know how to turn a girl's head," she teased.

"I hope so."

He set it down in front of her, waiting for her reaction.

"Isn't that pretty. Tiger lilies, right?" She bent over closer. "What's that in the middle?"

She picked up the jeweler's box.

Her eyes went wide. "For me?" And her hands trembled as she pulled off the ribbon and pried it open. "Oh my God."

"It's an engagement ring. Since we're supposed to be engaged, it seemed like the right thing to do. I, uh, hope you like it," he said gruffly.

But Bridget surprised him. She burst into tears and threw the box at the cake.

"What? What did I do wrong?"

"A romantic dinner and then a ring? How could you? It's so beautiful and it's all a big, ugly, disgusting lie! How could you do this to me?"

"Do what? I bought you a ring. What's wrong with that?"

Bridget tried to leap to her feet, but she caught her knee under the corner of the coffee table. Hooking it, she gave it a good push, and the whole thing lifted up on one side. She leaned forward, trying to regain her balance, but the heel of her hand came down on the rim of the cake plate.

As he watched in horror, the chocolate cake flipped up, like a huge, fat, messy tiddlywink.

Splat.

Before he could get out of the way, he got the full brunt of it. Cake, fudge, frosting, not to mention a whole tiger lily, had all plastered themselves down the front of his shirt.

Bridget just stood there, staring at the mess. A clump of cake slid off his shirt, plopping back onto the coffee table, and they watched its slow progress all the way down.

Finally she said, "I hope that wasn't a good shirt."

"Good or not, it's the only one I've got at the moment." Gingerly, he picked the lily out of the chocolate mess in his front pocket. After wavering for a moment, he set it over by the remains of the cake. "Do you have something else I could wear, just long enough to clean this up?"

"Oh, sure." She started to back up down the hall toward her bedroom. "I'm sure I must have... There must be something I can... I'll just see."

Tripp had no choice but to stay where he was, although he did, very carefully, peel off his shirt. And then he used the once-white linen to brush off the front of his pants. "God, what a mess."

Bridget came back, but she wasn't carrying any extra clothes. Instead, she had a stack of newspapers.

"I thought we could get this under you," she said, clumsily bending down to lay papers on the couch behind him, and to poke a couple of sheets under his feet. Obediently, he lifted first one foot and then the other.

Bridget took away his shirt, wrapping it in newspaper and carelessly tossing it aside. "Okay," she said breathlessly. "Now strip."

"Strip?"

"Your pants. They need to come off." She was kneeling, and her head was just level with his....

He clenched his jaw and looked across the room, out the window, anywhere but at the top of her pretty little head, just even with his belt buckle.

And then she started to undo it.

He caught her hands. "I think I can undo my own belt."

"Of course." She shrugged. "I just thought... Well, you needed to get out of them."

Her breath was wafting hot puffs of air against his belly button as he undid the buckle on his belt. Oh, God. This was torture. Unlike her other fiancé, Tripp was no saint. About two more seconds of her breathing on his bare stomach, and he was going to take off his pants himself and show her just what he had to offer.

Her hand brushed his fly. He went rigid.

"Sorry," she whispered.

"Maybe you could, uh, back up a little," he said gruffly.

"Just take them off," she breathed.

He looked down into her deep, dark eyes, and Tripp saw banked fires there that made it difficult to breathe. He saw the tip of her tongue dart out, once, to touch her top lip, and he knew that tongue was only a fraction of an inch from the front of his pants.

The images of her tongue and his... He shut his eyes.

"Are you in pain? You just groaned."

"Yes, I am in pain." Forcing himself to remain calm, he took her by the shoulders and pulled her to a standing position. All he meant to do was put some distance between them, but there she was, in his arms, breathing unsteadily, staring at him, and he knew she wasn't going anywhere.

So he kissed her.

He didn't bother to make it soft or nice. He just seared her with all the anger and frustration he'd been storing up. Damn it all to hell if she didn't kiss him back just as hard and mean and ferocious.

Her mouth opened to him, and he plunged inside. She was hot and delicious and she smelled like chocolate. No, that was him. It didn't matter. It was intoxicating.

She was moaning and pushing closer, pressing her mouth into his, rubbing the slippery silk of her blouse against his bare chest.

Swiftly, Tripp pushed his pants down and out of the way with one hand. They dropped onto the newspaper with a thud that startled them both. And them he grabbed her back, and kissed her again, with an unrelenting hunger that shocked even him.

Muttering something unpleasant, he pushed her backward into the couch.

"The chocolate," she tried.

"Don't care," he shot back, and fastened his mouth over hers so she couldn't talk.

She was shoving at his clothes and he was shoving at hers, until all he was wearing was his silk boxer shorts, and she was half-covered in her silk blouse. Tumbled together in the couch like that, surrounding himself with Bridget—it was fast and furious and the sexiest thing he'd ever done. He knew he had to pull back to breathe soon, but he didn't give a damn if he passed out at this point.

Gasping for air, she pulled back first. But her eyes were glued to his body, lingering on his chest, brushing over his arms and his legs, hungrily following a wayward streak of chocolate that painted a line across his ribs. She licked her lip. And then she bent to press her lips to the chocolate, to delicately flick the sweetness away with her little pink tongue.

He let out a sound of pure heat, of pure male agony. God, he hadn't planned to let things go this far. One more inch and they'd both be beyond the point of no return.

"Bridget," he tried.

"Mmm," she said, licking his chest.

"Bridget, I don't think we should do this."

"What?" But the moment was lost. He saw the strained, embarrassed look on her face as she sat up.

"I'm sorry," he said softly. Sorry? Yeah, he was plenty sorry. Sorry he'd interrupted her. Sorry he'd ever been born. "I didn't think . . ."

"I didn't, either."

"There's Jay to think of. I mean, you are engaged."

"Jay. Right."

She scrambled off the couch, hovering about ten feet away before he could protest.

Neither could think of a thing to say.

But Tripp was very aware that the pair of boxer shorts he was wearing did very little to hide the prominent evidence of his desire. "Do you have something else for me to wear?" he asked quietly.

"I—I couldn't really find anything that would fit you. You're a lot bigger than me, and I looked for something like a sweatshirt or a T-shirt, but I couldn't really find—"

"You don't have anything for me to wear?"

"Nothing but . . . well, this." She held out a robe. Her robe.

A plain cotton kimono, it probably came to midcalf on her. But as he held it up, he knew it would only do about knee-length on him. Still, it was better than nothing.

"Why don't you start cleaning this mess up?" he said. "There's chocolate everywhere."

"I know." Her gaze flashed to his chest, where he had been painted with a brush of chocolate frosting. His mind filled with the image of Bridget's mouth pressed to his flesh again, licking away that chocolate.

He couldn't bear it.

Hiding himself behind her robe, he mumbled, "I think I'd like to take a shower. Would you be willing to wash my clothes while I'm in the shower?"

"Well, I would. But I can't."

He sighed. "Why not?"

"Because I don't have a washer or a dryer."

"In the building?"

"Uh, no. I have to take my laundry out."

"Great," he said roughly. "This is just great."

"Look, why don't we rinse out the chocolate in the bathtub? We can hang your things up to dry."

"And how am I supposed to get home without my clothes?"

"Well . . ." Bridgie sent him a strange look. "I guess you'll have to stay overnight."

Chapter Eight

He was sleeping on Bridget's couch. Or trying to sleep. Just him, all alone.

No chocolate, although they'd checked the general vicinity to make sure.

No pants, no shirt. Just his boxers and Bridgie's robe. And no Bridgie.

This was what he was reduced to. Tripp Ashby, eligible bachelor, was finally engaged, and to a woman he was dying to touch, dying to make love to. So where did he end up? On her couch. And it was his own idea.

He was the one who'd been noble and idiotic, deferring to her white knight of a fiancé. Maybe it wasn't the right thing to do to make love to someone else's fiancé when that guy wasn't looking, but Tripp felt sure he could've overlooked it just this once.

Bridgie. The image of her mouth licking away that chocolate...

He punched the pillow, rustling around, trying to find a more comfortable position.

Surely, sometime in his life, he must've slept on her couch before. He pondered the subject.

There was that time when she came over to help him study for his Medieval History final, and they ended up falling asleep together. But that was his couch, not hers, and he hadn't even known they were sleeping together until he woke up.

He smiled. He remembered the expression on her face when they did wake up. Horrified. She'd leapt away from him, blushed seventeen shades of pink and made him promise not to tell anyone. She couldn't get out of there fast enough.

"But you know, Bridgie," he whispered into her dark living room. "If I had it to do over again, I might've tried harder to stay awake. And when you were all sleepy and cozy, I might've tried harder to persuade you to stay."

To stay. To let him kiss her. To let him make love to her. Right there on the dilapidated sofa in the basement of the house he shared with Deke.

But he couldn't think about how it might've been. It was too painful.

Sofas. Damn hard, uncomfortable places to sleep.

Tripp flipped over onto his back, folded his hands behind his head and stared at the ceiling. With Bridgie down the hall in a nice, soft bed, and him out here on a lonely, godforsaken sofa, it was going to be a long night.

But he'd no more than closed his eyes when he heard Bridgie calling his name.

"Tripp? Tripp? Are you awake?"

"I am now." He opened one eye. It was light in the room. Dim, but definitely light. "Is it morning already?"

"Yeah. But your clothes are still wet. Here, I brought out your pants so you could feel—"

She was holding them out in front of her, giving them the once-over, not paying attention to where she was going. One pant leg seemed to get tangled up with her leg, and she got stuck. Before she could catch herself, she fell straight forward, right over the side of the couch, right on top of Tripp.

"Oof," she said. She picked up her head enough to look him in the eye.

Above him, plastered to him, her body was soft in all the right places, soft and sexy as hell, and Tripp held on to her, unwilling to let her go.

"The way you've been behaving lately, maybe we should call you Tripp instead of me," he said lightly.

"What a klutz," she mumbled. "I'm not usually like this."

"I know."

She started to wiggle, to try to scramble off him, but that only made things worse. A tendril of her hair brushed his bare chest, her small hand skimmed his hip, and that was all it took. He went rigid. He let out a moan as her stomach slid down his stomach, grazing him right where it did the most damage.

"Uh, maybe you ought to . . ."

At first his motives were pure. He meant to move her away, to cool down the steam quotient and get them both out of trouble. But he made a mistake. When he adjusted his arms around her, bracing her against the back of the couch, he eased them both around. And suddenly he was on top.

"Tripp, can we . . . ?"

But he didn't want to hear her question. He could feel her small, slender body curving underneath him, into him. She was trembling, shivering, angling closer with every breath she took, and he knew suddenly that she was as turned on as he.

It was enough to make him break out in a cold sweat. With her pressed up so intimately, amazingly close, he couldn't think, couldn't breathe. And he couldn't be noble twice in a row.

So he did what came naturally, what required no thought at all.

It took only a few inches to bend down and kiss her, and he did it, savage and hot. All of last night's frustration came pounding out, as he delved deeper into her mouth, kissing her rougher and harder than he meant to. But, oh, she tasted good.

She was wearing a cotton nightgown, something white and demure, nothing like the nasty black number she'd had at the cabin. The cool cotton twisted between them, riding up over her thighs and her waist, and he could feel the slick heat of her bare skin as her leg wound around him.

He pushed more of the nightgown away, bending down to press his lips to her shoulder and her collarbone, to the soft swell of her breast, slipping his hand up under her hip. He found no barrier. Nothing—no panties—just soft, soft skin. He stifled a moan.

He splayed his fingers against her round, soft bottom, maneuvering her in closer, trying to ease the sharp hunger of his desire.

They were touching everywhere, but it wasn't enough. He wanted her, all of her. He had to have her. Now.

"Bridget?" He found her gaze. She looked dazzled, disoriented, but she nodded, very quickly. "Bridget?" he asked again.

"Yes. I said yes."

And then they both heard the front door of her apartment swing open.

They froze.

"There you are, ma'am."

"Thank you so much. What a lovely doorman you are. My son and my daughter-in-law will be so grateful you allowed me to come in," someone said pleasantly from out in the hall. "Good morning! Anybody home?"

Aside from the fact that he wasn't wearing anything but Bridget's bathrobe and a pair of boxer shorts, Tripp knew exactly what the two of them looked like, entwined like that on the couch. Most of her body was underneath him, her hair was a wild tangle on his pillow and one bare leg was wrapped around his waist.

Talk about compromising positions.

Quickly he detached himself, yanked his robe shut and vaulted over to the other side of the couch. Bridget still lay there, dazed, so he grabbed her wrist and pulled her to a sitting position. And then he reached back and jerked the strap of her nightgown into place.

Although he didn't think that little diversion was going to fool anyone.

One glance at Bridget, disheveled, breathing unsteadily, practically hyperventilating, and even an idiot could guess she'd just had the ride of her life.

But she looked beautiful. Good enough to eat, good enough to topple right back onto the couch and never let go.

"Just popped in to see how things were going," Kitty Belle said gaily, poking her golden brown curls into the room. Her bright little eyes skipped from one to the other. "And from the looks of you two, I'd say they're going just fine!"

"WEAR THE RING," he said between gritted teeth.

"No."

"Wear it, damn it."

"No."

"In front of my mother," he said ferociously, "I really think you should wear it. Especially after last night."

She crossed her arms over her chest and glared at him. "I won't wear it. Especially after last night."

"Are you two fighting over there? Newlywed squabbles, and you're not even married yet." Kitty Belle tittered at her own joke. "Sparks are flying!"

With Bridget's hand firmly in his, Tripp towed her over to where his mother sat. She didn't go willingly. This morning, all she wanted to do was hit him. Because if she stayed seethingly, blazingly mad at him, she didn't have to think about the wanton way she'd gone after him last night and again this morning.

If she hung on to her fury, she didn't have time to think about how sweet and nice he'd been last night, making that special dinner just for her. And that ring. If that wasn't enough to break her heart.

She didn't have to think about the way he looked in his boxer shorts, his beautiful athlete's body stretched out on display in front of her. All muscle, all sinew, all slim, elegant strength. If there had ever been a more gorgeous man, she hadn't seen him.

Damn the man. Last night, with that taste of chocolate, brushed just so across his muscled torso, like an added attraction, she had gone absolutely out of her mind. It was so embarrassing.

Last night. And then this morning. Even worse this morning.

He was going to make love to me. "No, he wasn't," she swore under her breath. There must have been some mistake. Her overheated imagination must have run away with her.

Because she certainly had wanted him to make love to her. *Tripp,* she had to keep reminding herself. *That was Tripp you almost took a tumble with on the living room couch. The man you've lusted after for so many years, you've lost count.*

She wanted him. Like just another one of the hot-to-trot tarts who were always chasing after him.

But she didn't want to be one of them. She had always prided herself that she was different, better, smarter, less ruled by passion, more ruled by her brain. She was the one with her eye on her future, on what a lifetime of trust and commitment could mean, as opposed to a few minutes of groping on someone's couch. Wasn't she?

Not when he kept sending her those smoky glances. How was she supposed to act like a human being, how was she supposed to keep her hands off him, when he insisted on looking at her that way?

It really wasn't fair. Even dressed in a chocolate-stained white shirt and rumpled, damp trousers, Tripp looked terrific.

"Terrific."

"Did you say something?" he asked her.

"No."

"Yes, you did."

"No, I didn't."

"Yes—"

"Stop fighting, you two."

"We're not fighting," Tripp said tersely. "We're having a discussion."

"Well, you know," Kitty Belle offered helpfully, "when passions run high, these disagreements happen.

Don't worry, children. It's a good sign. A very good sign that my decision is the right one.''

Bridget remained silent, glaring daggers at all of them. Kitty Bell was positively glowing. One moment she was paler than pale, hiding under thick makeup, and the next she seemed to be the very picture of health. Maybe it was part of her illness.

"Decision? What decision?" Tripp inquired.

"Oh, I almost forgot to tell you. And that's why I came, of course." Looking as if she had just personally hatched a golden egg, she confided, "You're going to be so happy. I've set a date!"

"A date for what?" he asked doubtfully.

"The wedding, of course."

"Next spring," Bridget interjected. "Or summer. I always wanted to be a June bride. Or how about Christmas 1995? Or Christmas '96?"

"Oh, but I can't wait that long." Kitty Belle pulled out her date book. "I've got it all set for November fifth."

"The fifth? But that's only two weeks away. Not even two weeks." Bridget's eyes were round with horror. "Tripp, stop this right now."

"I know you're worried, and yes, it is a very short time. But we'll make it," Mrs. Ashby said cheerfully. "After all, I don't have much time, so I have to make the most of what I've got. Leave everything to me."

"I don't want to leave it to you." She didn't want to leave it to anyone. She wanted to put a stop to it, right now.

"Your concern is sweet, dear, but completely unnecessary. I see now that you were right about keeping it small. Now we can do everything we want, and so quickly! Lucinda Gibson will lend us her conservatory, and we can have a string quartet in her gazebo afterward. Of course, your gown may be a problem, my dear." She frowned. "I'm afraid we're going to be forced to buy off the rack."

"I am not getting married in two weeks," Bridget hissed in his ear. "I'm not getting married at all. Tripp, do something!"

"I'm trying to think," he shot back in the same fierce whisper.

"So, all set for the fifth." Kitty Belle packed up her calendar and prepared to go.

"Okay, Mother, we'll go for the fifth." As the bottom dropped out of Bridget's stomach, as she flashed him a paralyzed look, he went on, "But not at Lucinda's. We want to get married at Lake Tahoe, don't we, Bridgie?"

"At Lake Tahoe?"

"That's right." He squeezed her hand so tightly, she let out a little squeak of pain. Right about now, she wanted to kick him. Hard. "That's where we fell in love, isn't it, darling?"

She narrowed her eyes at him. "Is that where it happened?"

He was selling her down the river. She distinctly remembered him telling her they would never have to go through with it. *I'm just asking for an engagement—a temporary engagement—not a wedding. Only a few months... Once she's gone, we can fold up our engagement and put it away, and no one will ever be the wiser. Don't worry,* he'd said. *I'll take care of it.*

Oh, yeah. He'd taken care of everything, hadn't he? At this rate, they'd be celebrating their tenth wedding anniversary before this "fake" engagement was folded up and put away.

"We have our hearts set on Tahoe." Tripp fixed a determined smile on his face. "We'll invite my buddies, since they're the co-owners of the cabin. That will take care of witnesses. And since it's Nevada, we can get a license in about five minutes. No problem."

"Are you sure you wouldn't rather go to the Cupid's Arrow Chapel of Perpetual Motion?" Bridget asked maliciously. "I'm not sure there's enough snow for the ski-by wedding, but we could definitely get Elvis."

"Oh, my word!" Kitty Belle gasped.

For the first time since they'd found out about her terminal illness, Mrs. Ashby actually looked as if she might expire at any moment.

"No Elvis," Tripp said firmly.

"No nothing," Bridget returned, just as firmly.

And then the phone rang.

"Don't decide anything without me," Bridget warned them. "I'll be right back."

But the minute she picked up the phone, Marie's annoying whine jumped out at her. "Ms. Emerick, where are you? If you weren't coming in today, you should've called to let us know."

"Where am I?" She glanced at the kitchen clock. Ten-thirty. Ten-thirty? And this was a Tuesday. She was due at Niles, Tweed and Sternham two hours ago! "I have plumbing problems," she made up on the spur of the moment. "My whole apartment is flooded. I'll be in as soon as I can."

She came charging back into the dining room, just long enough to tell Tripp and his mother that she had to go to work, and to let themselves out. What was wrong with her? A weekday, and she'd completely forgotten about her job.

She was losing her mind.

Struggling with the buttons on her blouse, she almost didn't hear Tripp slip into her bedroom. She would've known he was there, anyway. It was as if she had radar out all the time, tuned into his frequency.

"Look, I'm sorry," he offered. "There was nothing else I could do."

"Yeah, right. Where have I heard that before?"

He raked a hand through his hair. "You're right. It's my fault. I should've known the engagement thing wouldn't satisfy her. But she says she wants to see me married—to actually see my wedding—before she dies. That sounds reasonable."

Bridget shoved her arms into her suit jacket with enough force to knock herself off balance. "How could you say yes?"

But Tripp grasped her by the shoulders, holding her there at arm's length while he talked to her. She didn't want him to touch her; she was afraid she would weaken. She already felt herself melting and sliding.

"It won't be so bad, Bridgie," he said softly. "No strings—nothing either of us can't handle—just a small, quick wedding ceremony at the cabin, with a few hand-picked friends there who'll know the truth. You know, Deke and Ki and Steve. No big deal. And then, after everyone leaves, we'll spend our pretend honeymoon right there at the cabin, with no one to notice the fact that we're not gooey and in love like real honeymooners."

Not gooey and in love? *Speak for yourself, Trippett,* she thought mournfully. *No.* She wasn't in love with Tripp, and she never had been. So she'd lusted after his body from afar, and recently, not so far. Every woman at Beckett College had lusted after him. It was part of the core curriculum. But it was harmless.

"It'll be over before you know it," he promised.

"Over? Will any of this really ever be over, Tripp?"

"As soon as Kitty Belle . . ." His voice drifted away. He wasn't willing to say it right out, but they both knew what they'd be waiting for.

It was ghoulish and ghastly, but it was the only way.

"We'll get a quiet annulment, even quieter than the wedding." He smiled wanly. "No problem."

"Tripp," she said bluntly, "you've lost your mind. I can't marry you. I can't even be in the same room with you."

And with that, she swept past him and out of the room, sailed down the hall, pausing only to grab her coat and her briefcase from the hall closet.

Right behind her, Tripp kept talking. "It will be a vacation for both of us. You know it's beautiful up there. We can hike and ski and do a little boating. Even hit the casinos if you want to. You'll love it. You can take some time off from the firm, can't you? Didn't you say you were taking a leave of absence after Christmas to work on Jay's campaign? So just start it a couple of months early—get a vacation in before the campaign starts."

Bridget stopped. She leaned her forehead against the closet door, taking deep breaths.

"Come on, Bridgie. We're in this up to our necks. Can it really hurt to take the last few steps?"

"Yes, it can."

"Trust me." He spun her around and kissed her, a quick, hard, brave kiss that made her want to be brave, too. "We'll get through it together."

"We haven't done so hot together so far," she murmured.

"It will be different up there. Here, we're under a lot of pressure." He put an arm around her, pulling her closer. It was tempting to just snuggle in to his warmth and his strength. "There, it will be just us."

"Just us," she echoed.

What a terrifying idea.

NOT EVEN WORK could dull the emotional turmoil raging in her heart. She stabbed a pencil into her blotter, jamming it so hard, it broke in two.

Had it only been a few days since she'd sworn off Tripp for good? In this very office, she had promised herself she would put him out of her life. Only, somehow, he was more firmly embedded in her every thought, her every breath, than ever before.

The light began to flash on her phone, and she reached for it, welcoming the intrusion.

"Ms. Emerick, there's someone here to see you."

"Who is it?" she asked wearily. "If it's someone I need to see, I'd appreciate it if you could set up an appointment for later. Maybe tomorrow."

"But he's on his way in."

"Tripp?" she asked, half rising.

But it was Jay. He shut the door neatly, and then just stood there, watching her. His eyes were calm and pleasant, and he was even smiling, but there was a set to his jaw she hadn't seen before.

"Hello, sweetheart," he said smoothly.

"Hi, Jay." Bridget sat back down. She picked up the broken pencil and gave it another stab. "I saw the latest poll results on TV last night. You're up another three points. Looking good."

"Yes, the primary seems to be firmly in hand."

"Good." She waited a moment. "Is there something else? It's kind of unusual for you to stop by the office like this without telling me ahead of time."

"Actually, there is something." He removed a folded newspaper from his pocket and then laid it down on her desk. "Something unusual that has been brought to my attention."

"It looks like a newspaper."

"It *is* a newspaper, darling," he said kindly.

"And what's wrong with it?"

"Tripp Ashby is in it."

This was like pulling teeth. "So?"

"He's getting married. Or he's already married. Do you know anything about that?"

For one small moment, she actually considered telling him the truth. But she knew Jay. He was perfect. It would never occur to him to betray his fiancée this way, and it should never have occurred to her. She wanted to be as perfect as he was, really she did, but it was always a struggle.

It was a terrible truth, but it was so much easier to lie. So Bridget played dumb. "Should I?"

"Are you the bride?"

"Me? Is this a joke?"

"You tell me." He smiled again. "Read the story, Bridget. And then you can fill me in."

It was a column, not a wedding announcement, and she was relieved to see that at least.

"'Tongues are wagging about Tripp Ashby, son of Kitty Belle and the late T. M. "Tommy" Ashby,'" she read out loud. "'Is the scion of a prominent local family secretly married to a flashy brunette? This observer has heard it's a done deal, that Mr. and Mrs. Ashby did the quickie Vegas two-step, even though she's a complete stranger to those in the know on the local social scene. Who's the bride? And what's the big secret?' '' Bridget glanced up. ''But, Jay, this is a gossip column.''

''Exactly. Is that you?''

''The flashy brunette? When has anyone ever called me flashy?'' She hid a small smile. It wasn't hard to figure out the source of this story. Miss Ski Pants. Miss Ski Pants thought Bridget was flashy. And wasn't that amusing?

''I didn't think it was you, but still . . . There's more. Read on.''

She traced her finger under the next line. '' 'Other sources claim Tripp Ashby is still Chicagoland's most eligible bachelor, if not for long. Seems he's planning a wedding in a few weeks, and poor mom Kitty Belle is frantically working to pull it off. This version of the story features the same mysterious brunette as the bride-to-be. Let's hope somebody chez Ashby clears up the mystery soon.' ''

''It's suspicious, don't you think?'' Jay demanded.

The jig was up, but she wasn't giving an inch. ''What has this got to do with me?''

''Is it you, Bridget? I know you've been friends a long time, and that when he needs you, you have a tendency to come running.'' Jay considered her. ''I also know that I've been very busy lately, and you might have sought solace from an old friend to take up the slack. I hope it's not true, Bridget, although I would understand that it is partially my fault if it were. Is something going on between you and Tripp Ashby?''

''You can't be serious.'' She managed a laugh that sounded hollow, even to her own ears. ''Don't you think you'd know if I were seeing another man? And how could I possibly be engaged to two men at once? Why, it's preposterous.''

Yeah, right. Preposterous. Too bad it was also true.

She braced her hands on her desk, all ready to stand and make soothing noises for Jay's benefit. But as she rose, she happened to glance down at her left hand, in full display there on the desk, and she did a double-take.

Tiny stars danced in the periphery of her vision. Bridget fell back into her chair.

She was wearing the wrong ring.

Tripp's ring! How in the hell did that get there? She'd had it this morning when he was trying to make her wear it for his mother, and she remembered tossing it on her bureau when she went back to get dressed. In the hurry to get out the door, in her state of mental confusion, she must've picked up Tripp's ring instead of Jay's ring.

Talk about Freudian slips.

Quickly she stuffed her hand down under the desk where Jay couldn't see it.

''Is something wrong? You look very odd all of a sudden.''

''Nothing's wrong.''

But he peered closer. ''Something is wrong. Your face went white as a sheet, and your hand is shaking. See?''

''M-my hand?'' But of course, he meant her right hand. The ringless hand. ''I'm just upset. All these accusations of yours. Anyone would be a little on edge.''

''Darling, I haven't accused you of anything. But I'm not blind. I know how you feel about Ashby. Bridget,'' he said more sternly, ''I want you to tell me the truth. If I need to do damage control, I need to know now.''

Under the desk, she was struggling to get the damn ring off. It seemed to be stuck. "What did you say? I'm sorry. I wasn't paying attention."

"Are people going to be asking me questions about my fiancée and another man? Should I be prepared with answers?"

She had to tell him something. He was right. If this blew up in their faces, it would ruin his campaign. Jay had always been so patient with her, so giving, so selfless, that she couldn't risk his political career just on a whim.

As she tried to put her thoughts together, she could only say, "I can't explain what's been happening, Jay." That was true enough, wasn't it? She couldn't explain—not even to herself. "But I want you to know, I would never willingly do anything that might sabotage your career or your campaign."

"Okay. But what exactly are you saying?"

She had to get out from behind that desk. With her ring hand firmly clasped inside the other one, she stood up awkwardly. "I'm saying that I know I've been acting strangely lately. Irritable and uncooperative. Ever since...well, ever since I said I would marry you. I guess I've been mixed-up about what I wanted to do. Getting married is a big thing to think about, especially to someone like you, someone in such a prominent position. It's very—" she took a deep breath "—confusing."

Especially when there were two grooms, and marriage to either of them seemed like a one-way ticket to disaster.

"Don't tell me—"

"I'm beginning to think I said yes too quickly."

Jay's eyebrows shot up. "Are you saying you want to call off the engagement? Bridget, I really think that would be unwise. There is simply no way to make that palatable to the general public this close to the primary."

"I'm not calling it off," she rushed to assure him. "Not exactly. I just need some time to think things over."

"You can have all the time you want," he said kindly, "as long as you make the right decision. We belong together, Bridget. We're the kind of bright, committed people America needs at the helm. And together, we can really make a difference."

She had always thought what he said was true, for her as well as him. But now she wasn't so sure.

"If you think Tripp Ashby has more to offer you than I do, you're dead wrong," he said suddenly.

"I never said anything about Tripp."

It was funny. The one tiny Achilles' heel Jay had was his dislike of Tripp. She never had understood it, but she was beginning to. It wasn't Tripp; it was the way she felt about him. Jay was so controlled and so impassive that he just didn't understand her emotional attachment to Tripp. It frightened him.

Well, it frightened her, too.

Jay offered a serious devotion to duty. Tripp offered laughter and chocolate cake. Jay offered ambition and idealism. Tripp offered a chance to be reckless and crazy, head over heels.

And he also offered passion. It was no small thing. Tripp offered to quench a smoldering need that she had never once felt for her other fiancé.

Was it wrong to want that passion, just once in her life?

"It's not Tripp," she said slowly. "It's me. I need to put our engagement on hold for a few weeks, while I go away and get things clear in my mind."

"You're going away?"

"Yes," she returned swiftly, speeding up as she became more sure. "I've put in for a few weeks of vacation. I'm going to Lake Tahoe."

Chapter Nine

"Oh, yes, that's the one," Kitty Belle exclaimed. "Lovely, dear. Simply lovely."

Bridget gazed down at the white dress, feeling a bit awed by the whole experience. She'd looked at lots of magazines with Jay, but it was different when the dress was here, on her body. And it was different when Tripp's mother was offering extravagant compliments, cooing over her, actually being . . . well, charming.

"Do you really like it?" Bridget asked again.

"It's stunning."

She couldn't quite believe she and Kitty Belle liked the same dress. It was very simple, very Grace Kelly, according to the designer, with its fitted lace bodice and full, tea-length skirt.

She twirled in front of the full-length mirror in the hall, feeling like a princess. "Okay. This is the one. I'm sure."

"Wonderful. Now, dear, I need to speak with you about something else." Kitty Belle made a delicate grimace. "I can't make heads or tails of what Tripp tells me about your family. Now, I know your mother is no longer with us, but there's your father, two brothers, and two sisters, is that right? So are you using your sisters as bridesmaids?''

"Uh, no. I wasn't planning on having any bridesmaids.''

"None?"

"None.''

Kitty Belle blinked a few times, but she got back on track quickly enough. "Well, all right. I suppose. But when are they arriving, dear? Are they coming to Chicago first? Or just straight to Tahoe?''

"They're not. Either.'' She started walking, away from Mrs. Ashby. "They're skipping it. They're busy.''

"Busy? Too busy to come to your wedding? Why, the very idea!''

"We've never been that close,'' she lied. "You know, just grow up and head out the door and that's that.''

"But that's terrible.''

"Well, what can I say?''

"Say that you'll make up.'' Kitty Belle's eyes got misty, and she fingered the lace edge of Bridget's sleeve. "Your wedding would be the perfect time, my dear. Call up your father and patch things up.''

"It's a lovely idea, but I don't think so.'' Spinning on her heel, Bridget ran smack into Tripp.

"Oh, no! He's seen the dress! Quick, dear, get out of that dress.''

But Bridget couldn't move.

His eyes were a deep, moody blue as he quite resolutely set her away from him. They hadn't been speaking too much lately, as if he had decided some distance was the best policy. In fact, standing here in the hallway, with his hands on her shoulders, was the closest he had gotten since that other morning, the one on the couch.

But she wasn't supposed to be thinking about that. She couldn't stop thinking about it, but she had to find a way.

"Bridget, this is disgraceful. Go back in your room and get out of that dress."

There was no fighting Kitty Belle when she got stirred up. Dutifully, Bridget went over to hand the dress over to the designer patiently waiting in the bedroom, standing guard over a pile of dresses.

As she carefully stepped out of the white lace confection, she heard Kitty Belle exclaim loudly, "Tripp, did you hear? She's not having any bridesmaids and her father's not coming. Who will give her away? Tripp, this is horrifying."

"Don't worry. I'll take care of it."

Famous last words.

As Kitty Belle faded away, in search of new lists to conquer, Bridget marched out in the hall. "No," she said, staring right at Tripp. She raised her chin. "Don't even think about it. I'm not bringing my father into this mess."

"It looks strange this way, Bridgie."

"What doesn't look strange these days?" She swallowed around the lump in her throat. What with the dress and thinking about her father, she was awash in sentiment. "My father loves me, and he trusts me. I just can't do this in front of him."

"Okay. I understand."

"No, I don't think you do," she returned. "He raised me to be honest and to do the right thing. If he knew what I was doing, he would never let me go through with it. And besides, I don't want to disappoint him. I don't want him to know I'm capable of this kind of deceit."

"It's not like you're robbing a bank or killing someone."

She shook her head stubbornly. "To my father, it wouldn't be that far off. And he knows about Jay. He's met Jay. He likes Jay. He's so proud of me for marrying someone like Jay. How could I possibly explain what I've done?"

"If your father loves you, he'll understand. In fact, if your father really loves you, he ought to be trying to convince you not to marry that guy," Tripp said roughly.

"Lay off Jay. That's a very touchy situation right now."

"What isn't?"

She didn't answer.

"Bridgie..." He tried to catch her eye, but she purposely eluded him. "Bridgie, I need to know if you really want to go through with this. If the idea of marrying me is so abhorrent, even for a few weeks, then we'd better call it off now."

She caught her breath. It was almost as if Tripp's feelings were hurt. He was offering her an out. He was being gallant. She didn't know what to think. "I didn't say it was abhorrent, did I?"

"You didn't have to."

"Tripp, I..." Bridget lay a hand on his arm, feeling the fierce strength he held in check. "I care about you a lot. And God help me, I'm even starting to like Kitty Belle."

He gave a small smile. "I know. And she's starting to like you, too. She's really in her element with all these plans, isn't she?"

Bridget laughed. "Absolutely. I've never seen a woman more taken with the bridal registry at Marshall

Field's. And you know, it's hard not to get caught up in the enthusiasm. When she brought that woman with the dresses in here, and told me I looked stunning, well, I could've kissed her."

"It's terrible," he said in a husky voice, "but the lies we're telling are really making her happy."

"So you think we're doing the right thing?"

He shook his head. "I don't know. But a few little white lies never hurt anybody, did they?"

BUT AS THE DAY before the wedding dawned, Tripp found himself drowning in little white lies.

It was like a breath of fresh air to escape to Lake Tahoe, and he knew he'd made at least one right choice. If either of them had spent one more minute in Chicago, they probably would've killed each other.

Things were getting crazy here, too, of course, with all the last-minute details. Plus all three of his Stud buddies were expected any moment. But it was still a big improvement over the past few days.

Maybe it was finally the chance to do something, to get the damn wedding out of the way. Better than all that fooling around in Bridgie's apartment, while his mother treated Bridgie as though she were made of fine porcelain, and he wanted to wring her neck.

Was she the surly one? Or was he?

One minute she looked at him like she used to when she thought he wasn't looking, like he was her hero. And the next she was carping at him.

He could handle the carping—that was vintage Bridgie—but he couldn't stand the mournful glances, the screwy moods and the incomprehensible physical reaction he had every time she walked into a room. He'd known her for sixteen years, and he'd never lusted after her once. But now...

But now, all she had to do was look at him funny, and his body leapt to life.

He knew better than she did that he couldn't act on those feelings. He had good reason to believe she might just go along with it if he did. But he couldn't let that happen.

Not to Bridgie. She loved another man. She was engaged to another man. As long as he'd known her, she had been so clear about her future, and no matter how hard he tried to convince her that she didn't have to take on all the world's burdens single-handedly, she was bound and determined to be somebody, to make a difference.

But Bridgie was no politician. Blunt, uncompromising, quirky, she had always known she herself wouldn't end up as a senator or ambassador.

But Jay Philpott could. Jay Philpott was her chance. By marrying Jay, by helping Jay, Bridgie could make the impact she'd always wanted.

Tripp knew her well enough to have heard her talk about her dreams more than once. And marrying Jay Philpott put her a lot closer to her dream. Fooling around, pretending to be engaged to Tripp was bad enough, but if she slept with him...

Tripp was no fool. A senator-to-be's fiancée didn't sleep with another man without blowing her dreams to smithereens.

And so he did his best to give her her dream, to stay away, to hold back, which was never going to work after this sham wedding. How was he going to keep up the charade when he was weak with desire?

The worst part was, this was his own fault. It was his plan. Great plan. Safe, trustworthy Bridgie. Safe no more.

And whoever was at fault, he was sick to death of it.

But then he would see his mother, and he would remember what the whole scheme was for.

Just today, in the middle of the afternoon, he found her dozing in a chair in front of the cabin fireplace. Kitty Belle had always been so strong, so resolute, like a force of nature. And yet time and again lately, he caught her napping.

Looking down at the fine trace of wrinkles etched in her forehead, he knew suddenly that she had aged, sometime when he wasn't looking. Sure she was a pain in the neck, but she was also his mother. And his mother was getting old.

Kitty Belle was mortal. Kitty Belle was dying.

The finality of it took his breath away. In a few months, maybe even weeks, she would be gone. And there would be nothing he could do to fulfill her dreams.

Her eyelids fluttered open. "Tripp, darling, is that you?"

"Yes, Mother. Are you okay? Is there anything I can get you?"

"Oh, no, dear, I'm fine." She sat up straighter. "Well, fine, considering...you know."

"Right."

He edged away, but she caught his hand. He couldn't read her expression, but it was very intent. "Tripp, sweetheart, there's something I need to ask you."

This was awfully serious, serious enough to make him uncomfortable. "Okay."

"Are you really happy, with the way things have turned out?"

"I don't know what you—"

"Getting married, I mean. Are you happy with that idea? God knows you resisted long enough."

"Yes, I'm happy," he told her. White lie number one.

"And Bridget? This is what she wants?"

"Yes, she's fine." White lie number two. And number three brought up the rear. "We're in love, and we want to get married. What could be easier?"

She paused. "You're sure. Because I know I pushed unbearably and it really isn't fair to—"

"It's fine."

"If you're sure." She brightened then, as if she had decided to believe him, although she didn't quite rise from her supine position. "Have you convinced Bridget to call her father? There's still time to get him here for tomorrow, if we hurry."

"Bridget's father?"

"How can it be a wedding with no one to give the bride away?" She wrinkled her brow. "It's so unsettling to think no one from Bridget's family will be here. I don't like that, Tripp. I don't like it at all."

"If you want Bridget's father, then he'll be here," Tripp promised.

Now all he had to do was figure out a way to get a father for Bridget without Mr. Emerick, the high-minded plumber from St. Paul, finding out there was a wedding going on.

Looked like he was headed for lie number four, and the biggest of the bunch.

But if he wanted to keep his mother happy, he would produce a father to give Bridgie away. And if he wanted to keep his fiancée happy, he would leave her father out of it.

"HERE'S TO OUR old buddy, Tripp," said Steve Chambliss, holding up what was about number ten in his own personal stock of beer bottles. "May marriage make him a better man. 'Cause we all know it can't make him any worse."

His little joke was punctuated by the usual groans. They'd known each other so long, they had the routine down pat. Every time they were together, they drank beer, told terrible jokes, insulted each other and had a great time.

This time was a little different, of course, since one of their group was leaving the fold. Tripp was the second one, after Steve. But somehow, when the Studs were together, time had a way of standing still.

So they were throwing him an impromptu bachelor party, outside on the deck of the cabin they all knew so well. They would've been inside if they'd had their druthers, but since the wedding ceremony would be in there tomorrow, the boys had been banished to the deck. They didn't care.

A few more beers and they wouldn't know where they were, anyway.

"So here's to Tripp," Ukiah Jones, better known as Ki, interjected, offering a toast of his own. Ki had been drinking pretty steadily, and he was the shakiest of the four at the moment. He grinned. "Here's to good women, good lovin' and our good friend, Tripp, who's known plenty of both."

"Long may he wave," slipped in Deke Washburn, the good ole boy of the bunch.

"Well, he's not waving anymore," Ki protested. "He's getting married. Hanging up his spurs."

"You know Tripp never had spurs." Deke roused himself from his deck chair, reaching over to pass out another round of beers as Tripp collected the empties. "He's a pole vaulter. And everybody knows all a pole vaulter needs—" he winked "—is a great pole."

"You're sad, Washburn," Steve tossed in. "You've been using that same line on poor Tripp since freshman year."

"Aw, leave me be. The golden boy deserves it. I got plenty tired of all those women eatin' out of Tripp's hand."

"I think you've confused me with yourself, Dr. Feelgood," Tripp said dryly.

Deke's Dr. Feelgood herbal teas were famous worldwide, but so was his prowess with the ladies. None of the four had ever had problems with that kind of thing, which was another reason they'd called themselves Studs so long ago, but Deke was a law unto himself.

It was funny how different they were, and yet how well they all got along. Always had.

Steve was strong, sincere, forthright, an all-American man's man. Ki was a little slicker, a little smarter, a little more ambitious. When those wheels started turning, when he started poking behind the scenes of whatever crime he was writing about this time, look out.

And then there was Deke. He could charm the fur off a female grizzly bear. And probably had. He loved women. Absolutely adored them. All shapes, all sizes, all kinds. It was a perfect fit when he launched his line of teas and started convincing every woman in America that she wanted to taste Dr. Feelgood.

In this bunch, Tripp was the underachiever, measured against Deke's tea millions, Ki's true crime best-sellers and Steve's established carpentry business in San Francisco. They all had what they wanted and knew where they were going.

At first, they'd known him only as a jock, the kind of guy everyone looked up to because he could touch the rim in basketball, and touch the sky when he pole-vaulted. He loved it. For the first time in his life, he knew what it meant to be a regular guy, and not the Ashby crown prince.

And with them, for as long as he lived, it would always be that way. One of the guys. Who could ask for anything more?

"You're awfully quiet, Ashby." Steve raised an eyebrow. "Prewedding jitters?"

"Ashby nervous? Wait, I have to write this down. The Ice Man defrosts!" Ki said with a laugh. He chugged down a long swallow of beer. "Two seconds on the clock, Ashby at the line. Remember? How many games did we see end that way? And Tripp would sink his free throws, nothing but net, and Beckett College would notch another win."

"We never won," Tripp scoffed. "We had a terrible team."

"That's not the way I remember it. But hey, things have changed. This time, we're going to have to rewrite the ending." Ki tipped his chair back on two legs, and Tripp eyed him warily. Just how much had he had to drink? And was Tripp going to have to run over there and catch him? Unaware, still teetering on two legs, Ki went on with his little story. "Two seconds on the clock. Ashby has the ball. He's open if he takes the lay-up. He goes up... But wait. What's this? From out of nowhere, Bridget Emerick has just stripped him clean. And that's the ball game."

"Stripped me clean? I don't think so," he said with a laugh. "I don't think Bridget plays basketball."

"Yeah, well, I wasn't talking basketball," Ki returned, with a wink that looked more like a leer.

"Bridget Emerick," mused Steve. "Who would've thought you'd end up with her? When she called me to get the address to the cabin, I was pretty surprised."

Tripp flashed him a glance. "Why?"

Steve shrugged. "Just doesn't seem like your type. Don't get me wrong. She was always really smart, and that's great. But..."

"Yeah, I know what you mean." Ki rocked back in his chair again. "Funny girl, Bridget. What was it we used to call her? Can't quite remember. You remember, Deke?"

"Not really, but I sure do remember her. I thought she was an awful nice girl. Real... serious," Deke said after a moment. "Can't recall ever seeing her laugh. Real pretty, but real... serious. But I liked her."

"Yeah, well, you liked anything with two X chromosomes," Steve put in.

Tripp regarded them in stony silence, unwilling to discuss Bridgie. He had explained the situation to Steve, as well as he could, but he didn't know what Steve had said to the others. And it wasn't something he really wanted to have to dissect for their bachelor party entertainment.

"Yeah, well, the one thing I do remember is that she was always hot for you, Tripp, boy." Ki chuckled. "You always denied there was anything going on, but she was all over you like white on rice."

"Oh, she was not. We were just friends. At the beginning, she didn't even like me, thought I was a dumb jock." Tripp tipped back his beer for another swig. "She didn't like the rest of you guys much, either. And she sure didn't like the Studs thing."

"Well, calling ourselves Studs wasn't one of the brighter things we ever did. And whatever you do, don't tell Gwen," Steve grumbled.

"Married a month and already he's whipped." Ki shook his dark head sadly. "Watch out, Tripp. Next it will be you."

"Come on, Ki," Steve put in. "Quit giving him a hard time. You know it's not for real. Who knows? Maybe he'll find the real thing, and we'll all be back here in a year or two, giving him another bachelor party."

Tripp's jaw tightened.

"Hey, buddy, we all know the story." Steve leaned back against the railing of the deck he had built so many years ago, on one of their trips to the cabin. "It's okay."

"I think it's a really great thing you're doing, making your mama happy," Deke put in. "I always did have a thing for Miss Kitty Belle. My kind of woman."

The perfect set-up line. They might as well have said it in unison. Ki spoke first. "Yeah, but, Deke, they're *all* your kind of woman."

And the four of them laughed out loud, still enjoying their oldest, most tired jokes.

It punctured the tension nicely. Tripp relaxed, now that he knew they knew, and he didn't have to pretend anymore that there was anything normal at all about this wedding. But of course they knew. They knew him better than anyone. Anyone except Bridgie.

And when the evening was ready to wind to a close, they were all feeling pretty mellow. Deke looked like he was going to fall asleep right there in his lounge chair, and Steve stifled a yawn.

The Studs were getting out of practice at this carousing business.

They roused Steve and Deke, and the four of them lumbered over to the door into the upstairs part of the cabin.

"Well, none of us have a whole lot of practice at bachelor parties, especially bachelor parties where the groom has every intention of being a bachelor again very soon, but let me wish you all the best, old friend," Steve said fondly. He reached over and gave Tripp a hug.

"I hope you know what you're doin'." Deke offered his hand. "Good luck, pal. You're gonna need it. Matrimony is a very strange business if you ask me. And this one is stranger than most, seeing as how you're the groom."

"Wait, I remembered. Egghead. That's what we used to call her. Egghead Emerick. You guys remember?" Ki asked suddenly.

Bridgie deserved better than that stupid, unpleasant nickname. Anger blazed through Tripp. Even though he had always been the one who walked away from fistfights, the one who broke things up and calmed things down, Tripp had the overpowering need to punch Ki Jones in the face.

Stumbling a bit, Ki hung on to the door for balance. "Egghead Emerick. Isn't that a hoot? Tripp getting married, and picking Egghead Emerick."

Before Tripp could stop himself, he'd grabbed Ki by the collar and slammed him against the rough outside wall of the cabin.

That woke them all up.

Steve and Deke jumped in to pull Tripp away, but he held on, furious with Ki, furious with himself.

"Hey, what's this?" Ki held up his hands to show that he wasn't fighting back. "Slow down, Tripp. No offense meant."

"I swear, I will personally rip to pieces anyone who ever calls her Egghead again. Got that?"

"We got it, we got it," they murmured. "Come on, Tripp, buddy, calm down. You're getting married in the morning."

INSIDE THE CABIN, Bridget quickly moved away from the door. Her ears were ringing as she raced down the hall to her own bedroom.

Egghead Emerick. Isn't that a hoot? Tripp getting married, and picking Egghead Emerick.

She'd come up to tell Tripp it was getting late, that maybe he and his Stud buds ought to come in now, but she hadn't gotten any farther than the door when she'd heard Ki's voice from outside.

Isn't that a hoot?... Picking Egghead Emerick...

She hadn't minded the nickname back in the old days. She was glad she was smart and focused and a lot less silly than other women. Even now, it represented something important to her, and that was a willingness to be who she was no matter what a bunch of jackass men thought. Jay appreciated her intelligence. Jay appreciated her for what she could accomplish, whether she was soft and charming or not.

Whereas Tripp... Well, Tripp had appreciated her intelligence, too, at least as long as it kept him in school and on the track team.

But he had certainly never been attracted by her brain. In fact, until a few days ago, he'd never been attracted by anything else of hers, either.

Back in Chicago, just for a moment, she'd thought maybe Tripp was starting to feel something for her. When he'd kissed her, when he'd held her, even when he'd asked her if marriage to him was abhorrent, she thought she'd seen something in his eyes.

But it was impossible.

To Tripp and his buddies, she would always be Egghead Emerick, the too-earnest, too-solemn girl with the brain. The girl who was about as erotic as the economics textbook under her arm.

"So who cares?" she muttered, as she tossed herself into bed. "I've always known Tripp and I have nothing in common. He's a Stud, and I'm an Egghead. And never the twain shall meet."

Chapter Ten

"Come on, it's your wedding day," Tripp told her. He was obviously trying to be charming, and he was doing a good job.

It didn't hurt his case that he looked fabulous. He'd gotten his hair cut on the way to this wedding breakfast, so it was a little shorter, a little crisper. And it also shone lighter than usual in the bright sunlight on the hotel terrace. Strands of gold mixed in with the warm brown of his hair, making Tripp the golden boy she'd always imagined him.

And his eyes were so blue.

When he unrolled that effortless charm, it was quite something. He focused all his attention on her, flattering her, making small, private jokes for her. He did everything but cut up her food and feed her.

After about five minutes of that treatment, she was ready for the old, careless, irreverent Tripp. This one, this Stepford Tripp, sapped her strength.

Kitty Belle had arranged this breakfast, inviting the Stud boys, the justice of the peace—who, rather disappointingly, was a regular old judge of some sort and not an Elvis impersonator—the photographer and the happy couple. It seemed the least they could do to let his mother throw the breakfast, since she had so graciously accepted the end to the rest of her huge, elaborate party-giving plans.

Here, on the glass-enclosed terrace of one of Tahoe's smaller, prettier hotels, with all kinds of flowers blooming around them, Bridget began to feel like this was a wedding, after all.

It made her want to cry.

"Cheer up," Tripp cajoled. "Do you want people to think it's such a horrible fate to marry me?"

"It isn't exactly a walk in the park," she whispered back.

"I know just what will cheer Bridget up," Kitty Belle said gaily. She was drinking a Mimosa, splashing a liberal amount of champagne with her orange juice, and she seemed giddier than usual.

Bridget had a moment of worry. Was Kitty Belle supposed to be drinking alcohol with whatever medication she was on? But that was odd. She couldn't recall Kitty Belle ever taking any medication. But surely, for a life-threatening illness . . .

She had no time to finish the thought, because Tripp suddenly stood up, welcoming a rather grubby newcomer to their little gathering. Who was that?

Kitty Belle clapped her hands together. "What perfect timing."

"For what?"

"Why, for your father to arrive. Here he is now."

"M-my father?" she sputtered, giving this man the once-over. Holy smokes! She didn't know whose father this was, but he definitely wasn't hers.

"Surprise, darling," Tripp said, tossing her a meaningful look. "I brought your dad here from St. Paul, just in time to give you away."

Bridget felt her mouth drop open. Was this some kind of joke?

"Everyone," Tripp offered, "this is Bridget's father, Frank Emerick."

"Howdy, all," he said, hooking his weathered thumbs under the waistband of his polyester pants. "Proud to know you." He inclined his head at Bridget. "Howdy, darlin'. Awful glad this here boy of yorn arranged so's I could be here. Wouldn't want to miss my little gal's nuptials."

Did people really talk like that, or was this a put-on? He sounded like he'd just ridden over from "Buffalo Bill's Wild West Show."

There were wide eyes around the table, but the most curious glances were directed at Bridget, who still hadn't said a word to this father of hers. It was as if they were all waiting with bated breath to see what she would say.

But she hadn't a clue.

Luckily, Kitty Belle jumped in to fill the gap. "There's a little bit of an estrangement," she whispered loudly to the judge and the Studs. "But I'm sure they'll patch it up now that everyone's together again."

So this father impostor was plopped down right between Tripp and Kitty Belle, and he began wolfing down champagne and eggs Benedict like there was no tomorrow. Bridget squinted across the table at him, and he smiled back at her, revealing a gold tooth and a friendly disposition.

Still, she could swear she'd seen those grizzled cheeks and rheumy eyes somewhere before.

"Thank you so much, Tripp," she said with false brightness, "for bringing my father. Isn't that just too fun for words?"

"I was hoping you'd feel that way." But she saw the mischief in his eyes.

"Tell us, Mr. Emerick...or should I call you Frank?" Kitty Belle inquired politely.

"Oh, Frank's fine. That okay with you?" he asked Tripp.

"Fine with me."

"Okey dokey, then. Glad we got that squared away."

"Anyway, Frank, we're so glad to have you with us." Kitty Belle leaned over closer. "You must tell me about Bridget as a child."

"Great little gal. A real pistol." The old man launched into a story about gambling debts and using Bridget as collateral that was simply appalling. Nonetheless, she thought she recognized it from a Shirley Temple movie. If this really were her father, she imagined any prospective mother-in-law would have grave doubts about her gene pool.

But Kitty Belle drank it all in, murmuring, "Isn't that fascinating?" at appropriate moments.

Well, it was fascinating. It just wasn't remotely true.

The minute Tripp got up from the table, she did, too. She cornered him behind a potted palm, and she hissed, "Who is that horrid old man?"

"Your father, you mean?"

"He's not my father. He's nothing like my father!"

"He'll do for one day." Tripp shrugged. "Kitty Belle was really upset that you weren't going to have any family here, and the only way to calm her down seemed to be to produce one. As long as everything else about this wedding was a fraud, I thought a fake father was par for the course. Besides, the old coot is kind of entertaining. I figured contending with him might take your mind off whatever it is that has you so blue."

She blinked. He was right. The minute she'd been saddled with an extra father, she'd forgotten she was terminally depressed about this whole charade of a wedding.

"So where did you dig him up? Wait, don't tell me. He lost all his dough at a casino, or maybe his gold mine went dry. So out of the goodness of your heart, you gave him big bucks to be Dad for a day."

"Nope. Not even close. His name is Jedidiah Leland, and he runs the general store off Route 28." A crooked smile curved his narrow lips. "And it didn't cost anything. Well, not much."

"Rent-a-Dad. At least you didn't get the Elvis impersonator from Cupid's Chapel."

"I didn't think of that."

"Thank goodness. You know, no one with half a brain would ever think that man was a plumber from St. Paul," she chided.

"Kitty Belle seems to like him."

Bridget shook her head in disbelief. "She does. She loves him. Oh, Tripp, this is so awful of you."

"I'm just glad you're enjoying it."

"Enjoying it? I'm outraged! Now there are..." she counted quickly "—six people who think that man is my father. How will I ever live this down?"

"He's harmless, Bridgie," he said, angling an arm around her. "Kitty Belle is happy, the guys all know he's a fake and what do you care about the other two? They're hired help."

"Why don't I find that comforting?"

Over by the table, she caught sight of Jed, trying to hide a bottle of champagne in his coat pocket.

"You chose a petty thief to be my father," she grumbled. "Couldn't you at least have picked someone presentable?"

"There's always that Elvis impersonator."

She punched him in the shoulder, but she was smiling. And they were arm in arm as they walked back to the table.

THE WEDDING WAS OVER before it began. "Do you take this woman?" went sailing past, along with sickness and health and forsaking all others.

Bridget was so nervous, she knew the only way she was going to get through this thing was to hang on to Tripp, and hang on tight. She couldn't look at any of his Stud pals; she knew what they thought of her and this wedding. *What a hoot, picking Egghead Emerick.*

And she couldn't look at Kitty Belle without thinking of the reason behind the whole performance.

So she didn't have any choice. She looked at Tripp. She gazed into his eyes. She drank him in.

He didn't seem to mind.

Not for the first time, she and Tripp were a team. Just like when they'd pulled an all-nighter to get him through his history final, or when he'd boosted her up the ivy-covered wall of her dorm to sneak her back in after curfew, they had a common purpose.

And they also had a real bond—trying to keep a lid on the pack of lies they were telling.

Standing next to Tripp as the judge read their vows, Bridget could read his emotions as well as her own. They were both anxious, guilty, afraid that at the last minute someone would stand up and yell, "Stop this wedding! It isn't real!"

And yet she knew, too, that they were each glad they had a friend to lean on. *There is no one I would even consider doing this with—except you.*

He'd said that at the very beginning, but it was even truer now.

Kitty Belle had festooned flowers all over the cabin, but Bridget wouldn't even have noticed, except for the fact that Jed Leland, a.k.a. Dad Emerick, tripped over a miniature tree of roses and sent the whole thing flying, right before the judge launched into "the power vested in me" part.

"You can certainly tell he's your father," Tripp said for her ears only, as Steve and Ki tried to clean up the scattered flowers and leaves and Deke offered a steadying hand to old Jed. Meanwhile, everybody else just stood there, waiting to finish up the ceremony. "Something in the way he moves—definite family resemblance."

She should've been insulted, but she had to bite down hard not to laugh. It was the most ridiculous wedding that ever was, but she could hardly start chortling when Kitty Belle was sitting back there beaming and swooning with joy. It might be impossible, it might be torture, but seeing Mrs. Ashby so ecstatic almost made it worth it.

Besides, she got to lean on the most handsome man in captivity, even more gorgeous than usual in stark black formal wear, and she could pretend for a few hours that he really was hers.

It was perfectly acceptable for a bride to cling to her groom for support, to clutch at his warm, strong arm, to edge in as close as was humanly possible without sharing the same space. It happened all the time at weddings. Didn't it?

Everything else around her was a blur. The next thing she knew, the judge said, "You may kiss the bride," and Tripp gave her a funny, uncertain look. Bridget just waited, clutching her bouquet.

Finally, when she had all but decided he wasn't going to do it, he leaned over, framed her face with his hands and pressed his lips to hers in a sweet, small kiss that made her bones melt. She hung on, bouquet and all, kissing him back like there was no tomorrow, and she felt the surprise and tension rise in his body. Obviously, he had expected the kiss to be as big a fake as everything else about this wedding.

But she didn't care. She just put her heart and soul into that one kiss. How many chances was she going to get to kiss this kind of groom?

Somewhere in the periphery of her consciousness, she could hear Tripp's mother crying, "Look how in love they are. Isn't it wonderful?"

And then Kitty Belle started to sob and wail. The sound grew louder, it lasted longer, and Tripp pulled away from Bridget's embrace. Slowly, regretfully, he brushed a soft kiss across her cheek, and then he went to his mother.

"Are you all right?" he asked, clearing a path to a chair so Kitty Belle could sit down. "Are you feeling okay, Mother?"

"Yes, yes, I'm fine. It's just all the excitement," she whimpered. But then the tears started to flow again, and Kitty Belle sobbed, "Tripp, I've been waiting so long, and you're finally married. Finally married. I can hardly believe it."

There was a pause. And then Tripp said lightly, "I can hardly believe it, either."

Kitty Belle wailed even louder, as everyone ran around looking for tissues. Tripp patted his mother's arm, and Bridget just sort of hovered.

"Are you sure you're all right?" she asked gently. Kitty Belle seemed so agitated. No one knew exactly what her condition was, but it couldn't be good. What if the excitement of the wedding was too much for her? What would they do?

But her new mother-in-law assured them that she was really fine. She dabbed at her tears, she sniffled a little and then she sat up like the iron-willed aristocrat she was.

"Finish the ceremony," she commanded.

"Aren't we done?" Bridget asked, and the judge hurried to add, "Oh, I'm supposed to... May I introduce Mr. and Mrs. Thomas Michael Trippett Ashby."

And the Studs clapped politely, while old Jed gave out a big "Yahoo!"

With a sheepish smile, Tripp took her hand in his, flashing their combined rings at their entourage. Married. They were really and truly married.

Bridget gulped.

And then a catering truck wound its way up the mountain to dispense mountains of fancy food and drink, along with a harpist Mrs. Ashby had hired to provide background music. Bridget's Rent-a-Dad was first in line for refreshments, scooping himself huge helpings before he wandered away. If anyone noticed he was gone, no one said anything.

Bridget relaxed a little once he'd left; that was one lie put to bed without discovery. Although she thought Kitty Belle might want to know why he hadn't stuck around to kiss the bride, Bridget was eternally grateful he hadn't.

So she relaxed in the warmth of Tripp's attention, and she ate and drank whatever was put in front of her, which turned out to be quite a lot. Every time she turned around, Tripp was at her elbow, refilling her champagne glass.

She hadn't realized how thirsty she was. She hadn't realized what a relief it would be to get good and sloshed after living with all this unbearable tension.

Ki and Deke stayed long enough to offer a cappella versions of "Brown-eyed Girl" and "(I Can't Get No) Satisfaction," in honor of Bridget and Tripp respectively, which were much appreciated by everyone but Kitty Belle, and then they, too, prepared to depart, with Steve not far behind.

Even Studs had real lives to get back to, it seemed. The supposedly happy couple walked his old pals to the door to say goodbye.

She didn't realize exactly how much she'd had to drink, until she couldn't seem to get any words out past her slippery mouth. "Thanks for coming," she said slowly, working hard to get everything out in the right order. "I know it meant a lot to Tripp to have you here."

Beside her, Tripp gave her a reassuring squeeze. She hoped she'd said that right. It was like talking through cotton balls.

But if she was tipsy, none of the Studs seemed to notice. Or maybe they were feeling the effects of all that champagne themselves.

"Aw, Tripp, you know how we feel," Ki said awkwardly. He offered a hand. "Best of luck and all that."

Right behind him, Steve said lightly, "I should say congratulations on a job well-done, but I think you're just plain lucky, Ashby. You're getting a lot better woman than you deserve.''

Deke was less restrained than his friends. He grabbed Bridget, gave her a hot kiss and said, "I don't leave until I kiss the bride, especially when she's as pretty as this one.''

Dangling there in Deke's arms, Bridget giggled, but Tripp looked less than pleased. He pulled her forcefully back against him. "I'm the only one kissing this bride.''

The others backed off in a hurry, as Steve gave them a measuring glance. "I think you've been holding out on us, Tripp. This seems pretty darn real to me.''

Bridget tried to focus on the tips of her white shoes, but it was pretty far down there, and she was having trouble concentrating. What did Steve mean by that, anyway? But her brain was too foggy to figure it out. Meanwhile, Tripp made some offhand joke about Steve's delusions.

"Okay," Steve returned doubtfully. "That's your story—you stick to it." But as he slipped out the door, he leaned in long enough to whisper, "Who are you trying to fool, Ashby?" before he, too, departed.

"What was that all about?" Bridget asked, but Tripp didn't say.

He just pulled her into his arms and pretended they were dancing. "You're supposed to dance at your wedding," he muttered.

"Okay." She held on, trying to follow his steps, but mostly just sliding from foot to foot, spinning in a haze of champagne and confusion. She'd never heard of anyone dancing to harp music, but it didn't seem to matter. In Tripp's arms, nothing mattered. She smiled to herself, closing her eyes, hanging on, letting him carry her along on this dreamy dance to nowhere.

Kitty Belle and the judge were dancing, too, and there were so many flowers.... Pretty colors swirled around her. The pink of Kitty Belle's beaded dress, and the flowers—big pink roses and little white stars—with garlands and wreaths of greenery everywhere.

"I didn't want it to be green," she said stubbornly. "Who made it green?"

She felt her eyelids beginning to close, and then Tripp was there, like he'd been all night, to scoop her up in the nick of time.

His body was warm, and she could feel his heart beating, steady and strong, against her own. Maybe she should've swooned a little earlier.

Too much champagne, she thought dizzily. *Too much Tripp.*

"Wow," she managed, as he hoisted her and her beautiful white dress into his arms to carry back to his bedroom. She leaned her head down on the lapel of his dinner jacket. It felt cool against her cheek. "This was part of the fantasy. Do you remember? At my apartment? You called, and you were so sweet."

"Was I?" he murmured, bending his own head closer, nuzzling her hair.

Was he really nuzzling her hair? That was nice, wasn't it?

"Yes," she breathed, "you were. Sweet, I mean. You were going to send Jay packing, do you remember?"

"No, not really."

"Well, you were. And then you were supposed to sweep me up in your arms, and carry me down the hall, where we would make mad, passionate love amid the tumbled quilts, and our hearts would beat as one." She sighed with the sheer perfection of it. "Doesn't that sound great?"

"Certainly does," he said in a rough, strange voice. Clearing the door of the bedroom, he set her down carefully on her pretty white shoes. Her hands lingered on his shoulders, flexing against his shoulders, shamelessly using him for balance.

"Wow," she said again. She moved a shaky finger to trace the clean, hard line of his jaw. "Is this real, or am I dreaming?"

"You're not dreaming," he informed her dryly. He detached her hands and left her standing on her own two feet. "You're drunk."

She did feel a tad wobbly. "Nonsense. I'm not drunk. I don't even drink."

"You did tonight."

"You." She pointed a finger at him, but it wouldn't stay still. "You gave it to me."

He started to loosen his tie, to undo his collar, but Bridget teetered to one side and he stepped quickly to catch her. He murmured, "I guess I gave you a little too much, huh?"

"Guess so," she whispered breathlessly. She was smiling and she didn't know why. She just felt so heavenly. Daring and sexy and...heavenly. Looping her arms around his neck, she turned her face up to his. "You are so gorgeous. There ought to be a law."

"There probably is," he muttered. He lifted her up again, cradling her very nicely, until he deposited her carefully in the middle of the big brass bed.

And then he turned to leave.

"Wait." She sat up so fast, her head began to spin. With one hand at her forehead, she asked, "Where are you going?"

"I'm going to clear out the rest of our guests." But his gaze flickered over her. "Don't worry. I'll be right back."

"I wasn't worried," she said loftily.

His lips curved in a mocking smile. "Don't get into any trouble while I'm gone."

"What kind of trouble could I get into?" Tossing herself backward into the deep cloud of lacy white bed linens, she made a big whoosh with her skirt. "You know, Tripp, this is the best wedding I ever had."

"Glad to hear it."

And then he was gone.

IT DIDN'T TAKE LONG to pay off the photographer and the harpist, and then the judge offered to escort Kitty Belle back to her hotel. And that was that.

Hands in the pockets of his tuxedo pants, Tripp surveyed the damage. There were empty champagne bottles littering the living room and the kitchen, and the flowers were starting to droop. He really ought to clean up the table with the food on it. That was going to be a mess by tomorrow.

He really ought to, but he wasn't going to.

Ripping off his tie with one hand, Tripp undid the top button on his formal shirt with the other. He took a deep breath. No, the house could fend for itself. He had more pressing problems. Like what he was going to do with Bridgie.

He had to go back in there. He'd promised he would.

But it wasn't a pleasant prospect. Not with her all pliant and soft, all clingy and agreeable.

Hell. This was like being in Hell with the thermostat on high.

Her voice echoed in his ears. . . . *You were supposed to sweep me up in your arms, and carry me down the hall, where we would make mad, passionate love amid the tumbled quilts, and our hearts would beat as one.*

He was still trying to get his body to relax after that little speech. *Make mad, passionate love amid the tumbled quilts.* She was talking nonsense and he reacted like a stallion, raring to go. Where did she get this stuff, anyway? Did she really feel that way, or was she too drunk to even know where she was and who she was with?

He didn't know. He couldn't trust her, or himself.

And until he could, he wasn't going to touch Bridgie. One touch—that's all it would take.

And just like that terrible, terrifying morning on her couch, he'd be stripping off her clothes and making love to her in ten seconds flat.

No, he had to keep his hands off. He'd already taken advantage, every way but that one. She was his friend, and she trusted him, and he already owed her too much that he could never repay. What kind of man would make love to her under these circumstances, taking advantage yet again?

"Not this kind," he said under his breath.

She was supposed to marry a senator. She was supposed to go places and be somebody responsible and upstanding, and not somebody who slept with old friends just for the fun of it.

He was trying to be noble again. And he sure as hell wasn't very good at it.

Hell. That was the word for it.

Well, he might as well get it over with. Slowly he ambled back down the hall, easing the door open a crack. Cautiously, he swung it open the rest of the way.

He sagged with relief. She was asleep, passed out cold half off the bed. Her hair spilled around her, soft and dark against the white lace coverlet. Part of her dress, the puffy, starchy part of her skirt, was wedged underneath her, and she still had her shoes on.

He considered whether he ought to go now, while the going was good, or try to do something about the awkward position she was in. Would she care that she was wrecking her fragile dress? Already, she'd crumpled the skirt, and she was risking ripping the lace if she thrashed around while she slept.

She had looked so beautiful in that white dress, standing beside him in front of the judge.

Tripp smiled to himself. He hadn't been able to find the words to tell her, but she was simply breathtaking in that dress. It was very demure, with its high neck and long sleeves, yet tempting at the same time. The top was all lace, but it fit tightly to her body, and every time she breathed, he could see the gentle rise and fall of her breasts. He'd spent most of the day watching her breathe, wishing he could touch her, wishing he could mold his hands to her body as closely as that dress did.

He suddenly had a horrifying thought. Would she wear the same dress to marry Philpott? Did women do that?

Surely not. Women were sentimental about that kind of thing, right? But Bridgie wouldn't be sentimental about this wedding. Why should she? It was all just a sham.

And she was a frugal, commonsense sort of person. After investing in one dress, why buy another?

"Wear that dress for Philpott?" he growled. "Over my dead body."

Nonetheless, he couldn't let her sleep in it. She was going to be uncomfortable enough with the hangover she was working on, and adding a tight dress to the picture was really cruel.

Come hell or high water, he was going to have to get it off her.

"Bridget?" he tried softly. "Are you awake?"

Not a whimper. She snoozed on.

He came closer. "Bridgie?"

Nothing.

"Aw, what the hell?" he muttered. "As long as she's conked out, it's safe."

So he slipped off her shoes, and then eased her back up onto the bed, gently shifting her over onto her stomach. Carefully, he fiddled with the tiny buttons all the way from her neck to her waist.

"Damn dress," he swore. Either his fingers were very clumsy, or those buttons were very small. Finally, after an eternity, after he had seriously begun to think dresses were meant to be ripped, not unbuttoned, he got every last one of those little loops unhooked from all the little buttons.

His mouth went dry as he gazed down at her bare back. He couldn't resist drawing one finger down the line of glowing flesh revealed by the gaping dress. Her skin was so soft, so smooth, so warm under his finger.

"Ooooooh." She shivered softly.

He jumped back.

Slowly, bonelessly, she rolled over onto her side. The dress only partially rolled with her, slipping off one shoulder and catching on her arm. Her eyes still closed, she made a soft, sleepy little noise, aimlessly pushing away at her dress, as if she felt caught.

Tripp just stood there, watching her, unable to take his eyes away.

"Tripp?" she asked drowsily. "I'm...stuck. Can you...?"

And she held out her hand.

Chapter Eleven

"Tripp," she murmured again. "Stupid dress is stuck. Get it off."

What could he do?

He reached for her wrist. It should've been quick work to strip the dress off, but his hands were clumsy, and she was so limp, so loopy. As he struggled, she giggled. Eventually, he maneuvered her into a sitting position, and then, edging onto the bed next to her, he peeled her right out of her lacy prison, letting the top of her dress pool around her waist.

With one small wiggle, she was free of the whole thing. She kicked it casually off the bed.

"Ahhhhh," she said, sighing, leaning on him. "Better."

Better for whom? *Oh, God.* If he'd thought she was bad in the dress, he really wasn't prepared for her *out* of the dress.

She sidled up closer, and there wasn't much covering her body.

"Oh, Bridget," he groaned softly. "Why are you doing this to me?"

She didn't answer, just fastened her arms around him and kissed him on the neck, right under his ear. She kept kissing him, making incoherent little noises and snuggling into his lap, while he tried to figure out how to get himself disentangled.

He detached her hands several times, but she was very good at reattaching them somewhere else, somewhere worse.

Her white silk camisole left absolutely nothing to the imagination, although his imagination was awfully good. One thin strap tumbled negligently over her shoulder, revealing a swell of creamy skin. As his rapt gaze followed the curve, brushing over her breast, he saw the peak of rosy nipples through the slick fabric of the camisole. Tripp put his hands way out to his sides, afraid to touch anything.

And on the bottom. *Hell.* That was worse than the top. White lace stockings. A garter belt and panties that were barely there.

Who dressed women like this? Who dressed *Bridgie* like this?

"Bridgie," he said, steeling himself as he cupped her chin, "are you awake?"

"Mmm-hmm." Her eyes were open now, but they were still heavy-lidded. She slipped her hands inside his jacket, shoving it away. "Too many clothes," she whispered.

"I don't think so," he said unsteadily, but she was merciless, and with her smooth body climbing all over him, with her erotic little giggles filling his ears, his protests were halfhearted at best.

Before he knew it, she was all the way across his lap, plastered to the front of him, her breasts searing him through the cool silk of her camisole, through the heavy cotton of his shirt.

"Bridgie—"

"Oh, Tripp, you know what?" She stuck her finger across his lips, sounding very aggrieved. "You talk too much. No more talking. Just kiss me."

But she was kissing *him*. She had the sweetest, softest mouth, and she kept making greedy little moans that sent him right over the edge.

He tried to hold on to the fragments of his self-control, but how could he, with her small, warm hands sliding inside his shirt, her round, enticing bottom pressing into his lap?

His lap. He was so hard under her, it was painful. Aching for release, he knew he had to get out from under her before he died from frustration.

He tried to lift her away, but his hands grazed her hips, where slender ribbons on each side were all that held her panties together. One twitch of a ribbon, and she would be bare.

"Oh, yeah," he whispered, letting his fingers linger, flirting with pulling those ribbons and filling his hands with her.

But then she moved restlessly under his hands, edging around on his lap, and he ran into even more dangerous territory. One hand brushed the silky curve of her inner thigh, while the other spanned her round, firm bottom from behind. She pushed herself into his palm, and he felt her incredible heat, incredible wetness, through the silk of her panties.

"Oh, Bridget, you feel so good," he whispered. "How am I going to stop?"

"But we're not stopping," she said, with a very naughty little laugh. "I want you."

There was a light, a fire, in Bridget's deep, dark eyes, that he had never seen before. He knew she was a few drinks over her limit, but he didn't think those sparks came from a bottle. Her cheeks were flushed, her hair was a wild tangle of mahogany waves and her eyes were wide and impossibly dark. Bridget seemed consumed with passion, obsessed with need.

Tripp was feeling a few needs of his own, needs he was no longer sure he could deny.

And sitting up just wasn't going to do it. He nipped hungrily at her lips, pulling her more securely into his lap, fastening her arms around his neck. And then he fell backward into the bed, bringing her with him.

He pulled her up on top of him, so that her body straddled his, pressing her against him, against the one place he needed her touch more than any other. And when she let out a husky groan, he drank it in, loving the sound of Bridget's desire.

But he couldn't stand how slowly she was moving. Bracing his hands on her hips, he held her steady, and rolled her over. Like magic, he was on top. He grinned, bending down to drop kisses on her lips and her cheeks and her chin. She writhed beneath him. He couldn't ever remember making love to a woman as slippery and reckless as this.

He was struck by a sudden thought, a thought he did not want to deal with right now, when he was swept up and beaten up by pure lust, when he was having a great deal of difficulty remembering anything but Bridget.

But this was so unlike her. Calm, controlled, sedate Bridgie. Yet here she was, making incoherent little moans, throwing self-control to the four winds, getting on with some real steam.

It was so unlike Bridget that he had to stop, had to wonder if it was okay to do this. Hell. The last thing he needed was a conscience when every system in his body was on red alert and raring to go.

Maybe it was okay. Maybe she was caught up in a wedding night fever that she couldn't break. Possible.

Or maybe she'd been possessed by some evil, seductive impostor. Or maybe she was so wasted, she didn't know what she was doing.

But even as he hesitated, she was ravenous, pushing his clothes away, raining kisses, running her tongue over his chest and his ribs, inflaming him, engorging him, more than he thought possible.

And when she slid down one hand, cupping him through his trousers, fingering him ever so delicately, he knew he was going to explode.

"Bridget," he said through gritted teeth, "just how drunk are you?"

"I don't know," she breathed. "Does it matter?"

"There are rules about things like this, about taking advantage of someone who... isn't herself."

But she wasn't paying attention to his words. She stroked him then, with a surer, rougher touch, and he arched off the bed. He caught her wrist and gripped it tightly, inches away.

"Bridget, I can't do this. Not with you."

She froze.

Had sanity returned? If only it would. If only he could look into her eyes and see a thinking, rational being, one who would say "yes" right now and mean it.

Because, if by God that happened, he would be on top of her, inside her, in a New York minute.

"Bridget?" he asked slowly.

But her eyes were still cloudy, still confused. "You said you couldn't do this. Not with me."

"Not if tomorrow, when you remember, it will be my fault. I can't do that, Bridgie. It's not right. I..." He caught himself, just before the words *I love you too much for that* left his lips.

Of course he loved Bridgie. He had always loved Bridgie.

But not this way.

This was the real way, the whole way, the I-want-to-sleep-with-you-every-night, I-want-to-take-vows-with-you way. Tripp Ashby was notorious for never, ever getting close to feeling like this about anyone.

But he felt it. Shocked, astonished, he realized. He definitely felt it. For Bridget Emerick.

And he didn't want to make love with her unless she was in her right mind and fully participating. Scruples. At this late date. How inconvenient.

"Of course you don't want to do it with me. I heard what they said. Your Studs," she said angrily. Hot spots of color stained her cheeks. She reached out and slapped him hard, and he could hear a ringing in his ears. "Sure you had to get married. Too bad it couldn't be somebody more fun."

He shook his head, trying to regain his hearing. What had just happened here? One minute she was snuggling all over him, and the next she'd slapped his face. "I don't know what you're saying. You heard what who said?"

She detached herself from him with an elaborate show of pride, looking down her nose at him. Calmly, very slowly, she announced, "I seem to find myself rather inebriated at the moment and I apologize for any..." She hiccuped loudly. "Any inconvenience this may have caused you. But I think I'm going to be sick."

And then she leapt from the bed and ran out in the hall in her camisole and her garter belt.

He was up and after her in seconds, but by the time he got upstairs, she'd barricaded herself in the bathroom. She refused to open the door.

"It's better this way," he said quietly, his hand flat on the door. "I'll see you in the morning, okay?"

Silence was all that greeted him.

"What a wedding night," he muttered.

Dueling bathrooms. The bride was locked in one upstairs, while the groom marched downstairs to find one of his own. Six or seven cold showers sounded like a good idea.

BRIDGET HAD a wretched headache. She also had the most horrific case of total embarrassment she'd ever had in her life.

So if she had to wake up with a mouth full of sand and a head like a gong, why couldn't she at least have total amnesia about how she'd gotten that way?

But, no, she remembered every detail. She remembered the whole, bloody awful picture. She remembered crawling all over him like a lovesick fool, and him rejecting her.

I can't do this. Not with you.

Oh, sure. He was more than willing to make love to every cheerleader and pompon girl on the planet. To every bimbo with a bank account. But not to Egghead Emerick.

She remembered throwing herself into her own bed, still wearing that idiotic garter belt and stockings. But how was she supposed to know Tripp was going to see them? They were a present from Kitty Belle, who'd assured her that all the brides were wearing them these days. And Bridget hadn't had the heart to refuse such sinfully pretty things.

Now they were residing in the wastebasket. She'd thought about flushing them, but she didn't want to clog the drains.

Padding around in a much more sensible pair of flannel pajamas, she splashed cool water on her face and regarded herself blearily in the mirror. Her face was so pale, she might as well have been a vampire.

"At least vampires get to sleep all day," she mumbled. She hadn't ventured out of her room this morning, and she wasn't sure she was going to. "Chicken," she chided herself.

But what was the point?

If she went downstairs to the kitchen or the living room, she might run into Tripp. She might even pass by Tripp's bedroom, hereafter known in her mind as the Chamber of Horrors. And why would she want to chance that?

With the Studs and, most importantly, Kitty Belle, safely out of the cabin, winging their way far away from Lake Tahoe, there was no need to pretend anymore. Now she and Tripp could be pleasant strangers, inhabiting opposite ends of the cabin until it was time to go home.

Time to go home to her job and her fiancé. Her real fiancé. Jay Philpott. The good, honest, noble man she had betrayed in almost every sense of the word. And the fact that she hadn't actually, physically, betrayed him sure wasn't from lack of trying.

Bridget sat down on her bed and burst into tears.

But the hair on the back of her neck began to tingle. Lifting her head, she stilled. Was she supersensitive this morning, or was that really Tripp back there somewhere?

Quickly she jumped up and spun around, clutching a pillow to her midriff. "Tripp," she blurted. If she looked bleary and hung over, he certainly didn't. The swine.

Oh, he had a few shadows under his dreamy blue eyes. But that hardly interfered with his looks at all. The pig.

If at first her hair had tingled, now it was her whole body. She was standing there throbbing and trembling, unable to put last night out of her mind, unable to think of anything but Tripp's hands on her body, and her hands on his . . .

"What are you doing here?" she demanded in a voice that was more than a little shrill. "Or is it too much to ask to let me suffer in peace?"

"I'm sorry you're suffering."

"Then go away." She marched over there and tried to slam the door on him, but he caught it with his hand.

"Bridgie, we need to talk," he said tersely.

"I don't want to talk to you."

"You don't have a choice."

She had the absurd impulse to smash him with the pillow. Like that would've stopped him from invading her room and standing there, like a Greek statue, cool and immovable.

"I hate to bother you," Tripp said quietly. "I know you're not feeling well."

That was the understatement of the year. "I have a headache," she said, backing up awkwardly, still dangling the pillow from fingers that were just itching to smack him one right across the face.

"I can imagine." He gave her a tight, cynical smile. "You drank quite a bit last night."

"I am aware of that," she shot back. "Yet another disaster to lay at your door."

Tripp's brows drew together darkly. "My door?"

She ignored the danger signs. "Yes, your door. It's all your fault!"

"Yeah, well, I wasn't the one crawling all over you in a damn garter belt," he accused.

She felt all the color drain from her face. "I seem to recall you doing some crawling of your own, buddy boy."

"Well, what do you think I am, a saint? I'm not Jay. Old Jay would hide his eyes and walk away because he's such a stand-up guy. I did walk away, though, didn't I? Nothing happened, and it's completely because *I* walked away." And then he growled something under his breath, something that she couldn't quite catch, about never walking straight again.

"Don't talk about Jay," she tried. This time she did swat him with the pillow, although it was pretty ineffectual. "I already feel so guilty I can't see straight, and you bring up Jay, my poor fiancé that I've just treated like dirt, and he doesn't even know it. Well, thank you, Tripp Ashby, for yet another reminder of what a horrible, unworthy fiancée I am!"

"Look, Bridgie," he said kindly, detaching the pillow from her hand and setting it back on the bed. "You're not unworthy. So you got a little drunk and made a mistake."

"A mistake? More like a screwup of titanic proportions," she muttered.

"Everybody makes mistakes."

"Not Jay," she bit out. "And not me before I started getting involved with you."

"Yeah, well, get ready, because here's another one to blame on me." He ran a savage hand through his hair. "We have a problem."

Gritting her teeth, she asked, "What is it?"

"My mother."

Nothing new there. "What, did she miss her flight back to Chicago?" She glanced down at her watch. "She ought to be there by now."

"She didn't go."

That got her attention. "You're not serious! She didn't go? Why not?"

"She says she wasn't feeling well this morning." Tripp's handsome face was drawn and grim. "She says she doesn't think it's wise to travel right now, that her condition is deteriorating more quickly."

"Oh, no," Bridget gasped. "But she seemed fine yesterday, except for that episode right at the end of the ceremony."

"I know, but..." He broke off. "I've talked to her doctor a couple of times, but all he says is that every case is different, and that we can't predict what to expect. She could seem fine, or she could be progressively weaker and dizzier. She's definitely weak right now. And, Bridget, the thing is, she wants to stay here."

"Here, as in Tahoe?" She began to get a bad feeling about this. "Or, here, as in this general vicinity?"

"Here, as in this cabin."

"Oh, no." Thunderstruck, she thumped back down on the edge of the bed.

"Oh, yes. She needs to rest, she says, and she promises she won't bother us. She'll just sleep and sit in the sun. But she doesn't want to spend..." He took a deep breath and kept going. "She doesn't want to spend what may be her last days in a hotel. And I don't blame her."

"No, of course not."

"And it's really not that big a deal to move her into one of the upstairs bedrooms. They're all empty, all but this one, of course, and you'll have to vacate..." Tripp gave her a measuring glance, gauging her reaction. "She thinks you and I are sharing my room downstairs, of course."

"Of course," she echoed dully.

"And I'd like to make her as comfortable as possible." He held out his hands in a gesture of supplication. "It's getting to be ridiculous, all the compromises I'm asking you to make. It's not fair, and I'm sorry."

Bridget gazed down at her bare feet. "There's no need to be sorry. I agreed. Each step of the way, I agreed. I kept thinking..."

She'd kept thinking it was a lark, an adventure, before she settled into acting like a responsible human being for the rest of her life. She hadn't quite realized how painful this would be.

"So what are you saying?" she asked. "Am I supposed to move in with you, into the Chamber of—into your room?"

"Come on. It won't be that bad." He gave her a sardonic grin. "We've already been through the worst, don't you think? And we'll keep you away from the booze. I promise not to touch you, and to return you to your fiancé in one piece."

"Don't worry. I can control myself." She stood up, trying to be as cool and impersonal as she could. This was hard enough, when her brain kept feeding her the same scandalous phrases over and over. *He took off my clothes. He saw me practically nude. I touched him... everywhere.*

He was acting like sharing a room under those circumstances would be as easy as putting on brave faces to the world. In fact, he was more distant now that he'd ever been since the first days of their friendship. Apparently he didn't think it would be weird at all to share a room. But Bridget was terrified.

"Is Kitty Belle here now?" she asked.

"Yes, downstairs." His eyebrows were drawn together, and his eyes were a dark, moody blue. "I told her you were getting the rest of your things out of this room."

"Good cover. You're very good at thinking up lies on the fly, aren't you?"

"Yeah, it's a real talent," he returned, in just as snippy a tone as she had used.

So she threw her things haphazardly into a couple of suitcases, not bothering to be neat. They weren't going far. At the last minute, she remembered to retrieve the stockings and the garter belt from the wastebasket in the bathroom, just in case Kitty Belle chose this room. Wouldn't want her finding suspicious articles of clothing lying around in the wrong room.

And then she fled her sanctuary, luggage in hand.

Tripp was waiting outside, waiting to carry her bags downstairs. But as she shut the door behind her, they heard voices from down below in the living room.

Loud, agitated, excited voices. She and Tripp dropped the suitcases and ran to look over the railing.

"Where is she?" an aggravated voice demanded. "I want to see her, now!"

"She is on her honeymoon, sir," Kitty Belle retorted. "And don't take that tone with me."

Bridget was rooted there, stock-still, staring down at the newcomers. She couldn't possibly be seeing what she was seeing. "Oh my God," she whispered.

Tripp jumped down the stairs two at a time. "Come on, Mother. I'll take you upstairs where you can lie down. We can sort this all out later."

"But who is that man? Why does he want to see Bridget? And who is the other one?"

Tripp practically dragged his mother up the stairs, past Bridget, and into the last room, where Ki always stayed when he was at the cabin.

"Here," he commanded. "You rest, do you hear me?"

And then he slammed the door shut after her, and grabbed Bridget by the hand. Without brooking any objections, he towed her downstairs, down to where their new guests were anxiously awaiting them. Or at least anxiously awaiting an explanation.

"Bridget," the man said testily, "are you or are you not married? That woman just told me that you are on your honeymoon. With him!" he exclaimed, poking a finger at Tripp. "Is this true, Bridget Marie?"

She smiled weakly. "Hi, Dad."

It seemed the real father of the bride, the real widowed plumber from Minnesota, had just shown up.

"Look, you'll have to keep your voices down, so my mother doesn't hear," Tripp whispered hastily. "We haven't got time to explain, but you're just going to have to trust us. There is nothing wrong going on here." He looked more than a little guilty, chafing under Frank Emerick's stony glare. "Absolutely nothing," he repeated.

From behind her father, Jay Philpott made his presence known. Calm and collected as always, he pointedly ignored Tripp, gazing right at his fiancée. "Bridget, I think I deserve an explanation. I know you're not married, darling, so what exactly is going on here?"

"She can't be married," her father interjected. "She would've told me if she were getting married. I know my girl better than that."

Bridget had no idea what to say. Who did she lie to first?

"Bridget?" her father demanded. "Say something."

"Bridget?" Jay prompted.

There was a long pause, while she tried to think about the stars dancing in her periphery. Her worst nightmare was that either her dad or Jay would find out. And now they both had. What was she supposed to do? She felt like running for the hills.

"Dad, Jay," she said finally, in the calmest voice she could manage. "It's really wonderful to see you. Do you mind stepping outside for a second? We'll walk around back and you can see the mountains. It's really quite lovely here."

"We are more concerned about you than about the mountains," Jay said quietly. He continued to watch Bridget carefully, but when she took his arm, he did allow himself to be led outside.

She took them around the back, and then waited for the floodgates to open. She could feel Tripp at her back, offering himself up as a tower of strength, but she refused to lean on him. She'd gotten herself into this mess, and she planned to navigate her way out without his help or his interference.

"Get to it, young lady. What are you doing here?" Bridget wasn't sure she'd ever seen her father this angry, this hurt.

"Just tell us you're not married," Jay put in.

"She can't be married," Frank Emerick barked. "Not without telling me and her sisters and brothers. Running away like a common thief. She would never do that. The real question, Bridget Marie, is whether you're living here in sin with that uppity, pretty-boy snob."

Tripp stiffened behind her.

"She is not living in sin," Jay said coldly. "She wouldn't do that to me."

"Never did like that boy," her dad growled. "If you ask me, he never appreciated you. Always thought he was too good for the rest of us common folk."

"Daddy!" she protested. "Tripp never acted like he was too good for us. He and I were best friends. We still..." She faltered, but it was too late. "We still are."

"He took advantage of your good nature," her father insisted. "And he still is. Dragging you up here to this godforsaken place."

Jay gave Tripp a very chilly once-over. "Much as it pains me, Bridget, I tend to agree with your father. Your association with Mr. Ashby was very ill-advised."

"Listen, pal—" Tripp began, in a soft, dangerous tone, but she put her hand on his arm to hold him back.

"Please, no more trouble," she whispered to him. "Things are bad enough as they are."

Her father muttered, "Living in sin with a rich boy. Bridget Marie, if your mother were alive today, she'd turn over in her grave. You were raised better than that!"

"Daddy, I swear, we are not living in sin."

"Is that true?" Frank Emerick turned to Tripp for confirmation.

"Definitely," he managed around a fiercely clenched jaw.

"So you're either not living here..." But one look at her pajamas and bare feet made that unlikely. "Or you're married."

"Bridget, please tell me you're not married," Jay said softly.

She took a deep breath. "But I am. Married, I mean. Tripp and I are married."

"You are?" her father bellowed. "When Jay came to get me, spouting some poppycock about you running off to Las Vegas, I didn't believe it. My daughter, who has always been so smart, so responsible, running off to Las Vegas? I couldn't believe it. I still don't believe it!"

"It's Lake Tahoe," Jay told him.

"Same damn thing!" her father exploded. "Married? And without your family? How could you?"

As he readied himself for another volley, Bridget held up a hand for silence. In a panicky voice, she explained, "Yes, Tripp and I were married yesterday. But it's not what you think. It's just for show."

"Just for my mother."

"Just for a little while."

"And then we'll get an annulment."

Bridget added, "Because there's nothing going on that can't be annulled. Nothing of a marital sort of nature. We're just pretending."

"Just for my mother." As if they had practiced this act, Tripp finished up, "She's very ill, and we don't want to upset her. So for right now, it's important that we keep her in the dark, that we let her think this is a normal marriage, a normal honeymoon."

"A normal marriage? A normal honeymoon?" Jay demanded. He was definitely losing his trademark cool. "While you were already engaged to someone else?"

"But she doesn't know that," Bridget murmured. "Kitty Belle is dying. The one thing she wanted was for Tripp to get married. So we gave her that, as a gift. Was that so wrong?"

"Yes, it was." Jay backed up a step and looked away, at a tree, as if he'd rather look at anything but her. "How could you, Bridget? This is a disaster. This displays a phenomenal lack of judgment. I'm just appalled that the woman I wanted to marry could be so selfish, so shortsighted, so..."

"Human?" Tripp asked darkly.

Once again, she held him back. "I'm sorry, Jay. I did what I thought was best for Tripp and his mother. Tripp is my friend. And there wasn't anyone else."

Her father was taking a moment to digest this news. "Whatever foolishness you and this Ashby fellow have been up to, it's not his mother's fault. I don't suppose it would serve any purpose to disillusion a dying woman," he said grudgingly.

"Thank you, sir," Tripp said in a tight, uncomfortable voice.

"Thank you, Daddy. I'm sorry you had to come all the way out here." She hazarded a glance at Jay, wondering how this could possibly be fixed. He was hurt and disappointed, and it was all her fault. "But it was a completely unnecessary trip. Everything is fine. Everything will continue to be fine."

She linked her arm through her father's, drawing him and the rest of their little group back around to the front of the cabin. "Well," she said, standing next to their car. "I hope you can forgive me. Once you've had some time to think about it, to get used to it, we can talk all you want. In the meantime, have a good trip back.''

"Back?" Frank Emerick stilled. "What do you mean, back? We're not leaving yet."

"You're not?"

"Of course not," put in Jay. "We have rooms at the Pine Cone Resort. We're staying indefinitely."

"But you can't!" Bridget protested.

"Well, we are." Jay's expression was implacable. "I couldn't leave you here with *him*."

"I still don't trust him," her father grumbled. "When we're satisfied that you're all right, that this is on the up-and-up and you're not being taken advantage of, then we'll leave. And not before. We'll go check in at the Pine Cone and then we'll be right back here." Shaking a finger, he skewered Tripp with a ferocious glare. "I'm going to make sure there isn't any funny business going on with my daughter."

"There's no reason to stay," Bridget tried, but they were immovable.

"We're staying," Frank insisted. "If need be, we'll set up camp on your mountain here. I'm not leaving my daughter alone with the likes of *him*."

"But..." Bridget grabbed Tripp's arm. "What will we tell Kitty Belle? She thinks that crazy old coot from the general store is my father. And we certainly can't tell her Jay is my fiancé!"

"What?" her father exploded. "You told her someone else was your father?"

"Bridget!" Jay said, outraged. "Is there no end to the lies you're willing to tell?"

"All right, all right," Tripp began, in a very determined tone. "Calm down. This was all my fault."

"I know," Bridget said suddenly. "We could give them fake identities, too."

"Fake identities?" her father and Jay trumpeted in tandem.

"If Jed can do it, you can do it," she offered.

Tripp squeezed her arm. "Bridgie, that's a great idea. Your dad could be...oh, I don't know, your uncle. How about that? Uncle...Joe. What do you think?"

"I think you're all crazy!" Frank Emerick shot back. "Pretending to be someone else. I've never heard of anything so ridiculous in my life."

"If you want to stay, you can't be my dad, because Kitty Belle thinks I already have one," Bridget explained again. "You have to be Uncle Joe. Take it or leave it."

"This is outrageous!" he blustered.

"And I suppose I'm supposed to go lurking around as another uncle?" Jay demanded.

"Uncle?" Tripp said doubtfully. "Maybe he should be a brother."

"A brother? You can't be serious!"

"Well, you hardly want Kitty Belle to know who you really are, or anyone else in Lake Tahoe, for that matter," Bridget told him. "After all, this is a gambling mecca, which would screw up your image all by itself. And besides, how it would look for a prominent senatorial candidate to be hanging out in Lake Tahoe in some kind of ménage à trois with his fiancée and her other husband?"

"Ménage à trois? I didn't think my daughter knew about things like that! Where did you learn about things like that?"

"Daddy, it's not really a ménage," she explained, horrified. "It just might look like it to the voters."

It took a good half hour of wrangling and fighting, but she finally impressed upon them the importance of going undercover if they were bound and determined to stick around. Both Jay and her father were very stubborn men, and they insisted they weren't going anywhere. Which meant they finally agreed to be Uncle Joe and Brother Jay for the duration.

As she watched their rental car disappear down the winding road, Bridget reluctantly retreated to the Studs cabin, where even now, Tripp was probably carting her things down to the Chamber of Horrors.

"This is no way to run a honeymoon," she said under her breath. "No way at all."

Chapter Twelve

"Of course your family must stay for dinner," Kitty Belle announced. "I'm delighted they're all here."

She seemed to have perked up considerably since this morning, and she was even dragging tables and chairs around to make sure there was enough room for everyone to sit down.

"You know, Bridget," she mused. "Your uncle is quite charming. A little gruff, but just as sweet as he can be. I must say, your brother is very charming although just a wee bit stern, don't you think? And I really don't see the family resemblance there."

"He, uh, takes after the other side," she said quickly.

"Would you like to call them in, dear? They should be back from their walk in the woods by now." She peeked into the kitchen. "And I think Tripp is ready with dinner."

"But, Mrs. Ashby, you've set six places. There are only five of us."

"Oh, dear. I guess I neglected to mention that your father would be joining us."

"My f-father?"

"Yes, that's right." Kitty Belle smiled brightly. "It was the most amazing coincidence. I happened to pop down to the store out on the highway. I needed some moisturizer desperately. You know, it's so very dry up here—''

She didn't know which was more astonishing, the idea of Kitty Belle popping down the highway, or using moisturizer she'd bought over the counter at a dusty convenience store.

"And who should I run into but your dear father? So of course, knowing that your brother and uncle had turned up, I invited him to join us." Kitty Belle paused. "Is he similarly estranged from them, too, dear? He is a bit rough around the edges, isn't he?"

"My f-father?" Bridget repeated.

"Yes, dear." She pointed out the big front window, where a battered truck, trailing a cloud of black smoke, had just pulled up in front of the cabin. "There he is now."

And so they sat down together at the big round table, eyeing each other suspiciously, everyone trying hard to remember who they were supposed to be.

Jed Leland, the man from the general store, didn't seem to mind that no one knew quite what to make of him. Unconcerned to play another round as Bridget's father, he chowed down happily while Tripp was still bringing in dishes.

"Well, Dad, isn't it nice to see Uncle Joe and Jay again?" Bridget asked stiffly.

"Yes, of course, Dad," Jay said distastefully.

Old Jed's bushy eyebrows shot up to his receding hairline. "He's mine, too?"

"That's right." Tripp's eyes were dancing with mischief. "I guess it's been a while since you saw your son."

"Seems like forever, don't it, kid?" Jed asked cheerfully.

Bridget decided it was a good thing someone was enjoying this charade.

"Now, you're Bridget's uncle, correct?" Kitty Belle inquired politely, as she offered the real Frank a basket of bread. "So does that make you Frank's brother? Or are you Bridget's mother's brother?"

Her dad thought about it for a long moment, wrinkling his brow with concentration. Finally, after a long look at Jed, Frank allowed, "I can't claim any relation to him. I'm Mrs. Emerick's brother. Margie, who would be my late, uh, sister, yes, that's right—well, anyway, Margie was a real beauty. Bridget, and her sisters Patty and Linda, too, all take after their mother. Real beauties, every one." Proud of himself, he winked at Bridget.

"And isn't that odd?" Kitty Belle mused. "All the girls resemble their mother, and yet their brother has a very different look."

"Reckon the boy takes after my side of the family," Jed put in, yanking his polyester pants up over his gut.

Bridget kicked Jay, who said, "Who, me?" He took one look at Jed, the father he supposedly resembled, and began to choke.

Bridget lost track of the conversational threads after a while; it was just too tough to keep up. But it didn't matter. Kitty Belle seemed quite happy to chat with "Uncle Joe" and tune out the rest of their soggy attempts to be polite to one another.

In no time, Bridget's real dad was leaning in closer to Kitty Belle, telling her all his favorite plumbing stories about St. Paul, and she was tittering appreciatively.

"So you and your brother-in-law are both plumbers. Now isn't that interesting?"

"Me and my...?" It took Frank a moment to get the gist of that one. "Oh, me and my brother-in-law. Him over there. Right. Yes, we're both plumbers." He sent a searching glance to his daughter. "Are we?"

"Yes, you are," she prompted.

"Although I understand that Bridget's father has retired. Isn't that right, Frank?"

"Huh?" Jed said with a start. "Oh, sorry. Must've dropped off there. Retired? Why, yes, I am. Being a farmer, oh, sorry, I mean a plumber, well, that wasn't the life for me."

"And isn't it wonderful that Frank has retired right here to Lake Tahoe?" Kitty Belle informed them. "Why, he's running the general store out on Route 28."

"Is that right?" Tripp asked dryly.

But his mother had returned to her fascinating discussion with the real Frank. "Now, you haven't retired yet, have you, Joe?"

"Who? Oh, Joe. Uncle Joe. Right. That's me! No, no. I haven't retired. They'll have to bury me with my snake in one hand and my plunger in the other."

Kitty Belle tapped him playfully on the arm. "Oh, aren't you amusing!"

"If you were going to make me your brother, couldn't you have provided a more acceptable father?" Jay muttered ominously. "That man is beyond the pale."

"I'm sorry," she whispered back. "Do you think *I* like him?"

Thank goodness they were all the way across the table, and Kitty Belle was all wrapped up in their dad. She didn't seem to notice the heated discussion going on between Bridget and Jay.

"I'm sorry to break this up, but I think my wife is getting tired," Tripp announced, rising to his feet, signaling an end to this interminable dinner. "We had a long day yesterday."

"And a long night," Kitty Belle said knowingly. When the others turned to her, shocked, she shrugged unrepentantly. "They're honeymooners, for heaven's sake. They're supposed to be up all night."

Jay was bristling, her father was looking very suspicious, and Bridget felt her face flame with embarrassment. As she suffered, not sure what to do to make everyone stop glowering at her, Tripp pulled her to her feet, dropping an arm around her shoulders. He brushed a tender kiss on the top of her head. "Well, everyone, this has been great. We'll have to do it again soon."

Over my dead body, Bridget thought darkly.

Tripp began to clear away the plates on the table, and Bridget jumped to help him.

"I guess we should be getting back to the Pine Cone," her father remarked. He gave his daughter a meaningful look. "If Bridget is sure she doesn't need us."

"You're staying at a motel?" Kitty Belle asked, aghast. "Why, there's plenty of room here. We have two extra bedrooms upstairs, and as long as you and your nephew don't mind sharing a bath, we're all set."

"Now there's a good idea," Frank Emerick decided. "We can save some money and keep a closer eye on Bridget, all at the same time."

"I don't think so—" Tripp and Bridget chorused, but the ship that was known as Kitty Belle had already sailed.

With Frank trailing in her wake, Mrs. Ashby cruised up the stairs, chattering on about linens and pillows.

Jay hung back. As soon as the others were out of earshot, he bent over closer to Bridget. "I'll be right upstairs if you need me," he said meaningfully.

"Don't speak to my wife that way," Tripp snarled back.

"She's my fiancée."

"Not anymore she's not."

"Oh, yes," Jay said distinctly, "she is. Unlike your wedding, our engagement is no sham. One you and my fiancée have quit playing house, she will have a real life to come back to."

"I will?" she whispered. She hadn't been altogether sure.

"You will." Jay took her arm possessively. "Although Mr. Ashby here has done his best to ruin your life and my career, I think we can still salvage things if we're careful. Be careful, Bridget."

"Get your hands off my wife."

"Stop it. Stop it this instant. I'm not some bone to be fought over." She removed Jay's hand from her arm. "Go to bed, Jay. We'll talk in the morning." Softly, slowly, Bridget told him, "I know how hard you're trying to be fair to me. But let's just wait until tomorrow, okay?"

She and Tripp roused Jed and got rid of him, and then, wordlessly, they cleared away the dinner dishes. It was almost as if they were really married. Almost.

As soon as the last plate was in the dishwasher, Tripp led the way to his room. Their room.

Bridget stopped inside the door, her hand still on the handle, as she gazed at the big bed. One big bed. They didn't have any choice. To keep up the pretense, they were going to have to share this room. And that meant sharing the bed.

"Don't worry," Tripp said roughly, following the path of her eyes. He grabbed a pillow and a quilt. "I'll take the floor."

"You can't sleep on the floor."

There was a sharp, biting edge to his voice when he asked, "Do you really think I can do anything else?"

She flinched. "You're the one who said the worst was over. You're the one who said we'd be okay as long as I didn't have anything to drink."

"Well, that was before your damn fiancé showed up, shoving my nose in the fact that I've ruined your life."

"You haven't—"

"Save it, okay?"

Sleeping with her was apparently such a hideous proposition that he wouldn't even risk taking the other side of a king-size bed. Or maybe after last night's unpleasant lesson, he was afraid she would get a bit too friendly if they shared a mattress, and then they would both have to answer to her irate fiancé and father.

But Bridget knew better. She wasn't going anywhere near him. She'd learned her lesson. There was no way she was going to try anything with Tripp when her plans for the future were hanging by a thread.

"You don't have to sleep on the floor," she said angrily, skirting a wide path around him as she headed for the far side of the bed. "Don't worry—I won't touch you."

He lifted an eyebrow. "You think I'm worried about you?"

Bridget faced him down defiantly. "Well? What else? All the junk about us being okay if I wasn't drunk. Correct me if I'm wrong, but I assume that means you, oh Man of Steel, are not interested. So nothing's going to happen if I stay away from you. So I will. So end of problem. So sleep in the damn bed!"

"Sometimes, Bridget," he said between gritted teeth, "you are such a dope."

"A dope? I think I've got it exactly right. I *know* I've got it exactly right."

"Damn it, Bridget," he growled. Swiftly he advanced on her, stalking around the bed, trapping her. She backed up as fast as she could, but it was too late. She hit the wall.

And then Tripp grabbed her and held her fast, up against the hard, unrelenting wall. No harder than Tripp, though. Splaying her hands on either side of her face, he stared down at her, his blue eyes blazing.

She swallowed.

His feet were shoved around hers, his hips pressed into her. God, he felt good.

Abruptly, he said, "Still think you're right?"

"I don't know," she whispered.

"Damn you," he said again. And then he bent down just far enough to sizzle her with his kiss, fastening his lips to hers, delving inside, fast, furious, cruel.

Instantly, she was aroused, on fire. And he knew it.

"That's how it is between us," he said. "It has been for days. I'm trying to stay away from you, for the sake of your precious fiancé. I know you want your fancy life, saving whales, passing bills, married to that Boy Scout. It's what you want, isn't it?"

She swallowed again, searching his face. He was right. It was what she had always wanted. Her dreams were so much a part of her... How could she deny it? "Yes," she said finally. "Yes. I want to marry Jay. I want to be as good and committed and responsible as he is."

"None of those things are going to happen if you sleep with me."

"But—"

"He might be willing to forgive this little marital adventure, all for a good cause, as long as no one ever finds out." Tripp's face was so bleak, so harsh, Bridget wanted to reach out and smooth away the pain. But how could she? It was all her fault. "But a full-fledged affair? I don't think so. He would look down at his pretty little senator's wife and wonder who she was thinking of every time he made love to her. He would never forget, and never forgive. I wouldn't."

"You and Jay are very different people," she tried. "Besides, nothing has to happen. We already agreed that nothing—"

Tripp dropped her suddenly, wheeling and turning away. "I know better."

"Know better than what?" she demanded, rubbing her wrists. "Do you think you're so hot I can't share a bed with you and not fall all over you? Think again, Mr. Stud."

"It's not you," he said savagely, and she could tell he'd reached the end of his rope. "It's me, all right? Have you got that? I can't share a bed with you and not want you. I am barely controlling myself as it is. I feel like a damn animal, a damn tomcat on the prowl. And if I have to sleep next to you all night, smelling your hair, feeling you every time you turn, hearing the sounds you make when you dream—" He broke off, cursing under his breath. "I can't do it. I can't."

Bridget was stunned.

He switched off the lights, and she could hear the sound of his shoes, his pants, his shirt hitting the floor. Still, she was stunned. He rustled with his pillow and his quilt down there on the floor, and still, she didn't move.

Slowly, quietly, she found her pajamas, she dressed in the bathroom, and she crept back into bed. *I can't share a bed with you and not want you.*

This coming from Tripp? How could she believe this?

Hadn't they shared the same couch, all night long, at his college house? They'd fallen asleep studying for finals, and spent the whole night tumbled together on one narrow, uncomfortable couch, and nothing had happened. He never touched her. He was never even tempted to touch her, as far as she knew.

Hadn't they spent a whole night huddled together in the back of a van, sharing the same blanket, while one of Tripp's friends drove them to a concert?

Hadn't they shared a room on that blasted ski trip— two single beds, two single college kids—and nothing had happened?

Nothing ever happened. Not until the past few weeks, when she had suddenly found herself jumping on him at every turn. Sure, she could tell he was turned on. With men, it wasn't hard to tell.

But she thought that was just an uncontrollable physical reaction to the proximity of a woman, any women. She didn't think it had anything to do with her.

After all, *he* was the one who kept stopping things, not her. She'd thought he was being kind, turning her away, saving them both a whole lot of embarrassment. But now he said it was because he *did* want her, not because he didn't want her.

Men were very strange animals sometimes.

Bridget was still trying to take this in, to make some sense of it. Could it be possible?

Tripp, wanting her.

She could hear him down there, tossing and turning. Tripp, wanting her.

She had lusted after him from afar for the better part of sixteen years, and yet she had never acted upon it, because she didn't think it was right. Bridget Emerick was a woman who believed in love, not lust.

She sighed, trying to settle in. She loved Jay, right? She was going to marry Jay, right?

So why did she find herself wanting Tripp enough to throw away the rest?

"WHERE IS EVERYONE?" she whispered.

Tripp was extremely grouchy this morning, not surprising after another night on the floor. He'd spent the past few hours chopping wood or some other manly task, guaranteed to expend lots of hostility through sweat and exertion.

"I don't know," he returned shortly. He grabbed a towel and took off for the hot tub, muttering something about soaking his sore muscles.

"You haven't seen any of them?" Bridget called after him. "That's odd."

It had only been two days, but Bridget had gotten used to the fact that she would be spending her honeymoon—her pretend honeymoon—with a lot of chaperons. Yesterday, they'd been like the Brady Bunch, taking a picnic up the mountain a little ways, enjoying the clear, cold air and the fabulous scenery.

With everyone laughing and carrying on, it was very hard to remember how many lies they were keeping afloat, or to dwell on the fact that Kitty Belle might not be with them much longer.

The funny thing was she seemed very chipper, very happy, very, well, healthy. "This mountain air is doing me good," Kitty Belle proclaimed. She and Bridget's dad took a side hike of their own, looking for some species of fern or other. And although Bridget warned her father to be very careful, and to bring Kitty Belle back immediately at the first sign of any strain, everything went beautifully.

As a matter of fact, Kitty Belle seemed very taken with Frank Emerick. If Bridget didn't know better, she'd think the two were carrying on a flirtation. They always seemed to have their heads together, giggling about some private joke.

Today, they had disappeared completely. Which left the unhappy little threesome of Bridget, Tripp and Jay back at the cabin.

Bridget knew she was going to have to talk to Jay, to sort this out and create some peace. He had developed a major attitude problem—it was really weird, because she had never seen Jay behave like this, even though, of course, the situation was beyond bizarre, so who could blame him?—but every time he and Tripp were in the same room, they were practically baring their fangs at each other.

Perfect Jay was showing signs of imperfection. In a way, it was a relief.

But she knew she was going to have to talk to him alone soon, to take her medicine and make whatever major concessions he required to smooth things over. Because when her little idyll as a runaway bride was over, it would be time to go home and pick up the pieces, to turn back into the reliable, serious-minded

Bridget Emerick the rest of the world recognized. Too bad she was really dreading it.

Taking a deep breath, Bridget went to find him. He was in the living room, his hands in his pockets, moodily gazing out the window at the trees.

She took another heady gulp of air and prepared to do her duty. Better do it now, while Tripp was neck-deep in water, and unlikely to come running in and crossing swords with anybody.

But Jay jumped the gun. He turned, saw her and said, "Bridget, I really need to speak with you."

"Well, I need to speak to you, too, Jay." Bridget counted to three, looked him right in the eye, and started, "I don't know how to say this, Jay. You've been more than patient with me, and I really don't have any excuse, and I don't know how to ask you to forgive me..."

"Bridget, you know I will always forgive you, no matter what you do." He sighed. "Although this debacle has been more than I planned for, I'll admit that."

He was being noble and wonderful again, and she was miserable. "I'm so sorry, Jay."

He squeezed her hand kindly. "I know you are."

So he *did* forgive her. But she'd known he could. Didn't Jay always forgive everything? "I thought I could help Tripp and you would never need to know," she explained. "I know you must be very hurt. I didn't want you ever to find out."

He just shook his head sadly. "The truth would've come out sooner or later."

"I guess I know that now. I really made a hash of things, and I'm so sorry. But the last thing I wanted to do was let this affect your campaign. Whatever we have to do to make it go away, we will."

"I think…" He broke off. "I think you did what you had to do. I'm just sorry that *this* was what you had to do."

"I—I don't understand."

"Yes, you do." He smiled fondly at her. "Deep down, you understand perfectly. You tell yourself you've gone along with all this craziness as a favor to Tripp and his mother, but that's just a lie."

"It is?"

"Of course it is." Jay took her shoulders in his arms and gave her his most sincere, most concerned face. "Being here, watching you with him… Bridget, there's only one explanation for your actions."

She wasn't sure she wanted to hear this. Was it because she was crazy? Unworthy? Just plain stupid?

"It's because you're in love with him," Jay said softly.

"In love with Tripp?" she scoffed. "But that's not true! I admit, I've always, well, been attracted to Tripp, like a physical thing. I met him at a very impressionable age and he just got under my skin. But that's all it was, a physical thing. Tripp was never my type and I was never his."

"Maybe never before. But now…" Jay paused. "I'd say you two are definitely each other's types."

"No, Jay—"

"It's not me you need to convince," he said sternly. "It's yourself."

She was stunned. It wasn't true. Not even a little. "But why are you telling me this now?"

"Because I'm all packed and ready to go."

"Oh." She blinked. "Well, that's good. I mean, I do think it's better for you to go home, get moving on the campaign. As soon as I get back—"

"Bridget, have you heard a word I'm saying?"

"You're leaving. I'll be coming later."

He just shook his head.

"Are you saying you don't want me to come back?" she asked. "I would understand that, Jay. I mean, what I've done here certainly does change things, and if you want to end the engagement, of course I understand. Is that what you want, Jay?"

"No, actually, it isn't. If you were to decide tomorrow that you were unhappy here with him, I'd be happy to continue as we were before."

"You would?" But of course he would. Jay was too perfect not to be able to forgive completely, not to be able to see the future as more important than the present.

"But I don't think *you* would," he added.

"Listen, Jay, just because I've done a few irresponsible things doesn't mean that deep down—"

"Oh, yes, it does." Jay smiled, his six o'clock news smile. "Give yourself a break, will you? I know you want to be what you think other people expect. I know you think that duty and good taste require that you stay with me. But for goodness' sake, Bridget, think about what you *want*, will you? Look in your heart, and stop causing so much trouble fighting yourself."

"Fighting myself?"

But Jay picked up his bag, and then he was gone.

All his words were still swimming in her head, and she still hadn't made heads or tails of them.

But then another thought pierced her consciousness. Jay had left. And five on a honeymoon had just been reduced to four.

"TRIPP? ARE YOU AWAKE?"

"Bridget, why do you ask if I'm awake? You know

damn well I'm awake."

"That's the whole point. I can hear you thrashing around down there, and I know you can't sleep. And I just think you ought to come up into the bed with me."

"We've been through this. No."

"Please? You're crankier and meaner every day. And we both know why. Because you don't sleep. You lie on the hard old floor, and you're miserable."

A long pause hung in the still night air.

"Please? I'll stay way over on my side. You won't even know I'm here."

Silence.

"I promise," she said softly.

He muttered a very nasty epithet under his breath, he slammed his pillow down on the floor and then he strode over and jammed his long, lean body into the bed.

She knew he was turned away from her. She knew he was as cold and immovable as a block of granite over there.

"Tripp, I've been thinking, about Jay..."

"I am not going to discuss him while I am lying in bed with you. I know he trusts you, and I know you're trying hard to live up to his trust. I'm trying, too."

"But that's not—"

"Good night, Bridget," he growled.

It was so hard to picture a life without her dreams, with the sense of duty and obligation that had always hung around her shoulders. What would she do if she didn't have that golden future to look forward to?

What would she do if she gave it all up, like Jay suggested, if she tapped Tripp on the shoulder and told him, flat out, that she wanted nothing more from her life than to live in the suburbs with him?

And what if he told her she was crazy?

She gazed over at where his hard body formed a wall on the other side of the bed. *I love you. I think in my heart I have always loved you. But what do you feel for me?*

Could she make that move, could she tell him how she felt, without knowing? She had always been so secure in where her future lie. She was a careful, methodical person. Could she throw it away without being equally secure about the substitute?

Life had gotten entirely too complicated ever since she married Tripp Ashby.

Chapter Thirteen

Her hair was tickling his nose. Tripp brushed it away.

There it was again. He opened one eye, just an inch. Bridgie. Both eyes flashed open, wide.

Bridgie's body was curled up next to his, her head on his shoulder, her nightgown riding up far enough that her enticing little bottom was grazing his thigh. She slept there, within the circle of his arm, as sweetly, as trustingly, as if she did it every night.

Tripp brushed a thumb down the curve of her cheek, enjoying the rarity of an unguarded moment.

"Bridgie," he murmured, and she lifted her head sleepily.

Her drowsy smile lit up the room. She propped her chin on his chest. And then she snuggled back into him, and went back to sleep.

"Bridgie..." This was becoming a bit uncomfortable.

"Mmmm." Her leg tangled around his. "Be quiet, Tripp. I'm tired. There was this person tossing and turning and heaving big sighs on my floor most of the night, and I didn't get any sleep."

He smiled. "Oh, I see."

"Well," she said softly, "I hope you've learned your lesson."

He laid an arm around her, very carefully, unwilling to make a false move and scare her away.

She was his wife, for God's sake. Nobody would say a word if he dipped his head down, if he covered her mouth with his own, if he made love to her in his own bed in his own cabin, again and again, until they both fell apart at the seams. Until she knew, for once and for all, that she belonged to him.

Nobody would say a word. Except maybe Bridgie.

"Sweetheart," he murmured. He needed to hold her very badly. He needed to touch her and kiss her, and let her know how he felt. Because very soon she would leave him, and he would never know the joy of making love with his wife. "Bridgie?"

And then the door burst open.

Perched in the doorway, Kitty Belle stuck her hand over her eyes. "Sorry. I didn't see anything. Not a thing."

"Mother!" Scandalized, Tripp sat up, pulling the sheet up over Bridgie completely, shielding himself up to the chest. "What the hell are you doing? Didn't anyone ever teach you to knock?"

"I wanted to surprise you!" she said happily. "Now, Tripp, don't get all excited. I told you, I didn't see anything."

"You don't surprise someone on their honeymoon," he shot back.

"Oh, pish posh! I have a big announcement to make."

"Go back out in the hall, will you? Better yet, get some breakfast. We'll meet you out there in a few minutes."

As his mother finally consented to disappear, Tripp pulled the sheet back, revealing Bridget's rosy face. "It appears we are being summoned for a command performance," he told her. "Better get up, sleepyhead."

She muttered something unpleasant, but she deigned to hoist herself out of the bed, straightening her nightgown and marching haughtily to the bathroom to get ready.

"Oh, and Bridgie?"

She turned.

"You didn't do it."

"Didn't do what?"

He grinned at her. "You promised me you'd stay on your own side of the bed. You promised me I wouldn't know you were here."

"I lied."

And then she spun on her heel, leaving him alone in the big brass bed.

"I'M GOING HOME."

"To Ashbyville?" Tripp asked. "Are you serious? What does this mean?"

"It means that this mountain air has done me a world of good, and I'm well enough to travel."

"Well, that's wonderful. Isn't it, Bridgie?"

"Wow. It's fabulous." She crossed to her mother-in-law's chair. "Are you sure? You're really feeling that well?"

"Oh, yes, I think so. And I'm anxious to get home. I feel it's important to give the two of you some time for a real honeymoon." She winked broadly. "We need to get those grandchildren started, after all. You know how much I want to keep the Ashby name going, and now that my son is finally married, I can't wait to see my grandsons."

"Your grandsons?" Bridget was surprised. "Do you mean…?" But she could hardly ask her mother-in-law how long she planned to live. It was probably just wishful thinking, just a sweet dream for their future without her.

Tripp seemed to have missed the part about the grandchildren. He peered at his mother, as if there were something more going on that he couldn't see. "When will you leave?"

"Right away. All packed," she said cheerfully. "I've got a flight this afternoon."

"This afternoon?" Tripp stuck his hand in his pocket. "Well, I guess I'd better find my keys and get ready to roll. Whenever you're ready, I can drive you to Reno. Bridgie, do you want to come? Oh, and you, too, Uncle Joe."

"That won't be necessary," Kitty Belle said quickly.

"Mother, of course I'll drive you."

"But there's no need," interjected Frank Emerick. Awkwardly, he said, "When Kitty Belle told me she was ready to head out to Chicago, I thought maybe it was time I got back to St. Paul, as well."

"You're leaving, too?" Bridget looked at one and then the other. "But why now?"

"Well, I always said I would go as soon as I felt better," Tripp's mother said quickly.

"And I said I would go as soon as I was sure you were all right, Bridget Marie." Her dad gave her a gruff smile. "I guess I figured out, from watching the two of you together, that there was no reason to worry, none at all."

"Really?" Bridget said softly.

"Sure, honey." He reached out to ruffle her hair. "I know two people in love when I see them. I'm not that old and decrepit, you know."

"You're not old and decrepit at all."

His smiled widened, as her father stuck an arm around his little girl. "Why, I can tell just by looking at you that you're crazy about each other, and what's more, I trust him to take care of you."

"Thank you, sir," Tripp said somberly.

"What more could you ask?" Frank Emerick laughed. "The boy has a wonderful mother, plus he's a great cook, which is really a good thing, since Bridget is awful."

That got a crooked smile out of Tripp. "I know. Remind me to tell you about this one Thanksgiving—"

"Be quiet," she rasped. Quickly she pulled her father out of earshot, where they could speak privately. "Thank you, Dad. For going along. I know this hasn't been easy for you, telling all these lies, but it really has made Kitty Belle happy."

"Oh, I didn't mind so much. Once I got used to the idea." He cocked an eyebrow at her. "Once I saw how right the two of you were for each other. I admit it, I wasn't crazy about Tripp at first. You know, I like Jay. He's a good man, and I hate to see you lose him. But now I see things a little more clearly. Tripp loves you, baby. It's written all over him."

Bridget smiled wanly. She wished she knew whether it was true.

"We'll see you at Thanksgiving, right? Both of you? Your sister Linda will be making the turkey."

"I don't know, Dad. We haven't really thought that far ahead."

"It's just a couple of weeks away," he protested.

"I know, but . . ." She had to say it. "I don't know if Tripp and I will still be together in a couple of weeks. Once Kitty Belle . . . well, you know."

"No matter what happens with Kitty Belle, you two will still be together." Her dad gave her a confident squeeze. "Trust me. You'll be together."

"I don't know, Dad. I just don't know."

AND THEN THERE were two.

There wasn't much time left, only a day or two. It was a shame in a way, even though, left all alone, Tripp and Bridget weren't quite sure what to do with each other. The shadows in the cabin seemed longer, quieter, more forbidding. Time seemed to hang around them, unfilled.

He cooked her dinner, like always. She helped him clean up, like always.

The first day and then the second passed in this sort of edgy truce. Neither one seemed willing to confront the other and have it out.

Until finally, inevitably, they reached their last night together in the cabin.

And after dinner, after the usual ritual of cooking and cleaning, as the sun glowed pink behind the mountains to the west, they exchanged confused glances. What now?

"Hey," Tripp said lightly, "we've never had any problem keeping ourselves busy before this. Tell you what—I'll get the Scrabble game, and you get the dictionary."

It was a relief to fall into the old patterns. Scrabble. Over the years, they must've played a hundred games.

"I'll beat the pants off you," she promised. "I always do."

"Emerick, you are so conceited. Just wait till you see my seven-letter triple word score."

"Dream on."

Bridget lounged on the fluffy white rug in front of the fireplace, watching the embers die down, watching Tripp as he frowned at his rack of tiles.

"Will you hurry up?" she pleaded. "You must have some kind of word there."

He didn't even look up, just kept staring at his tiles.

Bridget sighed. In the morning, she knew, they would rise together for the last time, they would get into their separate rental cars and they would fly back to their separate lives.

As she stared into the dying fire, moodily contemplating the end of this wretched honeymoon, Bridget suddenly knew with crystal clarity what she was going to do.

It didn't really matter whether she went back to Jay or not, whether she did indeed take the high road for the rest of her life, or stayed earthbound with the rest of the mortals.

She could still have tonight.

She'd wanted Tripp Ashby for sixteen years, and this was her last chance. In the morning it would all be over, one way or the other. Her heart beat faster. Her face flushed with heat and desire. She was going to do it, and damn the consequences.

Even if she lost him forever, she would have this one night to remember. She wanted it. She wanted him.

Seize the night.

She sneaked a glance at him. Completely unaware.

"Tripp?"

"Hmm?"

Bridget reached over and knocked over his rack of tiles. Tiny wooden letters toppled into the rug.

His blue eyes blazed, reflecting the flames in the fireplace. "What are you doing?"

"I'm tired of this game." And she slid through the middle of the board, scattering letters everywhere, as she wrapped her arms around his waist. "What would you do if I asked you to make love to me right here, right now?"

He hesitated, for just a split second.

"I'm perfectly sober, and there's no one to interrupt us," she said quickly. She licked her lip, watching the fire in his eyes deepen. "Forget about the future. I don't care."

"I don't believe you."

"It's true," she insisted, and for the first time, it was. Whether or not she did the smart thing had ceased to matter. If this one small act threw away her future forever, she simply didn't care. "I want this, Tripp. I want it more than anything. Will you say something? Now? Before I lose my nerve?"

"Bridgie," he whispered, closing his eyes, gathering her close, breathing into her hair. "Do you trust me?"

She nodded.

"Is this really what you want?"

"It's what I want."

He tightened his hold, he knocked her back into the soft, thick fur of the rug and kissed her.

His mouth was so warm, and so demanding. It was as if he, too, knew they didn't have much time. He framed her face with his hands, and he dropped hungry little kisses on her cheeks and her chin, on her nose and her eyelids.

She had imagined so many times what it would be like if Tripp made love to her. She wanted him to be everything she had dreamed he would be. Her hero. Her golden boy.

Swifter, farther, higher. She'd seen him reach for the sky on the track field. She wanted to see that strength, that speed and daring, on this field of battle.

He didn't disappoint.

His whole body was one hard line of desire as he shrugged out of his shirt and reached for hers. "No, I can—" she tried, but he batted her hands away.

"I want to."

And then he ripped it away, ignoring the shattered buttons, ignoring the slashing, rending sound of torn fabric, as Bridget's breath caught in her throat. She was afraid. He stared down at her, at the curves barely contained by the lacy bra she was wearing, and he drank her in. Under his rapt gaze, with those smoky blue eyes radiating heat and passion, she felt more desirable than she'd thought possible.

Not quite sure she could believe what she was seeing, she murmured, "Do you want me, Tripp?"

"Bridget," he said roughly. "I want you so badly, I can't think of anything else. I want you so badly, I'm shaking with it."

Her mouth went dry.

Savagely, recklessly, he disposed of her blouse and tore away her bra. And he covered her hot, fevered flesh with his mouth and his hands, cupping her breasts, teasing her briefly, leaving her trembling with need.

She could feel him everywhere, and the pleasure, the pain, was exquisite. His fingers and his lips stroked and caressed her, they licked her, they flickered sparks over her shoulders, along the column of her throat, across the tops of her breasts.

But no farther. She was restless, impatient, anxious, melting inside.

She tried to wriggle closer, to reach for him, too, but he held her back, still taking his time, charting his own course.

Her breasts ached for his touch, for his mouth, and her nipples stiffened, tautened into impossibly hard little peaks. Tripp etched his kisses closer, but not close enough.

Desperate, she arched up into his mouth. "Please," she moaned.

And he bit down gently, and she moaned again, louder this time.

She lifted herself up off the fur rug, rubbing her jeans against his, greedy for the hard, heavy feel of him pressed to the center of her. She knew she was wanton, out of control, and she didn't care. This was Tripp. This was her fantasy.

But this was far better than any fantasy. This was real. Blazingly, scorchingly real.

"Get rid of this," he said huskily, trying to peel away her jeans.

She shed them herself, eager to feel more of him, reaching for his jeans, too.

And when there was nothing but skin between them, she took in the full, stunning picture of who exactly she was dealing with. Perfection. Not the idealistic, white knight kind. Tripp was real, hard, alive. He was a real man. And he was wonderful.

Tall, slim, lean, beautifully muscled, Tripp had the long torso and sleek arms of the athlete he had once been, still was. She ran her hands over his chest, his gorgeous, sweat slick chest, reflecting golden in the dying firelight. She filled her palms with his supple strength, mesmerized by the hard, strong curves of his arms and his back.

"You are the most beautiful man I've ever seen," she whispered.

"Be quiet," he said, nipping at her lower lip, wrestling her around until she was completely underneath him. His rigid arousal brushed her thigh, and she angled closer, wanting the feel of him under her fingers. But he caught both her hands in one of his, twisting them up out of the way.

"Tripp, please..." She needed to touch him. This was torture.

But he was merciless. "You're the beautiful one, Bridget," he whispered. His voice was tense, unsteady, as if he were having trouble breathing. "Do you know how much I love your hair and your eyes and the way your pupils get huge when I kiss you? I love the sounds you make when I touch you, here."

And he did touch her, there, and she offered up a husky whimper of heady desire.

"I love the way you move, and the way you breathe." He found her mouth again, and he kissed her, deep and long. "And the way you taste. I can't seem to get enough."

Poised there above her, his body fitted to her, he slid himself against her, back and forth, once, twice, just teasing her. She moaned incoherently, struggling to press in closer and harder, to find some point of relief.

But Tripp set the rhythm, and he wouldn't give in. Just barely brushing her, driving her mad, he held himself back. Every blood vessel in her body was pounding with the feel of him, every inch of her tingled and quivered. She was dizzy and weak, and the damn man was just out of reach.

A longer, more urgent sound escaped her lips. "Now," she begged, writhing under him. He stroked against her swiftly, sweetly. Again and again. Just right. Just perfect. Just Tripp.

Finally, at the exact moment she thought sure she would shatter into pieces, she clutched at him, she clutched handfuls of soft, white fur, and she cried out with blessed release. Everything went woozy. She was drowning in waves of passion, of knowledge, of Tripp.

But she needed to feel him with her.

"Tripp. Please?"

He knew what she wanted. His hands braced her hips, and with one thrust, he slipped inside. Sleek, golden, liquid, he felt impossibly devastatingly good.

She met each stroke, wanting more of him, taking all he had to give. Swifter, farther, higher. Deeper.

And together, together as they were always meant to be, they found their bliss. They touched the sky.

HE HADN'T PLANNED to spend his last night in the cabin buck naked on the rug in front of the fire. But what a way to go.

Bridgie's body was warm and delicious beside him, so soft, almost liquid, as she sinuously cuddled closer, tangling a leg over his, brushing his hair with one small hand. He closed his eyes, drawing her up against him, fitting her tighter, nuzzling her neck.

He wanted to make love to her again, right now.

And when they were done, he wanted to try it new ways and new places. He wanted to bury himself in her and never let go. He had never been so hungry, so greedy, for one body, for one woman. He could make love to her all day, yet he knew it wouldn't be enough. There was simply no way he could drink his fill of Bridgie.

Euphoria and confusion suddenly filled him. "I'm in love," he whispered, awed by the very idea. He was married to the woman he loved, and it was fabulous, it was wonderful, it was everything anyone could ever want.

If he'd known marriage could be like this, he would've done it years ago.

And if he'd known Bridgie could be like this, he would've taken her to bed years ago.

Tenderly, he looked down at the woman sleeping in his arms. His wife.

Holy hell. They were supposed to be at the airport in a few hours. She was leaving.

But she couldn't. He had to tell her first how he felt. He had to tell her something to make her stay.

But what? What could he say? *I love you. I want to stay married to you. I don't want to wake up alone ever again.*

God, it sounded idiotic. She was destined for greatness, and he was a regular guy. He eased out from under her, leaving her alone in front of the long cold fireplace. He had to think. He had to plan.

He found a blanket in the bedroom and he covered her there on the rug, tucking it in carefully so that she wouldn't get a chill. And then he jumped into the shower, hoping some frigid water would clear his head.

He had to figure out a way to convince her they had to stay together. But how?

WHERE WAS SHE? Fur under her fingers. Hard floor. A thin quilt.

She blinked open and looked around, getting her bearings. The living room rug? But of course. Tripp. Last night. Bliss.

Sighing extravagantly, she settled back down into the rug to nap a bit more. But wait a minute. If she'd made love with Tripp until the wee hours, and the stiff, well-loved feeling coursing her limbs told her that she definitely had, then what was she doing all by herself on this damn bear rug?

"Tripp?"

No answer.

She sat up, clutching the quilt to her bare breasts. They were sensitive, tender, from last night, and even grazing them with the quilt gave her shivers of remembered desire.

"Tripp?"

Nothing.

"Oh my God!" Flinging the quilt over one shoulder toga-style, Bridget jumped to her feet. "What if it was so terrible, he took off? What if I was so bad at it, he just couldn't face me?"

It had seemed terrific to her, like the stuff of erotic fantasies and sensuous dreams. But she had very little experience.

What if he knew better?

"Tripp?" she called again, ready to panic.

And he appeared in the hall. His hair was still wet from the shower, and it stuck up in funny spikes, as if he'd been raking his hands through it, again and again. His face was drawn and dark, and he looked very intense, very fierce, very mixed-up.

This didn't look good. Shower? As in, he couldn't wait to wash off the traces of their lovemaking? Mixed-up? As in, realizing he'd made a big mistake, and not sure how to break it to her?

Bridget didn't move.

"There's something I need to say to you," he began, in a low, agonized voice she wasn't sure she'd ever heard from him before.

She took a long, harsh breath. The Grand Canyon was ready to open up in front of her. But she would be brave. She breathed again, deeper still. "Okay."

"Bridget, I... That is, we..." He wheeled around, hit the wall with the flat of his hand and cursed under his breath. "About last night."

She squeezed her eyes shut. With all the courage she had, she made her voice sound casual, neutral. "Of course. Last night. What about it?"

"We got so carried away, we didn't think..."

"No, we didn't think. That's very true. We did not think." She began to pace, flapping her quilt back and forth. "But that's my fault. I mean, I'm the one who asked. So it's definitely my fault. And I knew we were leaving in the morning, and that was the end of it, and I went ahead and did it anyway, so you have nothing to blame yourself for, Tripp. Definitely my fault."

"It's not anybody's fault," he interrupted. "And that's what I want to talk about."

"What?" she cried. She was so confused.

"Bridget," he said, with a note of desperation. Advancing on her, he grabbed her by the shoulders. "We can't just leave. Not now. Not after what we did. I was hoping you'd see it, too. We have to stay married."

"What?"

"We got carried away. We didn't plan on this. But this morning, it hit me."

"What?"

"Bridget!" he shouted. "For once in your life, will you please listen to me? We were very irresponsible. We didn't use protection."

"This is about condoms? Birth control?" Now her head was really spinning.

"We can't go on pretending that nothing has changed." He released her abruptly, crashing a hand through his hair. "Everything has changed."

She felt tears of frustration well up in her eyes. "Will you just spit it out, please?"

"Oh, God," he muttered blackly. "I am making such a mess of this. This isn't how I planned to say it all. But, Bridget, we have to do the right thing now. We made love. We might have made a baby last night. And we have to be together, don't you see? It has to have a name. My name."

Babies and names. The almighty Ashby name. His mother wanted grandchildren. God forbid any sperm of his should go astray and make a baby he didn't have control over.

Bridget needed to sit down.

Her mind was whirling. Last night was a transformation for her, a revelation. She'd felt beautiful and loved. She'd felt as if she'd really looked inside herself, for the first time, and saw the love and the passion she had to offer. Forget about changing the world. She looked at Tripp and she wanted to be with him, to let the world fend for itself.

But, no. He looked and he saw babies. He saw duty. Obligation. The burden of carrying on his damn family name.

Everything she had just decided didn't matter to her in the least.

"I can't believe this," she whispered. She shook her head. But he was still there, still intense and fierce and mixed-up.

Still the biggest jackass in the history of the universe.

"I wouldn't stay married to you if you were the last man on earth," she declared, just able to stave off the tears. She had some pride, didn't she? Words were pounding through her brain, and she let it all spill out, not censoring one last, nasty crack. "You're an idiot, an idiot. If there's a baby, and it would be just my luck there would be after only one night, we will deal with it later. Much later. As far as I'm concerned, we've moved to divorce instead of annulment, but there is still no marriage. Not between us. We're the worst pair that ever lived. The Stud and the Egghead. What a joke."

"Bridgie, I didn't mean—"

"I've made a mistake," she mumbled, pushing past him. She slammed into the bedroom, trying not to hyperventilate. As soon as she could get some clothes on and heave her suitcases in the car, she was out of here.

Chapter Fourteen

The first thing she did was fire her secretary.

It was time to make positive changes, she decided. Out with the old, in with the new. Having cleanly and intelligently ended her engagement to Jay, she decided to bill more hours, stay at the firm until the wee hours every night, provide more service to her clients, get a better, nicer secretary, and maybe she'd even redecorate her apartment in her spare time.

Ha! What spare time?

She had an important job, and all kinds of responsibilities. Who had spare time?

She did. She had minutes and hours, piling up, spilling over her shoulders, dancing across her calendar. She would be looking at a contract, making phone calls, having lunch with a client—it didn't matter. Whatever she was doing, her attention would lag. She would stare into space. And all she could see was Tripp.

There ought to be a way to fill her schedule so full there was no space left for him, but it didn't seem to work that way.

"I was wrong," she said out loud, into the deep quiet of her office.

It would've been much better never to have made love at all than to remember so indelibly, and to face the prospect of never feeling that way again.

She put her head down on her desk, just to rest for a second. But her phone began to flash, its red light pulsing over there on the edge of the desk, and she hesitated.

What if it was him?

It wouldn't be. He'd had plenty of opportunities to contact her if he wanted to. And he hadn't.

She assumed he was in Schaumburg now, at his town house, with hot- and cold-running blondes. Trust Tripp to bring a cliché to life.

Tapping a finger next to the flashing phone, Bridget considered. It wouldn't be him.

Without giving herself time to think about it, she picked it up. "Ms. Emerick?" a female voice—definitely not Tripp—said in her ear. It was the temp sent up by the clerical pool. A very dim temp. She was calling from all of ten feet away. "I have a message for you."

"I'm right here," she said kindly. "You don't need to call me if you have messages. You can bring them in."

"Oh, okay." Clunk.

Bridget glared down at the receiver. Maybe she should've kept Marie.

The new girl flounced in and delicately dropped a small pink slip on Bridget's desk. As Bridget reached for it, the temp recited, "It was from a Mr. Ashby. He said to tell you that you left some things at the cabin and that he will box them up and mail them. Otherwise, he will contact you when it's time to file."

Bridget gritted her teeth. She didn't know which was more annoying—Tripp leaving personal messages with her secretary, or the secretary chanting them out loudly in her singsong voice.

"File what?" the girl asked cheerfully. "Like, file your income taxes?"

"No," she said, already waving her away. "Not income tax."

File for divorce, of course. He would contact her when it was time to file their divorce papers. She knew what that meant—as soon as Kitty Belle died . . .

"Wait," Bridget said, as the girl cleared the door. "Did he say why he was leaving a message, why he didn't want to talk to me directly?"

"Uh, no. I don't think so. Sounded real nice, though."

"Oh, he is," she said under his breath. "He's real nice."

TRIPP'S PACKAGE ARRIVED a few days later. Her wedding dress.

He really knew how to inflict pain, didn't he? Just hearing the first rustle as she pulled it out of the box, and she was assaulted with memories.

Whirling in front of Kitty Belle.

It's simply lovely on you, dear.

Do you really like it?

Standing next to Tripp in front of the judge, promising to love and honor and all that rot, while his blue eyes caressed her through the dress.

And after . . . There was the sticky part.

He'd peeled her out of that gown like she was a ripe banana. And when she was climbing all over him in her garter belt and stockings, he'd pushed her away.

I can't do this. Not with you.

That should have been her first clue.

She didn't actually know what had happened to the wedding gown after that. The last she remembered, she was kicking it unceremoniously to the floor because she was so hot to get out of it. Charming.

But Tripp must've rescued it, just in time to send it back and remind her of everything she wanted to forget.

She stuffed it back in the box, fully prepared to send it down the garbage chute, when her phone rang. No one ever called her at home except people trying to sell credit cards and carpet cleaning. So who would it be this time?

"Hello?" she asked warily.

"Hi, sweetheart. It's Dad."

"Oh, hi, Dad. This is about Thanksgiving, isn't it? To tell you the truth, I just don't think I'm going to be able to make it." She juggled the dress box with one hand and the phone with the other. "Sorry. But maybe next year."

"It's not about Thanksgiving, honey."

"Oh, okay." She waited politely. What else could it be?

After a pause, her father said carefully, "I'm in Ashbyville, honey. I'm staying at Tripp's mother's house."

"You're at Kitty Belle's? But why?"

"Well, you know, we got to be friends out at Lake Tahoe, and... But we can talk about that later," he hedged. "Right now, we were wondering if you could drive out here sometime." He paused. "Sometime soon. She really wants to see you, Bridget."

"Sure," she returned quickly. "Tomorrow's Saturday. I can come out tomorrow."

But as she set the phone back in the cradle, her mind was racing.

Kitty Belle's condition must have gone downhill fast. They'd been waiting for her decline, watching for signs, and now, all of a sudden, here it was. Bridget dropped to sit on her sofa, with the wedding gown box still in her arms.

It was weird how fond she'd grown of Kitty Belle after disliking her for so many years, and now apparently her father felt the same way. But it sounded like the end was near.

Kitty Belle had asked to see her. She probably knew that Bridget and Tripp were no longer living together, and she was going to try some last-ditch reconciliation with her dying breath.

Bridget closed her eyes. So many lies. So much pretending.

"Tripp," she whispered.

If his mother really was failing, he was undoubtedly devastated.

Maybe she would see him tomorrow. Maybe she could at least hold his hand a little.

ASHBYVILLE WAS a very pretty town, with a classic town square and a courthouse in the middle of things. The original Ashby Carriage Company faced the square on one side, as did a hole-in-the-wall café, an old opera house that had been turned into a community theater and a fire station.

Small town, Americana.

On this bright November day, Ashbyville was showing its best colors. The trees weren't quite bare yet, and the sun was shining, making the bricks and white clapboard of Ashbyville look very spiffy.

Bridget had a little trouble finding the Ashbyville home. She'd only been there once before, for Tripp's twenty-first birthday party, and he'd driven her out from the city.

That was a very long time ago, and a lot of water had passed under the bridge since then.

But a kind man at a gas station gave her directions, and she followed the main road around to a hill over-looking the rest of the town, and there it was. It had been home to prominent Ashbys for a hundred years, and it looked like it.

The house was imposing, all Georgian brick with fat white columns; Bridget experienced a moment of trep-idation as she pressed the bell.

And when the big white door with its magnificent brass fittings swung open, revealing her father, she re-ally did a double-take. "I certainly didn't expect you to open the door," she managed. "Or to have made your-self so at home here."

"Well, that's part of what we need to talk about."

"Can you give me a hint?" But all she could think of was that Tripp's mother had become so enamored of the plumber from St. Paul that she'd changed her will in his favor.

Either that or he'd taken a job as Kitty Belle's butler.

She couldn't decide which choice was more bizarre.

Her dad led her down the hall to a sitting room, opening the door, revealing Kitty Belle, perched in a pretty chintz chair. But she didn't look as if she were at death's door. As a matter of fact, she looked healthier than ever. Her hair was upswept in its usual elegant golden coiffure, and she was wearing another in her endless parade of tasteful pink suits, with pearls at her ears and her wrists.

"Sit down, dear," she said kindly.

"But I thought you were..."

"Yes, I know." Mrs. Ashby exchanged an uneasy glance with Bridget's father. He sat beside her, on the arm of her chair, and took her hand in his.

As she took the chair opposite, Bridget was beginning to feel like a grade-A stooge. A glimmer of what was really happening wafted into her brain, and she said slowly, "I think you'd better tell me what this is all about."

Kitty Belle licked her precious pink lipstick. "I don't know quite where to begin."

"Come on. Tell her," Frank Emerick commanded. "No more beating around the bush."

"Yes, dear."

Bridget's eyes widened. Since when did Kitty Belle go along placidly, with a simple "yes, dear"? This was so out of character as to be positively shocking.

Mrs. Ashby's cheeks were as rosy as her suit, and she definitely seemed to be having problems getting her words out. "Now, before I tell you the whole story, I want you to know, it was with the best of motives. I really did have your best interests at heart."

"You're not dying, are you?" Bridget ventured softly.

There was a tiny pause.

"Everyone dies sooner or later, my dear."

"But you're not sick, are you?"

Kitty Belle shook her head. "No, I'm not."

"And you never were?"

"Well, I had a sinus infection a few days before the wedding, but that's about it."

"I can't believe this! We thought you were dying!" Bridget shouted. "We made fools of ourselves because we thought you were sick, and now..."

She shook her head in disbelief. There were so many clues, and yet she hadn't wanted to see them, hadn't wanted to believe that she was making a mess of her life based on an even bigger lie than the ones she was telling. Here she'd been worried that her sham engagement, or the fake wedding, would somehow alert the cosmic lie-detector forces to come and punish her. At least she hadn't told anyone she was dying!

"You knew that the old coot Tripp dug up wasn't my father all along, didn't you?"

Shame-faced, Kitty Belle admitted, "Well, yes."

"And you knew who Jay and my dad really were?"

Kitty Belle nodded. "Your father is very bad at keeping secrets, as it happens. I think it took less than twenty-four hours before he told me who he was. It's one of the things I love most about him."

"Love?"

"Yes, Bridget." Her father clasped Kitty Belle's hand. "That's the other thing we needed to tell you. I've asked Kitty Belle to marry me. But we wanted to clear this thing up with you, first, so that there wouldn't be any old baggage between us."

"Once we decided we wanted to marry, well, I knew I was going to have to fess up."

"And you, Dad, did you know all along?"

"Actually, no, I didn't. It wasn't until we came back here that Kitty Belle confessed what she'd done." He gave her a stern look, but it was tempered with too much affection for anyone to take it seriously. "And I was very cross with her, too."

Cooing love birds. It was outrageous. "I can't deal with this right now." Bridget was still stuck back on the first betrayal. But her father and Kitty Belle playing at romance—well, that was way past too much.

"I know it's hard to understand, but it really was for your own good," Tripp's mother tried again.

"Oh, please!" Bridget jumped to her feet. "Do you know what you put your son through? He was heart-broken. He thought he was losing you! Did you ever think about what you were doing to Tripp?"

"I had to do it," Mrs. Ashby maintained. "He refused to get married. Thirty-four years old, and not even a step toward marriage or children—it's disgraceful. So I had to give him a push."

Bridget spun back around. She'd just had a terrible thought. "Have you told him? Does Tripp know you're not dying?"

"He does now," a voice said darkly.

They all turned. Tripp was lounging negligently in the doorway, as if he hadn't a care in the world.

Only the ferociously clenched jaw and dangerous look in his eye gave him away.

Bridget looked at him, and he looked at her. And wasn't he a sight to behold?

Everything they had ever done together in their entire lives came flooding back to her, almost like having an out-of-body experience. The good and the bad—it was there, flashing before her eyes.

She tried to remember to breathe, to swallow, to behave like a normal human being. Why was it that no matter how hard she tried to extricate him from her life, he kept coming back? She swallowed past a lump in her throat.

Whatever he had done, however he had treated her, the honest truth was that she wanted him back.

"WELL, MOTHER, you may not think you're dying anytime soon, but I think you may be surprised."

"Excuse me, dear?"

"Because I'm going to kill you myself," he said savagely. "With my bare hands."

"Oh, Tripp, settle down. Now, I admit, I shouldn't have done what I did, but it all turned out beautifully, didn't it?" Kitty Belle bestowed her most magnanimous smile upon them. "You got Bridget, and I got Frank. What could be lovelier?"

Except that he didn't have Bridget. "This is disgraceful," he muttered. He strode over to where his mother and Frank sat so complacently. "You have behaved so badly, Mother, that I can't even find the words to tell you."

"For someone who has trouble confronting people, you're sounding pretty good here," Bridget put in from the side.

He ignored her. If he looked at her, he would see all of his failures right before his eyes. He had made all kinds of promises to Bridgie, and they had all turned to dust.

Trust me. How many times had he said that? And how many times had he stomped on her trust? He knew she and Philpott had called it quits, and he knew why. Because of him. He'd ruined her life, and ruined his own, and he had no one to blame but himself.

"I think the thing that makes me the angriest is how you've treated Bridgie," he said, glaring at his mother. "She was the best friend I ever could've asked for, and you bad-mouthed her, you belittled her and then you manipulated both of us. How any father who gives a damn about his daughter could hitch up with you after what you've done... Well, it seems like a pretty pathetic way to be a father."

"Now just a minute," Frank Emerick bristled.

"Save it for someone who gives a damn."

"Tripp," Bridget admonished. "This is so unlike you. Yelling at two parents in one day."

"I guess I just got fed up." He jammed his hands in his pants pockets and glared out the window, into the garden. His mother's garden. Pretty to look at, snobby, with only the best seedlings allowed, that garden was the perfect symbol for Kitty Belle. "My mother has been on Bridgie's case for so long for not having the right bloodlines, it seems pretty rich for her to be hooking up with those same bloodlines now."

"What's this all about?" Bridget's dad asked.

"Oh, it's my fault," Kitty Belle admitted with a wave of one hand. "I admit, at first I didn't think Bridget was the right girl for you, Tripp, but that was years ago."

"Years ago? You were still singing that tune when you told me you only had months to live. What's it been? A month and a half?"

"Oh, I made that up," she insisted. "Actually, by that time, I thought Bridget would be perfect. She's always been in love with you—any fool could see that. Plus she's very sensible and smart."

Bridget was sitting there with her mouth open. Looking at her, Tripp thought he knew exactly how she felt.

"But I knew," Kitty Belle continued, "that if I pretended to disapprove, you would like her even better. A little reverse psychology."

"Do you feel as much like a prize chump as I do?" he asked, offering Bridget his hand.

But Kitty Belle refused to be daunted. "There was no harm done," she contended. "Now that everything's out in the open, you don't have to stay married anymore. Not unless you want to, of course."

"As it happens, Mother, I would love to. But Bridget has already turned me down," he said bitterly.

But he saw the look on Bridget's face. Sorrow, love, hope, and a burning need for another chance.

What had Kitty Belle said? *She's always been in love with you—any fool could see that.*

Except one fool—him. Was it possible she really did want to stay married?

"Bridgie, we need to talk," he muttered, and before anyone had a chance to protest, he grabbed her by the wrist and pulled her out of his mother's house.

"Where are we going?" she puffed, but he just kept walking, until he hit the town square.

There was a pavilion there, a small place that was just perfect for band concerts in the summer. Right now, it was empty, and it was private, and that was all he asked.

"Bridgie, look," he said, pushing her onto a bench. He hovered there, over her. "I screwed this up the last time, and I don't want to do that again. So here's the thing. I'm going to say this right up front, okay?"

"What?" she demanded. "What are you going to say?"

"I love you."

His declaration hung there in the air. She seemed frozen.

Maybe he'd already blown it, but he had to press on. "I love you, and I loved being married to you. It was the happiest I've ever been." He set his jaw. This stuff did not come easily to him, but he was doing his best. "Basically, the thing is, I'll do anything I have to do to make it all real, all official, all honest and sincere and genuine. I want to be married to you, for real."

"You love me?" she echoed, in total disbelief.

"Of course I do." As she hesitated, Tripp threw thirty-four years of good breeding and manners to the four winds. "The hell with it," he said, and he grabbed her and kissed her. "You love me, Bridgie. I know you do."

She hung on to the kiss, and her lips were as sweet and warm and tantalizing as he remembered. He could feel her beginning to surrender. But then she smacked him on the shoulder and vaulted out of his arms.

"You idiot!" she shouted. "Of course I love you. I've always loved you. Anybody who wasn't completely blind would've seen it a long time ago."

"You never told me!"

"I didn't know," she admitted. "Jay told me, your mother, my father... But I didn't see it."

"Me, either. But I'm not blind anymore."

And right there, in sight of the statue of the first Thomas Michael Trippett Ashby, in sight of several curious citizens of Ashbyville, Tripp got down on one knee.

He brushed a kiss across the back of her hand, he gave her the full benefit of his hottest gaze and he took a deep breath.

"Will you marry me, Bridgie?" His lips curved in a reckless grin. "Will you marry me all over again?"

And her smile took his breath away. "If I do, we have to do it right this time. I've got someone to give me away, and I've already got the perfect dress. Oh, and I have the perfect idea for where to go on our honeymoon."

"Anywhere everybody else is not," he said firmly.

"There's this cabin at Lake Tahoe..."

COMING NEXT MONTH

#561 HE'S A REBEL by Linda Randall Wisdom
STUDS #3
Ukiah Jones thought he'd spend the week before Christmas holed up in his Tahoe cabin, alone and secluded. But the cabin was occupied—by ex-spy turned mother Sydney Taylor and her two little charges—who made Ki play Santa and daddy!

#562 THE BABY & THE BODYGUARD by Jule McBride
When Anton Santa was hired to protect the three-year-old mascot of a family toy store, he didn't realize the pint-size client was the daughter of his ex-lover, Cynthia Sweet. Santa meant to keep his identity hidden and research the truth: Had he accidentally been hired to protect his own daughter?

#563 THE GIFT-WRAPPED GROOM by M.J. Rodgers
Noel Winsome was absolutely determined that her pre-Christmas marriage to a Russian mail-order groom would be in name only. But when Nicholas Baranov held her under the mistletoe, Noel wondered how long she could wait to unwrap her presents....

#564 A TIMELESS CHRISTMAS by Patricia Chandler
When he appeared in her courtroom out of nowhere, Miguel de Pima reminded Judge Dallas McAllister of a long-lost lover...one who'd been hanged on Christmas Eve a hundred years ago. This Christmas they had to find a way to reunite a town divided by hate, or risk losing each other...again.

AVAILABLE THIS MONTH:

#557 ONCE UPON A HONEYMOON
Julie Kistler

#558 QUINN'S WAY
Rebecca Flanders

#559 SECRET AGENT DAD
Leandra Logan

#560 FROM DRIFTER TO DADDY
Mollie Molay

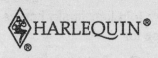

VOWS
Margaret Moore

Legend has it that couples who marry in the
Eternity chapel are destined for happiness.
Yet the couple who started it all almost never
made it to the altar!

It all began in Eternity, Massachusetts, 1855....
Bronwyn Davies started life afresh in America
and found refuge with William Powell. But
beneath William's respectability was a secret
that, once uncovered, could keep Bronwyn
bound to him forever.

Don't miss **VOWS,** the exciting prequel to
Harlequin's cross-line series, **WEDDINGS, INC.,**
available in December from Harlequin Historicals.
And look for the next **WEDDINGS, INC.**
book, *Bronwyn's Story,* by Marisa Carroll
(Harlequin Superromance #635), coming in
March 1995.

WED7

This holiday, join four hunky heroes under the mistletoe for

Christmas Kisses

Cuddle under a fluffy quilt, with a cup of hot chocolate and these romances sure to warm you up:

#561 HE'S A REBEL (also a Studs title)
Linda Randall Wisdom

#562 THE BABY AND THE BODYGUARD
Jule McBride

#563 THE GIFT-WRAPPED GROOM
M.J. Rodgers

#564 A TIMELESS CHRISTMAS
Pat Chandler

Celebrate the season with all four holiday books sealed with a Christmas kiss—coming to you in December, only from Harlequin American Romance!

CK-G

"HOORAY FOR HOLLYWOOD" SWEEPSTAKES

HERE'S HOW THE SWEEPSTAKES WORKS

OFFICIAL RULES — NO PURCHASE NECESSARY

To enter, complete an Official Entry Form or hand print on a 3" x 5" card the words "HOORAY FOR HOLLYWOOD", your name and address and mail your entry in the pre-addressed envelope (if provided) or to: "Hooray for Hollywood" Sweepstakes, P.O. Box 9076, Buffalo, NY 14269-9076 or "Hooray for Hollywood" Sweepstakes, P.O. Box 637, Fort Erie, Ontario L2A 5X3. Entries must be sent via First Class Mail and be received no later than 12/31/94. No liability is assumed for lost, late or misdirected mail.

Winners will be selected in random drawings to be conducted no later than January 31, 1995 from all eligible entries received.

Grand Prize: A 7-day/6-night trip for 2 to Los Angeles, CA including round trip air transportation from commercial airport nearest winner's residence, accommodations at the Regent Beverly Wilshire Hotel, free rental car, and $1,000 spending money. (Approximate prize value which will vary dependent upon winner's residence: $5,400.00 U.S.); 500 Second Prizes: A pair of "Hollywood Star" sunglasses (prize value: $9.95 U.S. each). Winner selection is under the supervision of D.L. Blair, Inc., an independent judging organization, whose decisions are final. Grand Prize travelers must sign and return a release of liability prior to traveling. Trip must be taken by 2/1/96 and is subject to airline schedules and accommodations availability.

Sweepstakes offer is open to residents of the U.S. (except Puerto Rico) and Canada who are 18 years of age or older, except employees and immediate family members of Harlequin Enterprises, Ltd., its affiliates, subsidiaries, and all agencies, entities or persons connected with the use, marketing or conduct of this sweepstakes. All federal, state, provincial, municipal and local laws apply. Offer void wherever prohibited by law. Taxes and/or duties are the sole responsibility of the winners. Any litigation within the province of Quebec respecting the conduct and awarding of prizes may be submitted to the Regie des loteries et courses du Quebec. All prizes will be awarded; winners will be notified by mail. No substitution of prizes are permitted. Odds of winning are dependent upon the number of eligible entries received.

Potential grand prize winner must sign and return an Affidavit of Eligibility within 30 days of notification. In the event of non-compliance within this time period, prize may be awarded to an alternate winner. Prize notification returned as undeliverable may result in the awarding of prize to an alternate winner. By acceptance of their prize, winners consent to use of their names, photographs, or likenesses for purpose of advertising, trade and promotion on behalf of Harlequin Enterprises, Ltd., without further compensation unless prohibited by law. A Canadian winner must correctly answer an arithmetical skill-testing question in order to be awarded the prize.

For a list of winners (available after 2/28/95), send a separate stamped, self-addressed envelope to: Hooray for Hollywood Sweepstakes 3252 Winners, P.O. Box 4200, Blair, NE 68009.

CBSRLS

OFFICIAL ENTRY COUPON

"Hooray for Hollywood"
SWEEPSTAKES!

Yes, I'd love to win the Grand Prize — a vacation in Hollywood —
or one of 500 pairs of "sunglasses of the stars"! Please enter me
in the sweepstakes!

This entry must be received by December 31, 1994.
Winners will be notified by January 31, 1995.

Name _____

Address _____ Apt. _____

City _____

State/Prov. _____ Zip/Postal Code _____

Daytime phone number _____
(area code)

Account # _____

Return entries with invoice in envelope provided. Each book
in this shipment has two entry coupons — and the more
coupons you enter, the better your chances of winning!

DIRCBS

"Really?" Bridget said softly.